A. D. SOREL

Black Sea Resolve

Krasnodar Rising

First edition

This book was professionally typeset on Reedsy.
Find out more at reedsy.com

To Brianna and Roya,
My rocks, my anchors, and my Northern Stars

1

Chapter 1: Andropov Rising.

MOSCOW, USSR
April 25th, 1978

The streets of Moscow at 7:30 in the morning were nearly empty. It is a gray day in April when the sun cannot break through the low clouds, and fog still clings to the streets of Moscow. In the backseat of his car, a Chaika, the vehicle used by the upper political class in the Soviet Union, Andrei glances through the window as the car speeds past Gorky Park, towards the Kremlin. People on the sidewalk throw a glance at the large Chaika, knowing that in the back of the vehicle, there must be someone important. Someone with strong ties to the party is going to the Kremlin.

Andrei Kirilenko, a prominent figure in the Soviet Union's Politburo, was one of Brezhnev's trusted proteges and one of those who orchestrated Nikita Khrushchev's departure from the leadership of the Soviet Union. With Khrushchev gone, Brezhnev led the party with a strong troika around him. Andrei is seeking ways to turn the Soviet Union's failing economy around.

Andrei rifles through his papers, holding information from the KGB and the Foreign Affairs Ministry, including summaries of events and analyses from Kabul and Tehran.

"*This will turn into madness.*" Andrei thinks. "*We cannot rely on any of these people. The Shah is all about the American dream and oil money and his riches, and the Afghan nekulturny goat herders are all about Allah. Without a strong fist there in the region, it will all turn to ashes, and they will be at each other's throats soon.*"

The car comes to a sudden stop at the gates of the Kremlin. The official guard salutes as they see the official party car. Nodding slightly, Andrei puts the papers back in his briefcase and looks at the guards. These are the toy soldiers. Trained to parade and to shine their uniform. However, no one knows when they last visited the firing range.

"Come on, Alexei, I don't want to be late," said Andrei to the driver.

"In a minute, comrade, we must obey all the checks."

Andrei walks through the doors into the presidium room, and two guards open the doors for him. Just like they always do, every Tuesday, when the meeting of the Politburo is scheduled. The meeting where all the decisions regarding the Soviet Union are made. The decisions driving the five-year plan. The plan that is put together by the members of the Communist Party.

He nods slightly, saluting the guards, and walks into the grandiose room from the Czar's time. He marvels as always at the beauty of the room, which is bright despite the gloomy rainy skies of Moscow on this day in April.

Sure, they knew how to build back then, he addresses no one in particular. "*They took from the people, but they knew how to build. And look at us now. We're enjoying the spoils after so many years."* Andrei walks towards his spot on the right side of the presidium table, shaking hands with Shcherbitsky and Pelše. He glances at Shcherbitsky.

You call yourself Ukrainian, but all you do is erase everything that makes us Ukrainians. Maybe one day, our time will come.

He glances around the room, taking note of who is not present and who is late. Andropov, not there. Brezhnev, not there. Chernenko, not there. Gorbachev, wait, Gorbachev is wringing his hands, and he looks tense. *"What is going on?"* Andrei is trying to think. *"What music was it playing on the radio? Was it Tchaikovsky? Neah, the radio was off."*

Yuri Andropov steps into the presidium room, followed by Konstantin Chernenko and Andrey Grechko. His face is set, determined. Clenching his cheeks and walking towards the head of the table. Clearing his throat, he looks around the room, assessing everyone.

"Comrades, I'm afraid I have grave news. Our beloved leader and comrade, Leonid Ilyich Brezhnev, suffered a stroke last night at 1 o'clock. He is in the care of our doctors at Voyennyy Hospital, but the prognosis is bad. Leonid Ilyich cannot speak or move, and it does not look like he will regain consciousness. I hope he will recover soon, and he will rejoin this spot here, helping us build the communist society we've all been dreaming of. Until then, with your permission and support, Comrade Chernenko, Comrade Grechko, Comrade Gorbachev, and I will continue the good work of Leonid Ilyich. Let's hope for his swift return and let's continue to work."

After a moment of silence, applause is heard in the presidium room. Hands are shaken, and shoulders are slapped. Kirilenko is making his way towards Andropov and Chernenko.

"Comrades, as you know, there's always a tough road ahead of us. It is always tough, and like always, we will succeed." Shaking hands with both, Kirilenko is making his way back to his seat. Appearances have been kept. *"They are having their troika now, and with Gorbachev following in his trail, at least he's young. But he has some ideas that will not sit well with Andropov."*

Andropov booms again. "Comrades, this is a sad day for us. I propose that we recess and return to our offices to get organized and prepare for the meeting next week, unless someone has something urgent to bring to the presidium."

Papers are shuffled, and chairs are grinding on the floor. "In this case," Andropov speaks again. "Let's hope for Leonid Ilyich's quick recovery and let's go back to work."

Andropov gets up and steps out of the presidium room, followed by the same people, Gorbachev, trailing behind them. Andrei gets up and looks around, the same faces, getting old, older and older every day, and yet clinging to power, with all their might. Each of them is trying to understand the new shift in power, and who can be trusted, who should be avoided, and who can be swindled for their political gain.

2

Chapter 2: Intercept over Sochi

SOCHI, Krasnodar Krai, USSR
April 26th, 1978

Vanea Gureevich hears the incessant ringing of his alarm clock, the familiar sound waking him. The clock shows 5:30 AM. Sitting up on the bed, he rolls his head side to side, stretching his arms while yawning. Vanea ruffles his hair as he gets up. Pulling the curtain from his bedroom window, he is bathed in the warm embrace of the morning sun. A few wisps of clouds hang lazily over the mountain tops, practically beckoning him to fly amongst them. Opening the window, he peeks over to the sea, just a thin layer of fog. Today is a good day to fly.

Stretching again, he talks with himself. "Come on, Vanea, get your ass in gear. You still have your daily 5 km run, shower, and get to the unit by 7. Get your ass in gear."

At 6:45, he drives his Lada Niva through the gates of the Sochi Airport, stopping sharply at the barrier so the guard could check his papers. "Good morning, comrade Major. How was the drive?"

"Good morning, Sergeant," Vanea replied. "The drive was good. It's nice to go out like this early in the morning. The best time to drive. Cold air from the mountains and salt from the sea. It's the best time of the day."

"Yes, it is," the Corporal replied. "Carry on, comrade, have a good day".

At 6:55, Vanea enters the unit locker room and begins to change into his VKK-6 flight suit. The flight suit that will help him against the G forces when he pushes his MiG-21 to 9 G's. Putting on the suit carefully, ensuring all zippers are in place. It fits well. He nods to the Sergeant waiting in the corner to get some help with the fittings, stretching his arms and then windmilling his hands to ensure that everything fits nicely.

"Thank you, Igor," he smiles at the Sergeant.

"Let's do a pressure test". Igor takes a hose and plugs it into the suit, inflating the lower part of the suit, which allows him to pull to 9 G's. Vanea groans and inhales, keeping the air in his lungs as he would strain for a G pull.

"One day, this thing will catch me by surprise, and I'm going to let one rip, Igor."

Igor laughs, "You will not be the first one or the last, and let me tell you, some of our guys have a bad diet".

Vanea bursts in laughter, "Tell me it's the Colonel, please tell me it's the Colonel, he has a gut already, I'm sure that when you squeeze him, there's no way he can hold it in."

Igor replies. "Vanea, I like this job, I like it too much, and I'm not that stupid. It's all good, your helmet? Is it good? Is the visor clean?"

Vanea smiles and replies. "You know I take care of that well. The visor is clean. The mask is fitted well. That's key out there.

Thanks, Igor. I like it when you're on duty with the fitters. We're always laughing. How many sorties today?"

Igor replies. "Just 8, they are saying that the fuel is scarce, two intercepts like yours, two reconnaissance flights, and four checks after maintenance".

Vanea spots one of his colleagues, another Major, "Good morning, Piotr, what are you having today?"

Piotr smiles and looks at Vanea. "Good morning, you are early. I have a reconnaissance profile, high altitude, Poti, Kobuleti, Kutaisi, then coming back. You know, I have to get my qualifications back after the Academy."

Vanea claps Piotr's shoulder. "I know, I was like that, after I came from Frunze, hang in there, a few more months and you'll get back into it. I have an intercept, a target briefed to come from Southeast. I take it that's you."

Both pilots laugh. "Will you maneuver?" asks Vanea.

"I'll give you a turn, or I will add a turn and a roll in there, but we will be high at 12 thousand meters. Not much happening there, and I'll be low on fuel," replies Piotr.

"At least put the sun behind you so I get some good film if I can find you," says Vanea.

"If you can find me." Replies Piotr. "Have a good flight out there and be safe, Piotr."

The little UAZ-69 puts along the taxiways of Sochi airport, moving towards the line of four MiG-21 that are sitting in the open, on the readiness line. The engine sputters from time to time, and the driver keeps revving it up as it drives along.

Vanea grins, "That's a bad carburetor, by the sound of it."

"I guess you are right," said the private. "I've cleaned the spark plugs, adjusted the pump, cleaned the jets and the venturi, but it's the damn float that's acting up. All of them are leaky, and they get flooded with gasoline, and the engine gets flooded. The mechanic took this carburetor apart last week."

"Maybe he had some spare parts after he put it back together." Laughed Vanea. "No worries, we're almost there. Pull there in front of the readiness hut."

"Yes, Major," Replied the driver.

Vanea gets out of the little jeep and slams the door once, making sure it stays locked, and slaps the fender of the UAZ to signal the driver that he is free to go. Stepping inside the readiness hut, a little five-by-ten room filled with couches, a table in the middle, with magazines and books spread all over. This is the room where pilots wait for the 5-minute take-off signal, located near the planes, ready to go into action. Two pilots are already in the room. One of them was snoring loudly on a couch covered in a ridiculous number of blankets, while the other was reading an Aviation Week magazine from six months ago, probably smuggled by some Aeroflot pilot.

"Good morning, Vanea, what are you doing here?" Asked the pilot.

"Good morning, Ivan Ivanovich. I'm scheduled for a readiness practice intercept today. So, I get to hang out with you guys until I get the call. How's the day so far?"

"Well, it's quiet, and it looks like it will be quiet the rest of the day. There are flights scheduled, but I'm pretty sure we won't get anything. I also don't think we'll be attacked today. It will be quiet."

Vanea nods. "Anything interesting in that magazine?"

"Yeah, they are canceling the B1 project."

"That's the Mach 2 bomber the Americans are planning, isn't it? The one with variable swept wings?"

"Yeah, that one." "And they put that on paper?"

"They do, turns out that being a spy means reading the papers, doesn't it. You are in the 110 today?"

"Yes, I am, I'll go and do the preflight. Get it out of the way."

Vanea gets out on the tarmac and walks towards the MiG-21 that's assigned to him, red numbers on the nose "110", the MiG is painted in the new camo colors, changing from the bright silver of the past, now with this matte color pattern, his MiG-21 looking more menacing than ever The crew chief walks towards him and throws a smart salute. Vanea salutes back, then shakes his hand.

"How's it looking?" Vanea asks the Crew Chief.

"It's all good and checked, it came with no problems after the last flight, the plane is fueled up, air tank is full, compressor is up, oil and hydraulics are full, batteries are charged and within specification."

The Crew Chief handed in the airplane notebook. Vanea takes it and starts looking at the maintenance records, flipping back a few pages to examine the previous records and the work that has been done on the airplane.

"Thank you, Senior Sergeant. Let's sign it now. This will be an alert takeoff. I won't have the time to do it when the phone rings."

Vanea takes his pen from the kneeboard and gets ready to sign.

"Major, don't you want to do the preflight first?"

Vanea smiles. "Sergeant, I'll do the preflight, but I can sign it now. I'm sure it's alright."

Vanea claps the sergeant on the shoulder and signs the logbook, showing that he trusts his Crew Chief and how he prepared the plane.

Vanea and the Senior Seargent start the walk around the

plane, Pitot tube, nose cone, intake, down the front landing gear, down the length of the fuselage, tracking down the left wing, pulling on the inner pylon, then going down and checking the left landing gear, up the wing again, pulling on the missile attached to the outer pylon, an inert R3R radar missile, no explosive and no rocket engine. Vanea continues to walk around the airplane, checks the central tank, the engine, and around the MiG, as he has done thousands of times before, and finishes his walkaround in front of the stairs to the cockpit.

"It's all good, Senior Sergeant, I knew it."

Vanea climbs up the stairs to the cockpit and starts preparing his office, straps, and air hose for the mask, as well as air for the Anti-G suit. Everything is set up to get in quickly. He leans over with his head down in the cockpit. He checks the pressure air lever, flicks on the battery contacts, and the plane starts to buzz to life. He then checks the battery level and presses the "Warning Lights Check" button.

"It's all good, Senior Sergeant," Vanea said, turning off the batteries and re-arranging the straps that he leaned on as he checked the cockpit.

"Do you want to leave the helmet here, Major?" Asked the Crew Chief.

"Neah, I'll put it on as I ran away, you know I got a wasp in my helmet once? I was hitting my head with my fists, trying to squish the damn thing against my head, and it stung me three times before I managed to kill it. Half of my head got swollen. I'll never leave my helmet out of the bag since then."

The Crew Chief stifles his laugh.

"Go ahead, Senior Sergeant, laugh out loud, just imagine how I was looking from the tarmac, rolling down the taxiway while I was bashing my own head with my fist." Vanea jumps down the stairs and clasps the Crew Chief's shoulder again. "I laugh at it every time I think about it. I'll go back in, I'll see you when the phone rings for me." Said Vanea.

"Do you know when they have you scheduled, Major?" Asks the Crew Chief. "No, it's an alarm when the target is in range. I think that's my target." Vanea points at the 2 MiG-21s lining up for takeoff in formation.

"Yes, they have to complete their mission and, on their way back, they scramble you," says the Crew Chief.

"That's what I'm thinking," nods Vanea.

Vanea walks back to the readiness shack, gets back in, and sits on the couch, stretching his legs on the table.

"All good?" Ask one of the other pilots.

"Yes, all checks out, 110 is a good bird." The other pilot nods and speaks.

"And the engine is quite new." Vanea agrees,

"Yes, just 157 hours, that's the sweet spot right now."

Vanea picks up one of the magazines on the table and thumbs through the pages, finding an article about the F-4 Phantom, and starts to read it, mouthing the words as he tries to translate from English.

"Sorry, guys, bad habit picked up from when I was a kid,"

One of the pilots laughs. "That's okay, Vanea, you look like a rabbit moving your lips like that, munching on a piece of lettuce." Vanea grins and shows the universal sign with two fingers up.

Vanea finished the article and put the magazine back, tilting his head back on the couch and closing his eyes, falling asleep in less than 40 seconds. One trick picked up from the training school. Not wasting a single second and getting as much rest as possible.

Vanea wakes up to the phone ringing, unsure of how much time has passed, and picks up the phone.

"Readiness hut!"

The voice on the other side thunders. "110, takeoff, runway 06, heading 1 5 0, climb to 10000 meters. Contact Sochi Ground control on 134.00, channel 10. Execute!"

"Confirm 110. Runway 06! 150! 10000 meters, Sochi ground control 134.00!" Vanea slams the phone down, grabs his helmet bag, and slams the door behind him as he starts to run towards the plane.

"Have a good flight, Vanea!" one of the pilots yells after him.

Vanea grabs the helmet from the bag and shoves it on his head, clipping the buckle under his chin. Helmet on and buckled, he starts climbing the ladder to his cockpit. The Crew Chief, already hooking up the ground power, has one foot holding the bottom of the ladder so it doesn't slip away from the plane.

Vanea jumps into the cockpit and pulls the straps over his shoulders, then starts to connect his mask to the oxygen tube, taking a sharp breath to ensure it is sealed properly. He connects the cables to the microphone and headset. The Crew Chief is already head down in the cockpit, next to him, doing the straps to the parachute and the chair, tightening them, waiting for Vanea to move back and forth in the seat and adjusting them again and tapping Vanea's helmet and giving him a thumbs up as he jumps down the ladder, pulling the ladder away and waiting for Vanea's start.

Vanea energizes the plane in the well-trained routine, batteries, pumps, the Mig starts to whine and buzz, coming to life, Vanea's hands move from switch to switch, going to the other side, fire extinguisher, APU, glances over the cockpit to see any faults, mashing the engine start button. Taking a glance at the clock, 1 minute since the scramble order, 2 minutes to go. The Mig starts to whine as air rushes through the turbine, spinning it faster and faster. Vanea's eyes are glued to the engine indicators, both needles moving, N1 needle increasing followed by N2 needle, and temperatures rising as the engine spins to life. Good start.

Glancing at the Crew Chief, Vanea gives him a thumbs up, makes the sign to unplug the power, and then points with his thumbs outward, sideways, making the sign to remove the chocks. His hands back in the cockpit, turning the rest of the equipment on, generators, cone, radios, and radar. Glancing at his gyro compass, he mashes the button to align it, waiting a second more after the gyro is aligned.

Looking back at his Crew Chief, cone cover, lanyards, pins, and chocks, he checks that all are removed. Giving a thumbs up again, Vanea pulls the canopy down, locking it, pressuring it, hearing the pressure valve sealing his cockpit, fully connected now to his Mig. The Mig that will be his world for the next hour will give him air, heat, and everything else he needs to fly all the way into the stratosphere.

He scans all the instruments one more time, checks the switches in the cockpit, pushes the takeoff flaps, and pumps the brakes a few times. The Mig hissed as the compressed air was released when the brakes were applied. Vanea checks outside, looking at the taxiway, and checks for no planes or trucks to interfere with his taxi to the takeoff position. *Ohh, the joy of radio silence.* Vanea mutters in his oxygen mask.

1 minute 30 seconds. He inches the throttle forward and releases the brakes. The MiG lurches forward, eager to go,

gathering speed already as he pulls from the apron into the taxiway. Vanea taxis quickly, turns the Mig around, and scans the airport pattern to ensure no planes are nearby. He stops short of the runway, looks at the tower, and waits for the red flare that will give him the clear order. Vanea glances down at the chronometer in the cockpit. 1 minute left. A whole minute just for himself. *"To get up and running in under 2 minutes, that's not bad, Vanea, not bad at all."* Vanea smiles under his oxygen mask as a flare with one red star pops up into the air from the tower, giving him the clear for takeoff sign.

Lining up the plane on the runway center. Vanea is rechecking the instruments, RPM, temperature, pressures, all looking good, rechecking the flaps, flicking the gear safety so he can retract the gear quickly after takeoff, one more glance at the rest of the instruments, whipping the controls to their full extent, stick and rudder, moving all the way, gripping the brake lever on the stick, Vanea pushes the throttle all the way, to the stop before the afterburner, feeling the Mig increasing the thrust, the brakes barely holding the plane still, head back on the seat, Vanea is releasing the brakes and pushes the throttle all the way up into the afterburner. The Mig accelerates down the runway, the thud of the afterburner igniting behind him, accelerating the plane even faster.

At 250 km/h, Vanea eases up on the stick as the Mig gets light on its wheels, the nose coming up. At 320 km/h, the Mig bounces on its fat tires as Vanea works the rudder pedals to keep it on centerline. One more little bounce and the plane lifts in the air, accelerating and climbing already. Vanea flicks the gear up, hearing the wheels being pulled up, he quickly pushes the flaps up button as the plane accelerates now through 450 km/h, he hears the thud of the wheels locked, glancing at the gear and flaps indicator in the cockpit, showing that all is up and locked, pushing the nose down a bit, letting the plane build speed, and turning right in a sharp turn, pulling the nose around, turning to heading 150. Vanea holds the plane level, 300 meters from the ground, the speed building up, 700, 800, 900 km/h, he eases the plane up, trimming it so it shoots up in the sky, grinning wide under his mask, the best feeling in the world now, zooming up at 900 km/h shooting all the way up, climbing like a rocket.

Passing through 6,000 meters, Vanea eases the nose down, maintaining the same speed through the climb, checking the speed and Mach number, and reaching for the radio channel selector. Vanea switches to channel 10, waiting for the Ground Control Intercept to come up on his frequency. Working through the contacts on his cockpit, Vanea turns on his reflector sight and puts the radar on standby, going through the warmup.

The plane goes through 8,000 meters, still climbing steadily, the radio crackles,

"1 1 0, Ground Control!" The steady voice of Sochi Ground Control comes through the radio.

"Ground Control, 1 1 0 receiving five by five," Vanea replies.

"5 by 5, 1 1 0 I have a single target, 145, 80 kilometers, 10.000 meters, target is coming to you, closing speed 2200 km/h. Intercept target!" the steady voice of Ground Control gave him all the information he needed to create the intercept geometry in his head, two objects, moving towards each other at over 2000 km/h. He needs to end up behind it, with enough closing speed to have a radar lock and a valid target solution.

"Ground Control, 1 1 0 received, intercepting target," Vanea replies, stabilizing the plane at 10.000 meters, glancing up at the periscope mirror on top of his canopy, seeing the white contrail extending for miles behind his plane.

"Ground Control, 110 requesting higher altitude, I'm showing contrails." Vanea knows that he will be visible from miles away with the white contrail behind him. Any pilot worth his salt will be able to counter him.

"1 1 0, approved"

Vanes pulls the nose up slowly, climbing up gently so he doesn't bleed any speed. The MiG zooming up, in the clear, bright sky, with a few wisps of cloud down below, Vanea can see the coast all the way to Sukhumi, even Poti. Shifting in his seat a bit, he looks up into the periscope mirror. He sees that there are no contrails behind him as he stabilizes at 12,500 meters. He flicks the switches for the SAU autopilot, the stabilize switch, then the recover switch. The Mig wags its wings as it steadies, flown by its electronic brain. Vanea sighs happily, relaxing now that the rush of takeoff is over and he has reached the target altitude for his intercept. His speed is now at 0.98 Mach, the engine running steadily, with 2500 liters of fuel remaining, and the central tank empty. *Plenty of fuel to have fun today.* Vanea thinks as he scans the sky in front of him, looking for the telltale contrail of the incoming target.

"1 1 0, Ground Control, target 145, 30 kilometers, 10.000 meters, closing! He's at your 11 o'clock. Continue intercept!"

Vanea replies quickly. "Received, 1 1 0 will continue intercepting the target" 30 kilometers, Vanea flicks the radar from standby to emitting, flicking through the switches on the armament panel, energizing the pilons, selecting the R3R missile on the outer left pilon, clicking the arming button of the gun, the thumping sound of the compressed air going through the guns without any ammo reverberating through the plane.

I have you now, Vanea smiles as he sees the dot on the radar, signaling a plane coming towards him at 25 kilometers, a little to the left. He interrogates the plane with his IFF and gets a friendly response. Not now. Part of this exercise is that you are not friendly now. Vanea works out the intercept geometry in his head, turning off the SAU autopilot, taking the plane back under his control, easing up on the right a bit to open up the separation between the two approaching airplanes. At this height and speed, it takes kilometers to make that intercept turn and still have the speed to take that shot. Diagrams drilled into his head during months and months of training, and so many interceptions. But, just as in the oldest times of aviation, from the moment two airplanes pointed guns at each other, the same principle remains. Who has the height, speed, and sun advantage wins in a fight. Vanea sees the contrail of the incoming plane and presses the transmit button on his radio.

"Ground control, 1 1 0, I have radar contact. I have visual!"

"Confirm 1 1 0, continue!"

Vanea pressed the radio button two times, acknowledging the orders from Ground Control.

As the planes are closing now, 3 kilometers in front of him, 4 kilometers lateral separation, Vanea pushes the throttle, all the way into the afterburner, hearing the thudding of the burners igniting and accelerating the plane over Mach 1, he curves the plane to the left, arching in an intercepting turn, curving down, and to the left, using the gravity to keep his speed up, arching towards the target, Vanea's eyes glued on the Mig in front of him, his SPO-10 RWR receiver start chirping. *"Ha! You saw me now, a bit too late."* Knowing that the other plane turned on his radar, but he is way out of the scanning range of the incoming MiG. Vanea gets out of his turn, the

MiG-21 in front of him, 4 kilometers away and a little higher up, gaining on him as it accelerates through Mach 1.3. He locks his radar onto the target, clicking the gun camera to record the upcoming intercept.

"Ground control, 1 1 0, radar lock on Mig-21!"

"Confirm, 1 1 0! Continue!" Ground Control replies.

Gaining on the Mig-21, 2 kilometers now, the radar indicates he has a firing solution, but he needs to get closer to the point where no plane could escape a missile shot. The plane in front of him wags its wings, the pilot looking for him. 10 seconds left now. The plane in front rolls right and pulls in a tight turn, trying to escape his shot. Vanea grunts as he follows into the turn, *Not making it easy, good! Come on, Piotr, show me what you got!* Vanea pulls harder in the turn, the nose of his Mig almost hiding the other plane in front from his view, the radar still locked on the target, while in that moment, the pilot in front continues with his roll on the right, flipping the plane upside down, rolling it still, and switching the turn the other way. Vanea curses in his oxygen mask, pulling up and rolling left, trying to find the other plane, the radar lock dropping as the plane slips under him, straining as he reaches 5 G's, pulling more on the stick and he sees the yellow lights blinking on his dashboard, high angle of attack warning indicators, *Careful now, careful, don't screw it up here* easing the stick he sees the other plane, still turning, afterburner on, glowing in the bright sky, curving the plane around in a turn, gaining on him slowly, still having some energy left, locking the plane again on his radar. Quickly glancing down at his radar screen, he saw that the missile was within the launch parameters.

"Ground control, I have a good lock, ready to shoot!"

"1 1 0 execute!"

Vanea flicks the trigger safety on his stick and mashes the missile launch button, triggering the gun camera to record a practice missile launch.

"Missile away!" Vanea reports.

"Confirm! 1 1 0 knock it off! Knock it off! Good intercept!" Ground control replies.

The plane in front of him gets level, wags its wings in front of him, and turns on a gentle turn towards Sochi. Vanea approaches on a tight formation flight, looking right into the cockpit, where he sees Piotr nodding his head at him and giving him a thumbs up. Vanea responds with his thumbs-up. Piotr wags his wings again and rolls inverted and dives down, continuing his flight plan. Vanea flicks the autopilot on and lets the Mig stabilize.

"1 1 0, Ground Control, what's your fuel?" Sochi Ground Control asks on the radio.

"Ground Control, 1 1 0 fuel is 1500 liters," Vane replies.

"1 1 0, continue to Sochi, RSBN 6, maintain 10.000 meters, stand by for additional tasking."

"1 1 0 received. Continue to Sochi at 10.000 meters, ready for additional tasking." Vanea replies.

"Not a lot of tasking, I hope, I don't have enough fuel for too much playing around." Vanea sets up his radio guidance, with the RSBN showing him the direction to Sochi, and steers the plane to match the heading for the return home, settling into his flight. He reduces the speed slightly, setting up his engine for maximum endurance. The distance marker is ticking away, getting closer and closer, now 30 kilometers. When the radio crackles again.

"1 1 0, Ground Control, fuel state?"

"1 1 0 is at 1.200 liters," Vanea replies.

"1 1 0 I have tasking for you!"

"1 1 0 receiving!"

"I have a target, low altitude. Turn left 0 9 0! Descend and maintain 200 meters. This will be a visual intercept, no radar!"

"1 1 0 received! Executing!" Vanea flicks the Mig upside down, curving down on a steep dive, turning East towards the sea, diving almost vertically towards his target, easing the dive as he passes through 5000 meters.

"The folks on the ground will have a good show today." Vanea thinks as he watches his speed, not wanting to break the sound barrier over the villages below him. Easing down more, under 1000 meters, skimming the ground now, going fast, 900 km/h, adjusting his radar altimeter to warn him at 150 meters, easing down more, hearing the beep of the radar altimeter, then easing up a bit at 200 meters above the ground. *"All I need now is a bird strike to ruin my day,"* Vanea thinks as he keeps pressing on.

"Ground Control, 1 1 0, request guidance to target!" Vanea asks Sochi Control where the target is, not energizing his radar.

"1 1 0, target is 0 7 0, 7 kilometers, 4000 meters, target is moving left to right, perpendicular to your direction."

Vanea continues scanning the sky ahead for the target indicated by the Sochi Ground and responds to the Sochi Ground.

"1 1 0 received! Intercepting!"

Vanea keeps scanning the sky, difficult to spot now with a front of white cumulus clouds over the sea at 2000 meters. Suddenly, he sees a dark spot moving between two clouds right at his 11 o'clock. 5 or 6 kilometers away.

"Ground control! Contact! 11 o'clock, 5 kilometers, 4000 meters!" Vanea announces on the radio.

"Confirm! Identify target!" Sochi Control barks the order at him.

"1 1 0 received! Identifying!" Vanea replies, glancing at his fuel, still plenty, pushing the throttle into the afterburner, and curving the plane up in a turn to approach the plane passing in front of him. Looking at the plane in front of him, with its stubby nose and skinny wings, swung open. *Ha! That's a Su-17 from Gudauta!* Vanea grins, closing fast on the plane and lining up for what would be a perfect gun shot. No radar, the plane in front of him was utterly unaware that a fighter lurked behind it.

"Ground Control, 1 1 0. I have a Su-17, no ordinance, I have a gun solution!" Vanea says on the radio.

"1 1 0, good intercept. Good job, that was quick! Break and return to Sochi. That was textbook. The 17 did not know you were there."

Vanea grins under his oxygen mask. "Ground Control, 1 1 0 returns to base. Thanks, don't tell them I was there. I want to send them the picture. I got their tail number on my gun camera."

"Ground control received. You are clear to switch the radio to the Sochi tower. Nice working with you 1 1 0."

"1 1 0 switching to Sochi Tower. Nice working with you, Sochi Control! See you at the debrief!"

Vanea and his Mig are now settled on their approach to Sochi, with gear down, flaps down, and 400 km/h needles aligned on his ILS.

"Tower, 1 1 0 on final, gear down and locked," Vanea announces his landing.

"Clear to land 1 1 0, wind 083 at 4 m/s, number one for landing!" the tower replies.

Vanea descends on the landing approach, conducting his final checks in the cockpit, including gear, flaps, SPS blower, and brake parachute. He eases down his Mig, slowing down further as he reaches the runway outer marker, the familiar buzz of the marker on his headset. Slowing to 370 now, easing down, always hard to gently land a 10-ton airplane at 360 km/h, holding the plane there as he passes the runway threshold, a few meters left now, holding the nose up, bleeding all the speed and the lift left on his swept delta wings. Touching the airbrakes and extending them as the Mig touches the ground, the all familiar squeal of tires hitting the tarmac as the Mig settles on the runway, slowing down now, Vanea mashes the parachute button and he is greeted with the familiar jolt as the drag parachute extends and slows him down more, holding the nose up more, then easing the front wheel down, braking now, flaps up, speed brakes up, looking at the soldiers on the side of the runway that will retrieve the drag chute.

"1 1 0 drop your chute, turn left on the taxiway," the tower gives him the order to vacate the runway.

"Received, parachute and left on the taxiway." Vanea flicks the parachute safety button, then presses it, glancing in his mirror to see the parachute drifting away, pressing the brake lever and turning into the taxiway, seeing in the distance his parking spot, the Crew Chief, ready for him, waving at him, already directing him into his parking spot. Vanea taxis on the tarmac, turning sharply on the parking spot where the Crew Chief is waiting for him, chocks ready in his hands. Vanea holds the brakes as he pulls the throttle back, stopping the engine. He hears the sound of his Tumansky engine slowing down, ticking away as it turns slower, coming to a stop. Vanea turns off the plane, his hands dancing over the contacts and switches, unlocking the canopy and opening it, as the Crew Chief already puts the ladder on the aircraft.

"How was it, Major?" Asks the Crew Chief.

Vanea removes his mask and grins at him.

"Senior Sergeant, it was perfect! It was a perfect day to fly, with a good intercept, and the plane worked as expected. Nothing to report. Thanks for giving me a good bird."

The Crew Chief smiles and glances at the telltale needle on the accelerometer. "You pulled 6 G's on it?"

"Yeah, up high, couldn't pull more at that altitude." Vanea smiles.

"Don't worry, I took good care of your plane". Vanea slaps the side of the Mig, now free of his straps and connections. Coming down the small ladder, getting the maintenance logbook, and signing the plane back to the Crew Chief.

"Thanks a lot. Time for debrief now." Vanea shakes the hand of the Crew Chief, takes his helmet off, and ruffles his hair, sweaty and pressed against his head from the helmet. Spreading his arms wide and taking a deep breath while looking up at the blue sky. Smiling as he thinks. *It's never enough. The moment you come down on the ground, you want to go back there. It's never enough.* Climbing into the UAZ.

"Let's go to the Squadron building, time for debrief."

3

Chapter 3: Tanya's tea

Krasnodar, Krasnodar Krai, USSR
May 27th, 1978

Tanya, an 18-year-old girl, yells from the shower.

"Daaaad, what's colder than cold water in the Soviet Union?"

Tanya's dad bursts out in laughter and yells back. "Hot water?"

Tanya's mom, a plump, short woman in her late 40s, comes quickly into the living room.

"You two will get in trouble, and all the neighbors will hear you. And that's not something we should be yelling about."

Tanya yells back. "What if it's true, Mom?"

Tanya's mom goes to the bathroom door and talks to Tanya. "Tanushka, darling, you are going to catch a cold. Do you need another towel? I'll go and turn on the stove, I'll warm up the kitchen, and you can dry your hair there. Just don't catch a cold now, in the middle of May, I know you will get out with your hair wet and will come back all snotty and coughing."

Tanya replies, "Thank you, Mom, I'll be alright. I have two

robes here, I'll bundle up. I swear the water was warm, and then it sputtered once and just turned freezing cold."

Tanya steps out of the bathroom, bundled up in two bath robes, vigorously towel-drying her hair. "Ohh, Tanushka, poor thing, you are shivering."

Her mom comes closer and rubs her back. "You know how the pipes and the central heating are in this building, I could've had some warm water for you, go in the kitchen, the stove is on, it will warm up quick."

Tanya replies, "I'm fine, Mom, I'm fine now, I just got cold there, but I had to rinse the shampoo."

Tanya emerges from her bedroom half an hour later, dressed in a summer dress, her curly blonde hair falling to her shoulders. Tanya is a tall, willowy girl. Her years of running track in school are evident in her posture. Her dad looks over his glasses and grumbles.

"Shouldn't you be studying? You hate working at the textile plant, and it's bad for your health, and you had the grades for the University."

Tanya rolls her eyes like every young girl when her dad is telling her about studies, sitting next to him on the sofa. "Dad, I'm beat, that's all I ever do, I go to the factory in the morning, you know I pick the morning shift, and then I come home and grind my nose in all the textbooks. You know I wanted a few years of work to see how it is, and to help you out a bit, you, Mom, Grandma, and Grandpa."

Tanya's dad sighs, "Tanya, you know we don't need anything, and all you give us, I'm saving it for what you will need in the future. You may want an apartment, a car maybe, when you have a husband."

Tanya laughs, "There are no husbands in the textbooks dad,

and I know you could use some money now, finish the roof on Grandpa's house, we haven't been on a vacation for the past 3 years, since you start to work on your weekends on that house, you could finish it early, maybe I'll move to the countryside and become a peasant girl. But dad, tonight I want to go out, Mischa's having a tea with some other friends, and every once in a while, I need to get my nose out of those books."

Tanya's dad smiles, "Tanushka, you have the hands of a piano player, not a peasant girl. The last time you had dirt under your nails and liked it, you were 9 years old. But you're right, go out and have some fun, just be careful and don't be late. And I will never want you to think that we need your help."

"You don't. I want to do it, and I want to feel what it is like to earn something before returning to studies. Don't worry, you will be the proud father of an engineer in a few years."

Tanya's mom joins in the conversation from the kitchen. "I could be the proud mother of a doctor!"

"Mom, you know I faint when I see a drop of blood. What a good doctor I would be, maybe a proctologist," Tanya replies.

"Young lady! That is not funny! And you have no idea how much you would faint if you were to become one. And what kind of tea is that, and who else is coming, and what are you youngsters doing there, are the parents home?"

Tanya smiles and answers, "There is tea, I'm sure of it."

"And what else?" Her mom keeps drilling her with questions.

"There's wine and vodka and there's juice too, Mom, you know how it is. You know I rarely drink. I need to listen to some music and talk to some people my age."

Her dad joins in. "What music are you kids listening to, all that Western rock and roll?"

Tanya nods, "All kinds, Dad, some it's good, some it's not so much, there's this band they all sound like girls, Bee Gees they are called, the girls like them, but they sing so high they sound like girls."

Tanya's dad snorts in laughter, "Westerners, no wonder."

Tanya smiles, "It's not like that, it's just music, and they must be good, but there's ABBA and the Beatles and the ones I like, Led Zeppelin."

"I like ABBA," Dad replies.

"No, you like the blonde singer, not their music."

"Noooo, the brunette, she's a good singer." Tanya's dad winks at her as he hears his wife from the kitchen.

"Nikolay! Maybe she can cook your favorite piroshki! And I'll go sing."

Dad replies. "I wouldn't change you for 10 ABBA's, my sweet piroshki. And Tanya, anything else you and your friends are doing when you have your tea?"

"Not much, Dad, sometimes we dance, sometimes we play cards, sometimes we listen to the radio."

Nikolay lifts an eyebrow. "What radio station?"

Tanya glances sideways, "You know, the one you listen to sometimes, Radio Free Europe, but we do it quietly, and we all gather round and listen to it. They have good music sometimes."

"You don't do it for the music, though, you and your friends are too young for that, why do you care?"

Tanya draws herself straight. "But how could we not, Dad? It's us, we must know, the young ones who could still change something. How come, in here, where we have gas, coal, and oil, there is no hot water? How come we have all the farms and record production every year, and there are empty shelves in the store and barely any food? How come you are still waiting to get your car, but there at the Party headquarters, everyone has two?"

Nikolay shushes her. "Tanya, careful, with that radio, it takes one person, and all of you could end up in jail or worse in Siberia, counting trees, be careful, as to all that, I don't know, but life is hard, and always has been, and some people are luckier than others."

"Yes, Dad, but just because things are always like this, it doesn't mean they have to be. That's why it's up to us, the young ones, that maybe one day we could do more and change it for the better, for us and you and for the ones that will come after us."

Nikolay draws himself straight on the couch, "And how will you change all that? How would you fix it?"

Tanya sighs, "I don't know yet, but that's why I'm going to the University, and I'll become an engineer, and I will design a boiler that will give perpetual hot water to the whole Soviet Union, so hot that we will melt Siberia and revive the Mammoths, I'll have two as pets, the woolliest and the most stinky of them."

Tanya throws her arms around her father's neck and kisses him on the cheeks. "But until then, I'll go with my friends, I'll be careful and not do anything stupid, I promise."

Nikolay smiles. "Go, go, my idealistic daughter, we'll talk about your boiling Mammoths later."

Tanya hugs and kisses her mom, "I'll be back before 10:30, don't worry."

She locks the entrance door behind her, and they can hear her footsteps down the stairs, going quickly, five stories down the stairs.

Nikolay sighs, "These kids, they are spoiled, they don't know, and they don't know how hard it was before. She's trouble, this one."

Katya comes close to her husband, "Maybe they know more than we do. Kids are different these days. I just hope she's safe."

Nikolay replies, "She will be, they are just kids, nothing will happen to them, oh, you heard? On the same radio, Brezhnev is dead or very ill. They played somber music a few days ago, but no news came out, so maybe he is sick."

Katya furrows her eyebrows. "There are other old folks there to take his place in a heartbeat, you know, what she asked there, those are good questions, but not the kind of questions you should be asking out loud."

Tanya walks home, a few hours later, walking quickly from the bus station towards the tall towers where she lives, looking down as she tries to avoid a puddle from yesterday's rain. Three men are walking towards here, dressed in the well-known Militia uniform, one man wearing an officer's hat, and the other two regular conscripts.

"Good evening, Miss. Identification, please! Isn't it late for a young lady like you to walk home?"

Tanya fumbles in her bag for her identification papers, looking up at the Militia officer questioning her.

"It is not late, it's just the right time to walk, and how do you know where I am going?"

The officer smiles. "You live right around the corner in that building, Tanya Ivanisevic, isn't it so?" The officer takes her ID card and looks at it. "See, I was right, you live right there, and now that we clarified that, may I ask where you are coming from?"

Tanya draws herself up and looks the officer in the eyes. "I was visiting some friends, and we got together for some tea, you know how it is, a lot of girls gossiping and having fun. Is there a problem with that?"

The officer continues to smile and returns her identification papers. "No, Miss, there is no problem, just that you have to be careful what you are gossiping about."

Tanya tries to smile. "It's just girl talk, dresses, boys, and such, what girls usually talk about."

The officer moves sideways and gestures for her to continue her way. "Thank you for your cooperation, Miss. Have a safe walk home."

Tanya starts walking and then turns her head towards the officer. "Thank you, why would I not be safe? In the end, you are here and identifying everyone?"

The officer smiles again, a weird, creepy smile. "No, not everyone, just the ones that matter and the pretty ones. Good night, Miss."

Tanya steps into her building's hallway, closing the heavy metal door behind her, and presses her back against it, taking a few deep breaths. Her hands tremble, and her chin quivers, as she is stressed after the encounter with the Militia officer. She talks to herself. *That was KGB, and not Militia, oh Tanya, why are you so weak and give in to fear? Even if you didn't do anything wrong, you are scared of them, such a weak girl you are.* Tanya exhales deeply, drawing herself up, and shakes her blond curls. She takes a few deep breaths and goes up the stairs, climbing quickly to the 5th floor, and opens the door to her apartment.

"Mom, Dad, I'm home!"

Tanya's mom comes and hugs her, "How was it, Tanushka?"

Tanya hugs her back, "It was good, Mom, we talked, danced a bit, had some tea and some wine. Nothing special, just when I came home, there were some creepy Militias that ID me. They always give me the creeps."

Her Mom rubs her shoulders. "They creep out to everyone, that's their job. Think nothing of it. Dad is sleeping already. Are you hungry?"

"No, Mom, thank you, I'll go to bed, I have to go to work in the morning. Good night."

Her Mom looks into her eyes and hugs her again. "Sleep well, sweetheart."

4

Chapter 4: A day at Tyndall AFB

Panama City, Florida, USA
May 27th, 1978

James is driving down the 98 highway, heading south towards Tyndall Air Force Base, in his Chevy Laguna, the Laguna purring at 70 miles per hour. Diane, his wife, sits in the right seat, shifts slightly, and says.

"Darling, isn't it a bit too fast? We're nearly there, and do you want to meet the cops in Panama City already?"

James puts his hand on her knee, "Honey, they don't put cops on the bridge. It's hard to stop someone on the bridge, and you block the traffic. You should be able to spot the base from here, isn't it?"

Diane looks towards the base, "No, they have trees, all I see is one of those big round things."

James replies, "That's a radome, to protect a radar antenna from all the rain and wind around here."

Diane smiles, "Look at you, talking like you are a pilot, you know, I can already see that you are changing your color, you were turning gray in that five-sided gray building."

James grins, "Well, flying a desk for the past 4 years will do that to you. Gosh, I was dreading it in there, and all the brass, all the time, me, a poor Major saluting all the time. I was dying inside."

Diane gets his hand from her knee and squeezes it. "I know, but it's what you have to do, a future Colonel has a better chance to go all the way through the ranks with a stint in the Pentagon. And now, you will go to fly again, and I'll be the one dying inside every time you get diverted somewhere, or there's bad weather. Unless you don't want to salute anymore and go to airlines, you know it's a good option."

James smiles, "Yeah, five blokes in the cabin, trying to make a fat pig to fly, while 300 folks in the back are drinking and snoring away."

Diane frowns a bit, "Can't have it all, darling, I know what I signed up for, I know how worried I was with your two tours in Vietnam, and with all the Thuds that went down, and with all the friends that we lost. I know how down and gloomy you get when you are not at Mach 2 with kicking the fire and lighting the tires. But I hope you know that there's one more soul there that goes through things as well."

James smiles and squeezes her hand in return while navigating the highway exit, slowing down and downshifting while still holding Diane's hand in his.

"It's kicking the tires and lighting the fires, and it is rarely Mach 2, although Mach 2 is fun, nothing as crazy as you may think, but it's fun. Also, I was thinking, why just one soul? Why not make it two souls?"

Diane's eyes widen, her beautiful brown eyes drilling into

James's face, taking in his profile as she tries to understand more, unable to see his eyes through the dark sunglasses.

"What do you mean?" Says Diane.

She bit her lower lip and pursed her lips, her chin quivering, understanding what he was trying to say.

"James Boyd, are you saying what I think you are saying?"

James grins big, "Diane, love, I've been through two tours in Vietnam, right after we got married, Washington was a drag, and it wasn't a place to raise a kid there, but here, now, this should be a good one, and I know you want it, and I don't know how good I will be with kids, but I think it's maybe the time to think about it. I know I like the technological process of making them."

Diane smiles while trying to hold down her tears, putting her head on James's shoulder while running her right hand over his chest.

"James, you naughty man, you'd better stop with all that technological process. I think you will make a wonderful father, and you are right, my parents are close too, from Tallahassee to here, it's quite close, we'll have some help."

"Don't plan the nursery room just yet, love, we still have a bit to sort through."

Diane laughs, "Nursery room, I even picked the college in the last 20 seconds."

James smiles again, "At least someone's organized, let's see when the U-Haul will come here from Washington, what we will find, and how quickly we will find our stuff."

Diane pats James's chest, "Like that's ever been your problem. You will go there on your squadron, brief, fly, and hang out with the guys, and you will shoot your watches while sitting at the bar, and I'll be the one unpacking boxes and such. You guys always do that, and the girls come and help."

"Well, I'll try to help, but you know how it is, you are my wife, the Air Force is the mistress."

As they drive parallel to Tyndall Air Force Base, James points at the flight line. "Look, that's what we're flying. The F-5E."

Diane lifts her head, trying to get a better view of the flight line. "They are small, they look a bit like the ones you used to fly in training."

James nods. "Yes, the T-38 and the F-5 are brothers, sort of. This one is the newer variant."

"It's a small airplane, not like the Thud or the Phantom. You don't even need a ladder to climb on this one."

"Yes, you do," James replies. "It's a smaller aircraft, nimbler, but it's fast and can pack a good punch."

Diane nods, "And this squadron, what's the mission, because you told me that the air force is working on some newer planes, the 14, 15, and 16?"

"426th Tactical Fighter Squadron will work mostly as a training squadron for all the countries that will buy the F-5, this is a cheaper plane, so there are the Swiss, Canadians, Austrians, Iranians, that will come here and train with us and get certified and learn from us, we work with them and we train them, also, we can be used as an Aggressor squadron."

"What's that?" Asks Diane.

"Both the Navy and the Air Force want the crews to train against other aircraft. Remember, in Vietnam, we had no idea how to fight against MiG-17s and 21s or against their tactics. Now, as Aggressors, we will study those tactics and act like bad guys, so from time to time, I'm going to kick some guys down. That's why the 426th is made up mostly of veterans with one or two tours, men who have been there and done that. We'll make everyone smart against the enemy."

Diane smiles again, "I like that, you get to be the meanie, and you will not get deployed in hot areas."

"You know how it is, darling, they may send us over to these countries that are buying them to help them set up and train, but no, the squadron should stay here and not be deployed in combat."

James pulls in front of the barrier at the main entrance of Tyndall Air Force Base, and the guard comes closer and gives a smart salute, asking for papers. James reaches into his glove box and pulls out his papers. Years of service had him well-organized, with orders and his USAF ID card. The guard salutes again and waves to the guard shack to raise the barrier.

"Welcome to Tyndall, sir! Drive that way, and the billeting officer's office is right there on the left, park right in front of it, and he will sort you out."

James nods, "Thanks a lot, it's good to be here."

James and the MP guard both look up as a flight of three UH-1 Hueys, followed by two big Chinook helicopters, thunder over the base, flying fast, turning North, and going away.

The MP looks down, "I heard that one way too many times in the jungle."

"Me too," James replied. "One of the best sounds ever."

The MP looks at him curiously, "In the jungle, sir?"

James nods and puts his hands together like pulling an ejection handle from between his legs.

"Yeah, I had to get out of a Thud fast, and I was in the bush for two days before they picked me up in Laos."

The MP salutes again. "I'm glad you made it, Major. Please drive through."

"Thanks again," says James as he puts the Laguna in first gear and gets going through the barrier.

James holds the door open for Diane as they get out of the billet office, almost an hour after they got there, James holding a big welcome package folder with everything they need to know for the next few days, and all the rest of the forms and paperwork that they will have to fill in.

A voice yells from a few feet away. "Badger! Hey Jimbo, you guys made it. How are you doing, mate?"

Diane and James climb down the three steps in front of the billet office, and James walks towards his fellow pilot. Ronald "Banjo" Davies, a former squadron mate from his first tour in Vietnam.

James pumps his hand and then gives him a quick hug. "Hey, Banjo, it's good to see you. How are you doing?"

Ronald turns towards Diane, shakes her hand, and then hugs her. "Nice to meet you, Diane. I'm Banjo, Ronald Banjo. I heard a lot about you."

Diane smiles and replies. "Good to meet you, too, Banjo. I heard about you a lot. You guys have been through a lot."

Banjo laughs, "I'm sure half of it is not true, and the other half I don't remember, or we should not talk about it."

James pats Ronald on the back, "How's the O-Club here?"

"It's nice, the Heritage club, it's quite nice," Ronald replies. "I tell you what, let us go and see our place and sort out a few things, freshen up, and we'll meet at the O-Club later and have a cold one,"

James tells his old buddy. "You guys are going to live right across the road from us, and Jayne, my wife, knows you are coming and she's waiting for you. She heard the stories as well.

She'll help you out. We're a tight unit here, and we're taking care of each other. Go and sort things out, and we'll see you all later, and you get to meet the folks too."

Ronald shakes James's hand again and goes towards one of the hangars. Diane takes James's arm and pulls him closer. "You know, I think I like it here, I'm just curious about those things we should forget about, you don't have any of those stories, James, do you?"

James opens the Laguna door for Diane to get in the car, "Stories, I forgot about any stories, darling."

Diane laughs, "You are a very smart man."

A few hours later, Diane and James step inside the O-Club. Ronald turns around and sees them. He clinks the bottle of beer in his hand with a fork to make everyone quiet down.

"Everybody! Here comes the Boyds. James Badger and his lovely wife Diane."

The crowd cheers as Diane and James step in, making their way towards the bar. James shakes hands along the way, introducing Diane to everyone. Some new faces, some old pals, and some foreigners too. James spots a Swiss uniform shaking his hand.

Diane leans over to him, "I will not remember a single name."

James whispers in her ear, "It makes two of us. I know you are tired, we'll not stay long."

"No, I'm not, people are warm here, I love it. And I can see the light in your eyes, you go and meet all the guys and shoot your watches."

James wraps his arm around her waist as they navigate between two tables. "There will be time for tall stories soon, no worries."

James finally gets to the bar where Ronald waits with his wife, Jayne.

"You guys made it. How do you like it so far?" asks Ronald.

"It's good, it's a tight group here, and the club is nice."

James turns towards Diane, "Anything from the bar, dear?"

Diane thinks for a few seconds. "I'll have a Shirley Temple, but we should find a table."

Jayne takes Diane's hand. "I got you, girl, we have one here. Let the guys do their thing, you know how they are."

James looks at Diane and Jayne as they fade away in the crowd and turns to the bartender, "Two Shirley Temples for the ladies over there, and two, errrhmmm, and two Wild Turkey shots."

"Coming right up," says the bartender. James pushes one of the glasses to Ronald and takes the other one.

Ronald lifts his glass and clinks it on James's, "Nice to have you here, and it's good to see you."

James lifts his glass. "It's sure damn nice to see you too," he drinks the shot in one and holds the glass in the air, looking around, and sees at the end of the bar a small table with a white cloth and a lit candle burning on it. He and Ronald go to the small table and tap their glasses on it, saying almost in unison.

"And to the ones that should be here, but they are not." Their ritual at the Missing Man Table.

James and Ronald go back to the bar, and James asks. "Okay, so tell me everything. How's the flying here? Who do we share the base with?"

Ronald responds, "It's just us here and 7th Cav, they still fly the old Huey and Little Birds and Chinooks, still low and still pretty much crazy, they have some old heads in there, but most of the guys just caught the tail end of it, with Saigon and all that. But here, it's us, and we have plenty of birds. It's not just us. It's the guys we train, too. They are not NFGs. The guys we train have good hours on other planes, so they are mostly good folks, just the culture is different, but you will learn soon enough."

James nods. "That's nice, so we don't babysit them a lot."

Ronald shakes his head, "We do, but we work tactics with them, formation, we spend time on the range a lot, and from time to time we go to the desert to Nellis to play the bad guys."

James lifts his eyebrows. "How is that?"

Ronald beams, "Oh man, you're gonna love it. You have your clearance, right?"

James nods. "Yeah, I have all the paperwork done and everything."

Ronald continues, "There are some nice toys in the range at Nellis, we have some SA-2's and SA-3's, so during the big Red Flag exercises, we go full on, with SAM sites, and Soviet tactics, we fly low, we get GCI, intercepts and such and we get to thump a lot of new pilots and fight with a lot of planes, even the new ones they are testing now. It's quite cool and we come on top most of the time."

James grins. "That is cool! How's the Colonel?"

Ronald pauses a bit and thinks. "He's alright, flies a lot, and I like that about him, but he's salty, you're gonna get chewed on your first day. Everyone does. I guess he's a bit salty because he knows we're never going to be deployed."

James thinks for a second. "You are right, we're the fighter squadron that doesn't get to fight for real, man, we're getting old, we're dinosaurs."

Ronald laughs, "That's a bunch of bull. There are four squadrons like ours, three here in the US. We and the other squadrons are probably the best pilots in the whole Air Force. Perhaps the guys at Nellis have more training, and the Navy is doing the training at Top Gun. If it were up to me, and it hits the fan again, we could go in a few days, and we would do a better job than anyone else."

James listens carefully. "It's not like anything is brewing anywhere." Says James.

"There's always something brewing. I heard that some honcho in Russia is dead or dying."

James replies. "But there, they have other Honchos lined up, one after the other, no?"

Ronald laughs, "They don't tell me, buddy, they don't tell me. Let's go back to the ladies. You look dead tired. What time do you meet the colonel tomorrow?"

James sighs, "Zero seven hundred hours, and yes, I'm tired. Let's have some dinner, and I'll go crash."

Tyndall AFB, Florida, USA
May 28th, 1978

Major James "Badger" Boyd raps his fingers on the Colonel's door and hears the "Enter" from the other side. He steps into the office and throws a smart salute.

"Good morning, Sir, Major Boyd reporting for duty!"

The Colonel salutes back and glances at him. "At ease, Major, welcome to the 426th squadron. I've reviewed your file, and you've done well so far. You'll continue to do well here. Just keep everyone safe around you. The folks you are training are good, but they don't have your experience. Also, there is a cultural shift around here, but you will learn from the rest of the guys."

James nods. "Understood, Sir."

The Colonel taps his fingers on the table and looks at James again. "Also, I understand this is your first day here. But find your iron quick, on the flight line, we are in flight suits, but when you are in your uniform. I want it spotless and not a single crease on it. On your way out, ask my assistant where the nearest barber is and get your haircut accordingly. Dismissed!"

James salutes again and walks out, doing that awkward walk so you don't turn your back to your superior. He gets out of the office and finds his way to the fitting office to get his flight suit in order.

Ronald intercepts him as he is walking by. "You got chewed?"

James smiles, "Yeah, I did, my uniform is not right, and my hair is long, like I'm a hippy or something."

Ronald laughs, "It's part of the welcome package." I'll show you around. I'm on the schedule today, and tomorrow I'll give you a check ride, then you'll go to work. When was the last time you were up?"

James keeps walking next to his friend. "Last week, I got checked in the F-5 and I got a few hours in it."

Ronald nods, "You'll get proficient quickly."

James nods. "Can't wait to get back up in the air."

5

Chapter 5: Amir's training flight

Tyndall AFB, Florida, USA
June 5th, 1978

James is going through his kneeboards and flight plan, working through the briefing of his training mission with Amir Ghasemi.

"Alright, Amir, this will be a sortie with you and me, a two-ship element. You've been in the range before. It's a bit of a trek from here to Avon, but we have plenty of fuel, and our divert will be there at Avon."

Amir nods.

"You have our flight plan and our frequencies. Any questions?"

Amir responds. "No, Sir, it's all clear."

"Come on, don't Sir me anymore," James replies. "We will be carrying two training bombs on our inner pylons and two rocket pods with inert loads. We still have to go through all our arming and preparation before our runs. We'll do four runs in range. First, once we are clear in range, we will bomb as an element. Trail formation. I'll lead the first run, then you will lead the second, and then we'll switch to rockets and repeat the process. I'll lead the first run, then you will lead the second. Separation and the way you come down the *chute* in your bombing run are crucial. Don't come too close to me, and if you hear Knock it off on the radio, you disengage, and you go level and turn left. I'll rejoin with you. Any questions?"

Amir shakes his head. James continues his briefing,

"What's the mils and speed, and dive angle we recommend for a rocket pass?"

Amir thinks for a second. "11 mils, 400 kts, 1500 ft release."

James looks down and thinks for a moment, "*Remember the cultural thing, you can't tell him he is wrong, he'll get all worked up, especially here with his mates, and it will be on his head the whole flight.*"

James lifts his head. "That will work, but I would say we go with 14 mils, you know, if you stay with 11, you will have to press at a lower altitude or come down at a higher dive angle, and you may end up hitting the ground. Put it there on your kneeboard and go with 14 this time, okay?"

Amir nods and scribbles on his kneeboard. "Thanks, I'll do that."

James smiles, "All will go well, and you will be flight lead."

Amir beams and smiles. James continues,

"Alright, we have 1 hour and a half until takeoff time. Let's get going."

James's flight, callsign Tiger, is approaching the Avon Firing Range.

"Tiger flight check!"

Amir responds. "1-2 check,"

James continues, "Avon, Tiger 1-1 with 1-2 with you."

Avon responds, "Identified Tiger flight. Continue to IP"

James confirms, "Roger, continue to IP. 1-2 come closer," James instructs Amir to close his formation.

A few minutes later, Avon comes on the radio, "Tiger flight, you are clear in range, target is marked with red smoke at your 11 o'clock, bomb run, clear in hot!"

James responds sharply. "Clear in hot Tiger flight. 1-2 trail formation!"

Amir responds, "Trail formation Tiger 1-2"

James cranks his head, watching Amir getting in formation behind him, and getting enough separation, he monitors the target range, red smoke bellowing from the edge of the circular marked target, he lets the target pass on his left, right when it lines up with his canopy bow, double checking the armament switches in the cabin, adding a dash of burner to help him in the turn and roll the airplane left, pulling over the horizon, and diving towards the target, the same way he did it so many times in training and over Vietnam, lining up his sight on the target, looking at the smoke for wind direction and adjusting a bit to the right, flicking the Master arm switch.

"Tiger 1-1! In! Hot!"

Avon replies, "Clear in hot!"

A few seconds later, Amir's voice comes on the radio. "1-2 clear in hot!"

"Clear in hot!"

James comes down the chute, altitude going down quickly, passing through 4000 ft, down even more, adjusting his sight over the target, holding it steady now, 2000 ft, he mashes the release button and hears the clinking sound of the bomb being released, pulling out of the dive, nose on the horizon and pulling left in a tight turn, looking over the shoulder to see the effect of his bombs, the white puff of smoke from the training bomb inside the bullseye of the target, he spots the other plane pulling out of his dive, a little lower that briefed, the bombs scoring wide of the target.

"Tiger flight is clear of range," James says on the radio.

"Tiger flight, BDA, Tiger 1-1, 25 meters south, that's a bullseye. Sierra Hotel! Tiger 1-2 150 meters North of target."

James replies, "Roger Avon, 1-2, you have visual with me?"

Amir responds, "1-2 visual."

James continues, "Form up on me, we will continue to IP, 1-2, make sure you don't bust through the briefed hard deck. Make sure you account for the wind direction on the next run."

Amir clicks his microphone twice, confirming. As they rejoin and continue to set up for the next run, James comes on the radio, "1-2 take lead, I'll follow you. Avon, Tiger 1-2 has the lead."

Avon replies, "Roger, Tiger 1-2, target is at your 11 o'clock. Wind is 280 for 4 QNH 1015, clear in hot!"

Amir replies, "Roger, clear in hot! 1-1 trail formation!"

James clicks his microphone 2 times, setting up in trail formation behind Amir's plane, watching his attack run, seeing that Amir is losing a lot of speed pulling into the target, coming down a bit too shallow, and adjusting his run so he doesn't get too close, he mutters to himself, *Come on Amir, come on, work it out.* Watching as Amir corrects his dive and gets back down the chute. *That's it, that's better!*

Hearing Amir on the radio. "1-2 in hot!"

Hearing Avon replying, then checking in hot as well. Watching Amir's training bomb separating from the plane, and working his target, dropping his bomb, pulling level and over the horizon, starting to join with Amir's plane as he waits for the BDA report,

"Tiger 1-2 BDA bombs North 50 meters, that's a bullseye Sierra Hotel! Tiger 1-1 30 meters South!"

James joins in. "Sierra Hotel 1-2! Sierra Hotel!"

Knowing well that Amir will understand that Sierra Hotel means "Shit hot" in the USAF, and can't get a better praise than that!

Amir and James are back in the briefing room after their flight. The bomb and rocket passes were completed, making for an overall successful flight, although there was a slight challenge at the end. They almost got diverted due to an incoming storm, but in the end, all was well, and they landed safely.

"What do you think, Amir? How would you evaluate this flight?"

Amir thinks for a few seconds and goes through his notes. "I think it went well, Major Boyd. We hit the targets with bombs and rockets as we were briefed and ordered."

James takes a deep breath, "Indeed, we did, but Captain Ghasemi, if you drop a 500-pound bomb 600 feet from the target, the only damage that you will do is to give them a mild scare. In the books, it is a hit. However, in reality, that was not so good."

Amir looks into James's eyes. "It is difficult to judge all the variables and drop consistently."

James smiles, realizing that he finally gets to Amir, "Yes, it is, and I have to tell you a secret, we use a method, it's called TLAR."

James smiles again when Amir looks at him inquisitively. "That's not in the manuals."

James responds, "No, it is not, it means That Looks About Right. You come on these bomb runs trying to stick to the manuals, but you have to play with all these variables, the wind blows from the left, then you aim a bit on the right, you know that"

Amir nods. James continues, "You are too slow in the chute, the bomb will drop short, so aim a bit further, if you are a bit faster, aim a bit shorter, the same goes with the altitude, and you have to figure it out when That Looks About Right, TLAR."

Amir thinks about his flight, and James can see that he is reliving the flight in his head.

"But Amir, listen to me, you are a good pilot, but you have to be critical of yourself. Going about it that we hit the target and follow the orders won't take you there. Each flight, you must go and look hard at all your mistakes and at the ones you fly with, and do you know why?"

Amir looks down, "No, I don't know why."

James continues, "How are things back home in your country?"

Amir responds with a surprised look on his face, not sure where the conversation will lead. "They are good, but just like anywhere, there is unrest. Not all the people are happy with how the Shah is running the country."

James nods, "So I've heard, so there could be unrest, revolution, even war maybe, there's always a war somewhere."

"There could be, indeed, there could be a war with Iraq," Amir replies.

James gets closer to Amir, "So if you are not critical now, and you don't train right and you don't face where you are and how to get a little bit better all the time. When that time comes and you don't hit that target right, and you don't take care of your squadron mates, and you don't challenge them to get better. Then, when you write that letter to their wives or mothers, when you lose a squadron mate, would you say that? Would you say that you did not do your best? Would you say to that mother that you could have pushed her son to be better? But you didn't?! That's why we do it this way. We all make mistakes, and we will continue to do them, and we're not perfect, but that makes us get better, each flight a bit better than the earlier one."

James clasps Amir's shoulder, "Come on, Captain Ghasemi, you are a flight lead now, how will you lead your flight?"

Amir lifts his head and looks at James. "I'll lead them right, and if I have to write that letter, I hope I will be able to say that I led them right, God willing."

James smiles, "Inshallah, Amir, Inshallah, let's go get some food."

They stepped out of the briefing room. Two sweaty, tired pilots walking side by side, step for step.

Neither spoke.

Each was lost in the words just said. Amir thought of the letter he might one day have to write, and whether he'd be able to live with the truth inside it.

James thought of the letters he had written, and whether, looking back, there was anything more he could have done.

6

Chapter 6: Andrei's dilemma

MOSCOW, USSR
June 5th, 1978

Andrei Kirilenko sits at his usual spot around the presidium table in the big room in the Kremlin palace. Looking towards the head of the table, where Andropov is arranging his papers, holding them in his hand and tapping the edge of the stack on the table to get them all straight. Viktor Cebrikov, a new face in the room, the former Deputy Chairman, has now been appointed Chairman of the KGB. Andropov takes a quick look at his wristwatch, then up at the clock on the wall, clearing his throat with a cough, bringing the room to attention.

"Comrades, it is time to start our meeting. First, you are all aware of the state of Leonid Brezhnev. Unfortunately, Leonid, although stable for now, will not be able to recover and continue to be a strong leader for our party and the Soviet Union. It is noted now that the leadership of the party will continue in this format, and the *Politburo* will remain in this state until the next congress in 1981. Until then, comrades, we have work to do, and I must say, with great concern, that we are behind schedule on our 5-year plan. This will be further reviewed in the weeks to come. However, I want all of us to look back at all our republics, from the Pacific to the Baltic, from the Black Sea to the North Pole, and see how they collectively become stronger and better, and to build a communist society by the end of this five-year plan. Nothing is impossible if we lead the working people right!"

Applause erupts from the room, everyone knowing that they must show infinite support to the new leader of the Communist Party.

Andropov surveys the room and puts his hands up to calm the applause.

"Let's get back to our agenda, Comrades." Andropov silenced the room.

"Afghanistan, this is becoming problematic for us, with Daud dead and this revolutionary movement. We fear that the country will turn back towards a religious ruling, and with the events in Iran, we may not be able to dictate what is happening in the region. Pakistan is leaning more towards the Americans, and the same way with Iran."

Andrei Gromyko, the Minister of Foreign Affairs, speaks up. "The revolutionary movement in Afghanistan is holding strong for the moment. However, it does not seem that there will be much progress without our support, and the tribal movement in the mountains, the Mujaheddins, will cause problems. They are fanatics, and they are already calling for *jihad* against any external influence. We must face the facts, but a military intervention will be needed there. Diplomacy will not work there, and with all the influence we can muster and all the help from our colleagues in the KGB, I'm afraid we will not be able to succeed. A strong religious movement there will potentially influence the Muslim population in our neighboring provinces, Tajiks and Turkmens especially."

Andropov looks across the table towards Dimitri Ustinov, the Minister of Defence. "Comrade Ustinov, what would it take to be able to normalize the country?"

The entire presidium room smiles. They all know that the term 'normalization' was coined by Brezhnev after the military invasion of Czechoslovakia in 1968.

Ustinov responds, "To *normalize* the country, we will need three to four motor rifle divisions, plus the aviation support with helicopters and front-line bombers. We could achieve that readiness in 6 months with the right resources."

Andropov looks inquisitive at Ustinov, "Three to four motor rifle divisions, Comrade Ustinov? We're going to Afghanistan, not Berlin. I believe that three or four tanks should do it there. The Afghan army is non-existent, isn't it?"

Ustinov responds, "Comrade Andropov, the terrain is most difficult, we could start with a smaller force, however, I'm afraid that we will get bogged down in the terrain and we will suffer massive casualties for little progress, in my opinion, having a force that could press on all the passes and all the points, will not allow the Mujaheddins to react in any way, and we will continue this action quicker. Also, having that established, it will give us the option to continue, if needed, towards Iran or Pakistan."

There is silence in the room, hearing that possibility. Andropov continues, "What would be the reason for that, Comrade Ustinov?"

Andrei Kirilenko looks quickly around the room and realizes that not all the faces appear surprised. This has been discussed before.

Ustinov continues, "Comrade Andropov, with the political situation in Iran, we could control more than half of the oil reserves on the planet. The Soviet Union has an abundance of oil, but we're experiencing difficulties extracting it, and we are relying on foreign equipment for our oil fields. Having a strong presence in the Gulf will enable us to meet the world's energy requirements. This will be a good position to be in. However, this is just an option that is worth considering. We could achieve this in 8 to 9 months."

Andropov looks towards Cebrikov, the new leader of the KGB. "And how will the Secret Service support this?"

Cebrikov clears his throat. "We have certain assets in Kabul. However, in the mountains with the tribes, there's little we can do to develop, and an asset there is almost impossible. In Iran, we already have an action underway with the mullah, but the situation is highly volatile, and we cannot guarantee much support. However, intelligence and information are easier to come by from Iran, where almost everything is for sale."

Andropov shifts back towards Ustinov, "And what preparations will we need? What is the readiness?"

Ustinov shifts in his chair and looks down at some of his notes. "Our readiness level is quite high, with all the units ready to go into action at a moment's notice. However, we will need to have sufficient supplies of fuel and ammunition to sustain this kind of effort. This will go way beyond our estimates we have for training."

Andropov asks the Minister of Oil, Fedorov. "Can we sustain these requests?"

Fedorov, obviously ready for this question, answers quickly. "Yes, Comrade Andropov, we can sustain this request. Our levels are not great, with extraction being difficult due to the weather conditions in the fields of the far East, but we have sufficient reserves to sustain it. We can move oil from Ukraine and Krasnodar towards the Afghan border in time."

Kirilenko jumps into the conversation. "Comrades, those reserves in Ukraine, I have checked recently, are for agricultural use, for the farmers to be able to harvest in the summer. If we are moving these out now, how are we going to be able to put food on the table?"

Ustinov jumps in. "For the good of the Soviet Union, Comrade, we will find a way."

Kirilenko replies quickly, "It's the same for Krasnodar, you will take resources from Georgia and Ukraine, for a potential push in Afghanistan, and who knows what else? Comrades, to me, this is a big risk, and with a lot to lose, the Persian Gulf is already quite unstable as it is. Why risk it more? And how will the Americans react?"

Gromyko, the Foreign Affairs Minister, jumps in. "The Americans lost all the will to fight after Vietnam. All their military branches are demoralized and not willing to fight. By the time they pose a threat, we could achieve this."

Kirilenko slaps his hands on the table, "Comrades, we're talking about starting a new world war, when we barely have enough food to feed our people. We supply from Ukraine and the southern regions to the entire Soviet Union, but this is barely enough. We had 2 years with bad crops, we're planning to import grains from Canada, is it smart to start this adventure?"

Andropov silenced the room. "Comrades, these are all good points, and I tend to side with Andrei here. This is rushed and not wise. However, Comrade Ustinov, this plan of yours may have some benefits. I want you to work with your Deputies and the Chief of Staff to present a more elaborate plan, which will serve as an option. Comrade Cebrikov, you should find a way to create a diversion, a *maskirovka*, and maybe tie NATO, UN, and the Americans up in other problems, then this can be decided later."

The Politburo continues to work on other issues for several hours. As the meeting ends, the members start to walk out, often in pairs, talking about issues and how their staff should continue to work on various tasks. As Andrei walks out, Arvīds Pelše, the Party Control Deputy, tugs on Andrei's elbow.

"Andrei, I noticed how tired you are after this meeting. I recommend that you join me at the steam bath tomorrow morning. It is so reinvigorating, and it clears your head of all the thoughts. I will be there at 7 o'clock in the morning, before going back to Latvia. It will do you good to join me."

Andrei nods and continues walking towards the exit, aware that this is an invitation to a secret meeting, or perhaps a place where he will be instructed to step down. Andrei thinks to himself, *"If I worry about it, would it help?"* and keeps walking towards his car.

The next morning, at 6:55, Andrei steps into the steam bath, his head heavy from the previous day, from all the thoughts going through his head, and from too many glasses of vodka, but *banya* will clear all that, with its invigorating steam and heat, will clear ones head, and who knows, what other set of thoughts and worries this day will bring. Andrei gets into the empty steam room and sits down, head hanging low, waiting for the sweat to come, getting warmer and warmer. A few minutes later, Pelše comes into the room and nods.

"Comrade Kirilenko, I'm glad you took my advice. A bath is always good. It cleans our bodies and cleanses our heads and our thoughts, and we all need cleaner thoughts, don't you think?"

Andrei lifts his head, his face already covered in sweat, smiling towards Pelše. "Good morning, Comrade Pelše. Indeed, it was a piece of good advice, and yes, we always need a clean head. In our position, it is always required."

Pelše sits in front of him and pours a bit of cold water on the hot rocks, the hissing of the steam covering their voices. No listening device will ever survive in the heat and steam of a *banya.*

Pelše continues to speak, "Especially after the conversation yesterday, don't you think?"

Andrei looks up, "It was a hard conversation yesterday, and I think I was right to say what I said."

Pelše looks into Andrei's eyes, his face hard and set, wanting to know more. "And that's all you had to say?"

Andrei meets Pelše's eyes, thinking that this could end with him dead, or worse, in Siberia. "What I had to say, what I want to ask is this! If we finished building the Communist society that we all dream and talk about all the time, if our people are living in prosperity and all the workers have equal rights and all that they need, if we have so much to give away that we can talk about changing nations that most of our people can't even find on the map, either Afghanistan, Iran or Angola. Are we so good in our own backyard that we can talk about others? Because I know the people! Because I've been there! Because I know how much work we have in front of us! Shouldn't we focus here? For us?"

Andrei clenches his jaw a few times and then sighs. The

first sweat is done, as the *banya* tradition says. Getting up and walking towards the cold room, stepping inside there in silence with Pelše behind him, neither speaking, both caught in their own thoughts. Andrei groans as he pours cold water on himself, the shock of the temperature and the stress of this conversation making his heart pound in his chest. Thinking about how many decisions have been made like this, two old men, talking with hidden meaning, neither of them willing to show their hand, neither of them wanting to show weakness. Andrei smiles and thinks. *This is almost comical, if it weren't for the rest of the lives being changed here.* Walking back into the hot room, he pours more water over the hot stones, gets some branches, and slaps them across his back. Pelše is behind him, doing the same thing. When Pelše speaks again, he uses the patronymic name.

"Andrei Pavlovich, what people are you talking about, the Soviet Union people or the Ukrainian people? Because some of them have it worse than others. And yes, I had to support the workers in Angola, not that I wanted to, but I had to."

Andrei turns around. "Arvid Yanovich, people should be equal in the Soviet Union, and I would like to know where this is going?"

Pelše smiles, "I want to know how big of a patriot you are Andrei, and now I know, and I would also advise that maybe you and I should focus on our people, you on the Ukrainian people and I on the Latvian, and I know that other leaders are doing the same, in the Baltics, in the East, and down South."

Andrei looks at Pelše, "That is high treason!"

Pelše smiles, "Yes, it is, and how would you call taking the means of harvesting the crops, putting a country in hunger? Tell me, Andrei, how would you call that?"

Andrei sits down, going through another sweat in the *banya.* "That decision is on all of us, equally." Andrei is emphasizing the word *equally* at the end of his sentence.

Pelše puts the herbs down, "It is, but if I had the chance to serve My People better, I would do it, even if I were to be called a traitor."

Andrei smiles with a sad smile. "That's the act of a true patriot, Arvīds Yanovich. I hope I will have the same strength."

Andrei shakes Pelše's hand and walks out of the *banya,* getting dressed and walking out of the steam bath, looking left and right, half expecting to be picked up right away by the KGB agents, walking towards his car, and getting in the back seat, talking to the driver,

"Let's go to the airport, Alexei,"

The driver replies, "Right away, Comrade Kirilenko, good bath?"

Andrei smiles, thinking that the driver is most likely a KGB informer. "Yes, Alexei, it was needed, and guess what, I ran into Arvīds Pelše, and we managed to clear some work problems too, and find a way to send some kids from Odessa to a vacation camp in the Baltic, while some kids from Riga will come to Odesa."

The driver smiles and looks at Andrei through the rear-view mirror. "Then it is a good day already, Comrade Kirilenko."

Andrei nods and quickly writes down that the first thing to do is to organize this camp with the kids and inform Pelše about this conversation.

Andrei walks into the antechamber of his office in Kiev, greeting his secretary, "Good evening, Nadia. I trust everything was all right while I was gone to Moscow?"

Nadia springs from her desk and walks towards him with a stack of paper, letters, and communication that Andrei must read through. "Yes, Comrade Kirilenko, everything was alright. I have the mail and some reports for you. Anything else you need?"

Kirilenko walks into his office with Nadia in trail, turns around, and realizes he has not held the door open for her.

"Sorry, Nadia, long days. I shouldn't forget my manners."

Nadia blushes profusely. "No worries, Comrade Kirilenko, it's just a door, and I can walk just fine. It was open already. No need to hold it. Do you need anything? "

Kirilenko sits at his desk, "Yes, a coffee and add a splash of vodka to it, maybe two splashes. Also, call the Chief of Staff for Ukraine and tell him to come here within the hour. Who else do I need? Yes, I need the Chief of Power and Energy, the Chief of Agriculture, and all three of them. Tell them to come with their situation and reports. Whoever comes first, send them in. I will see them separately."

Nadia scribbles quickly on her scratchpad. "Anything else?"

Andrei responds, "No, that would be all, thank you."

Nadia opens the heavy wooden door of Andrei's office and steps in, "General Radzievsky, Comrade."

Andrei gets up from his desk, "Please come in, Alexei."

He shakes the General's hand and invites him to sit down.

"Thanks for coming in such a hurry, General." Andrei sits down on the chair in front of his desk, crosses his legs, and relaxes in the chair.

"Well, Comrade Kirilenko, I figured that if you wanted to see the readiness reports, you could have asked for them through a courier, so this must be more than that."

Andrei smiles, knowing that General Alexei Radzievsky is a person who goes straight to the chase.

"Indeed, General, with our change in leadership, we may soon need your expertise and valour."

The General lifts his eyebrows, "Here in the Kyiv district?"

Andrei continues. "The Politburo is contemplating a heavier action in Afghanistan and maybe continuing to Iran. You were the Chief of Frunze Military Academy. I'm curious to know your view."

The General thinks for a few seconds. "It could be done, some may think that it is a wise move, it could open the door to the whole Middle East, but will we succeed where the Brits and the Russian Empire fell before? That area is a tough country. But if this is the order, we will find a way. However, this is not in the Kyiv military district."

Andrei nods, "Thank you for your input, General. You are right, this is not in our military district. However, I fear that if something does not go right with this move, your troops would be the next ones to go. Our soldiers here, in *our* military district, under your command, have an exemplary readiness level. They would be the first choice for replacements or to sustain that offensive. Don't you think so?"

The General nods, "Indeed, it would be a smart choice. Here in Kyiv, we're not protecting a land border. We have a buffer and the Black Sea, so, indeed, we could move and support. Comrade Kirilenko, you seem to have a knack for military actions."

Andrei laughs, "General, you know what I did best in the Great Patriotic War? I was a lousy soldier, according to some, but I was good at logistics. I moved factories, increased production, and increased the morale of the soldiers, and that made a huge difference at the front. So, I'm looking at this from a logistical perspective, if and when our help will be needed. Why not make sure that we are ready to go at a moment's notice? This way, we will be able to make an impact."

Andrei pauses for a moment, then continues. "I would like you to instruct the rest of the Staff to increase the readiness level, to increase the fuel and ammunition supply, even if we have to go past the needed quota. I'll approve it and do this quickly."

The General asks, "Are you certain of this action, Comrade Kirilenko?"

Andrei responded and shrugged his shoulders. "I'm not, but my gut feeling tells me that there will be something, and you know that old saying. I would feel bad to be in my bedroom in my underwear and have a living room full of surprise guests, and I would feel better to be dressed well and have nowhere to go."

The General laughs. "Comrade Kirilenko, with your permission, I will use this phrase in the future."

Andrei smiles, "Be my guest, General."

Andrei gets up, and the general follows, shaking his hand and walking him towards the door. "Thank you, General, and I will keep you informed as soon as I know more. I'm sure Ustinov will say the same thing. We must be prepared for whatever may happen. Just keep that in mind."

Andrei invites Comrade Sidorov in, shaking his hand as he walks through the door. "Thank you for coming in on such short notice, Comrade Sidorov. I trust you are doing well."

Sidorov responds while sitting down. "Comrade Kirilenko, you are welcome. I was about to go to inspect a vegetable greenhouse that's entering production close to Odesa, when I got your call 5 minutes before leaving."

Andrei nods, "Comrade Sidorov, I appreciate your quick response, and I'm sure that the Comrades in Odessa will wait for your inspection. Will these greenhouses work?"

Sidorov nods vigorously, "Comrade Kirilenko, yes, they do. We control the heat, humidity, and light, ensuring the vegetables grow at the fastest rate and produce more. We also control the pests better. Overall, in a greenhouse, we see an increase in production per hectare. of over 300%."

Kirilenko listens intently and looks surprised, hearing that number.

Sidorov puts his hands up, "And Comrade, before you ask, no, we cannot have a greenhouse for grains or corn, it doesn't work that way."

Kirilenko laughs, "Everyone asked you the same question?"

Sidorov smiles, "All the time, Comrade, now what can I help you with?"

Andrei gets quickly to the point. "Our crops this year, we cannot control the weather, but let's do everything in our power to make sure that the harvest is done right and proper. And spare no effort. Also, people in the villages have their small personal land plots, aren't they?"

Sidorov looks surprised, "Indeed, they are, each family has a personal lot of 1 acre."

Andrei continues. "Have we calculated how much they contribute to the total food in Ukraine?"

Sidorov thinks for a second. "It is hard to calculate that volume. However, you would be surprised, it's close to 50%."

Andrei smiles. "That's brilliant, so with a little support from us, that could increase?"

Sidorov beams, realizing where this conversation is going. "Comrade Kirilenko, I've said it for many years, we could feed the country from those lots, if we extended them a bit."

Kirilenko puts his hands up. "Comrade Sidorov, I cannot do that, but what I can do is to ask you to help them as much as possible, if they need fertilizer, or any additional support that we can give them, and make sure that our *kolkhozes* are producing as well. It could be huge for us."

Sidorov nods vigorously, "Comrade Kirilenko, thank you, we will do that, thank you."

Andrei gets up, signaling that the meeting is over. "Also, Comrade Sidorov, from our granaries, requests that are coming from Moscow, or requests that are coming from the army districts outside of Ukraine, delay those, if you cannot, defer them to me."

Andrei shakes Sidorov's hand. "And this does not leave this office. Goodbye, Comrade, and have a safe trip to Odessa."

Sidorov nods. "Goodbye, Comrade Kirilenko."

Andrei invites Volkov, the Energy and Power Chief. "Come on, Comrade, please do sit down, and thank you for coming in on such short notice."

Volkov sits down with his stack of reports in his hands, "Thank you, Comrade Kirilenko. I trust you are doing well, and your trip to Moscow was fruitful."

Andrei smiles. "Trips to Moscow are always fruitful, but, just like any other task that is completed, it will create two other new tasks. With the new Party Leader in place, we will have to adjust a bit on how we deal with the power and energy here in our Union. I trust that we are making progress with the new sea oil platforms?"

Volkov looks through his papers and responds, "Yes, as of last month, the two platforms are extracting, and the volumes are good, and the crude is very well, we can use it for high quality gasoline and jet fuel, the refining process for this will be quicker and more simple, this also means that the crude we extract from the land, that's high on Sulphur, we can use that for mazut and diesel fuel, more suitable for agriculture and power and heating plant."

Andrei claps his hands. "That's excellent news, Comrade. You did a good job, and I trust that these rigs are ahead of schedule?"

Volkov smiles, "Thank you, Comrade, but to be honest, we were lucky. It was easier to drill than expected."

Andrei laughs. "Comrade Volkov, that's still your merit, and you should take the praise. On another topic, with our change in leadership, we must support all of our people in the Soviet Union, however, let's make sure that we stockpile now what we need for agriculture and harvest when it comes to diesel and gasoline, and also, let's make sure we stockpile what we need for the army needs, once we have those levels met, we can help others, if you are having any problems, please delay them and send them to me. Understood?"

Volkov looks through his papers, understanding that stockpiling the levels means that no fuel will leave Ukraine for many months to come. "Understood, Comrade."

Andrei claps his shoulder as he walks him out of his office. "Once again, congratulations on the oil rigs coming into production, Comrade. You served the Soviet Union like a true hero."

As Volkov walks out, Nadia steps into the office. Kirilenko runs his hands through his hair, then puts his hands behind his back and stretches. "Nadia, place a call to Pelše in Latvia. I need to give them the good news that we sorted out the camp for the Latvian children to come to Odessa in the summer, like we discussed yesterday."

Nadia nods and walks out, "Right away, Comrade."

Andrei picks up the phone. "Hello, Comrade Pelše? ......Yes, Comrade, as we discussed yesterday, the camp for the 50 Latvian children to come in the summer to visit Odessa is all set up..... We will pick the 50 children with the best grades from Ukraine and send them to Latvia for your summer camp, and they will have the time of their lives."

Andrei listens to Pelše on the other end of the line, and at the end, he says. "Comrade Pelše, I like your approach and how all the people in the Soviet Union should be united, and I agree with everything you said today. Goodbye!"

Andrei puts the phone down and runs his hands over his face, growing weary and tired from the early morning, from all the thoughts and plans within plans going through his head. Thinking to himself, *"Could I do it? Could I bring the Union to an end? Me, Pelše, and others? How would we be judged? But you heard them, we could feed our people, we could keep our people warm. Our people!"* Sighing deeply, still in his thoughts. *If this office is bugged, and it probably is, would they figure it out, and how quickly would they report it? Did I say too much? No, I did nothing of the sort; I'm just getting ready and planning ahead, like any good leader would do......back in the War, we all fought together, we had an enemy, now, is it us? The enemy within? Some old fools who did some heroic things many years ago, do that still give us the right to lead, and to change people's lives?* Slapping his hands on the table. *Come on, Andrei, you think too much.*

Getting up from his desk, "Nadia, please phone for the car to get ready. I will go home. The old man is tired and hungry."

Nadia responds, "Right away, Comrade, Comrade, if I may ask, I know since the loss of your wife Masha, it must be hard. Do you have any food at home? Could I be of any help?"

Andrei stops and looks at her. "Nadia, you good soul, stop worrying about an old man. I don't need much, and I have everything I need. It's late, and I'm sure your kids and husband are waiting for you. Go home."

7

Chapter 7: Andropov's demise.

MOSCOW, USSR
August 7th, 1978

A few months have passed since Andrei's conversation with Pelše, and to his surprise, he remains in the same position and is still a member of the Politburo. Back again in the Presidium room. Week after week, the Politburo holds its meetings, decisions are made, actions are taken, and orders are given. It's August now, and everyone is praising the harvest, which is one of the best so far in Ukraine. Andrei smiles when he hears the praises, knowing that so far, Sidorov has kept to his word.

"At least we fed our people." Andrei thought to himself.

Ustinov, the Minister of Defense, clears his throat, his turn to speak,

"Comrades, some months ago we discussed the situation in Afghanistan, and we plan, and we prepare, and nothing comes of it. And two days ago, the Shah of Iran declared maximum political liberties, free speech, and Western-like freedom. To me, a military man, this is the work of American Imperialism, and it's like we are having the enemy at the door. In Turkey, they have their missiles and their bases. Soon this will be in Iran, Comrades. We may already be surrounded. While we sit and talk, the enemy works."

Before Andropov responds, Andrei Gromyko, the Minister of Foreign Affairs, raises his hands, and Andropov makes a sign to him, allowing him to speak.

"Also, on the 5th, an attack in Islamabad killed four Palestinians, and the Iraqis orchestrated this. The whole region is a powder keg."

Andrei laughs and tells the room. "Comrades, and we're planning to bring the biggest matchstick."

Getting serious, he looks at Ustinov. "This could be a tremendous advantage, but could also lead to a larger conflict. But we need to balance it right,"

Ustinov replies. "We know their capabilities. We could be anywhere in the Persian Gulf in two weeks once we clear the mountains in Afghanistan." Andrei nods in understanding.

Andropov looks around the room and begins to speak, in a deep, measured voice, ensuring he is heard.

"Comrades, Comrade Ustinov, I want to know the minimum military force needed for the Afghanistan action. Just Afghanistan. I am concerned that with such a large presence, we may prompt the Americans into taking rash action. Also, I would like your General Staff to confirm our readiness level. I propose we start this operation at the end of August."

The room becomes silent, and Marshal Ustinov glances down at one of his papers. "We can achieve our objective. The mountain passes will close in November, but we have the Salang Pass tunnel, and we will capture that first."

Andropov looks deeply concerned and stressed. Applause

starts from the room, and a voice yells.

"Glory to the Soviet Union and its people!"

He smiles, looks up, and joins in applauding with the rest of the Politburo. "This, Comrades, will be another great victory for the Soviet Union and the workers everywhere."

Andrei looks at Andropov, overwhelmed by the weight of his thoughts, as he remembers his friend Leonid Brezhnev, who sat in that seat just a few months ago. The same worries and stress had consumed him, and now his friend is gone, finally at rest.

Andropov ends the meeting, and as the presidium room empties, Andrei sees Pelše next to him, shaking his head.

"Poor Yuri!" said Pelše, using Andropov's first name, "Poor Yuri, not able to say 'No' with a full heart and not able to say 'Yes' fully, such a burden this is."

Andrei shakes his head, "Indeed, but what do you do when both options are neither good nor bad? How do you find balance?"

They are walking out of the room together, and Pelše smiles and turns towards Andrei, "Comrade Kirilenko, those kids, they returned from Odessa, the happiest kids ever, they had the time of their lives at their summer camp. That was such a good idea, and we should do that more often."

Andrei gets surprised for a second, then quickly reacts with a big smile, "Indeed, I have checked as well, and the kids from Kyiv had the best time in the camp in the Baltics, you are right, Comrade, this should become an annual tradition."

Andrei keeps walking, understanding the clue that Pelše just gave him. Thinking to himself, *"We shall see, we shall see."*

Andrei is sleeping in his Party hotel room, the same room he has used for many years in all his travels to Moscow, making it feel like a second home. He hears the phone ringing, and he lifts himself from the bed. He looks at the watch on the bedside table at 4:30 in the morning. He picks up the phone.

"Kirilenko! ....Yes, I will be there in 30 minutes."

He puts the phone down, then picks it back up and calls the reception. "Kirilenko here, room 102, I need a car in 15 minutes, to the Kremlin! ......Yes, you have multiple requests? .....Then you could put us in the same cars, we're going to the same place."

Kirilenko puts the phone down and heads to the bathroom to get ready, lost in thought. *"If it were war, they would have sent a car. If I were arrested, they would have sent a car. Then it's something else."*

Andrei walks back into the presidium room, five minutes before the meeting should start, Marshall Ustinov at the head of the table, and the room fills quickly. Ustinov looks around the room and speaks,

"Comrades, I regret to inform you that tonight, Comrade Andropov suffered a massive heart attack, and despite all the medical efforts, he died at 3:17 AM. He was a great patriot and a great leader, and I hope he rests in peace."

Marshal Ustinov puts his head down and observes a moment of silence. After a minute, Ustinov continues,

"The preparations for the state funeral will start right away, and the ceremony will be held in four days. As one of the most senior leaders of the party, and with the upcoming actions in Afghanistan, with your permission, I will take the role of the General Secretary."

Applause starts in the room, and everyone joins in. Andrei surveys the room quickly and thinks, *"Gorbachev is too young, he would've made a good Secretary, but not with his views and not now, Cebrikov, he's too new, Shcherbitsky he's too wild, Ustinov does not have a Troika. And he is rushing the State funeral for his army to go to Afghanistan, and maybe for full mobilization."*

Andrei claps harder and louder, looking at Ustinov and nodding his head in approval. "Comrade Ustinov, congratulations. You will be an esteemed General Secretary and a strong leader for the Soviet Union. However, I have a proposition to make. Change is always hard, and change in leadership is even harder. Unfortunately for us, we have had to make too many changes lately. With our full support in mind, wouldn't it be better for us to present our common view and reiterate our plan and commitment to the local party leaders? I believe that this way, we will have more support from all the workers in the Soviet Union and present a strong front to the rest of the nations that look up to us. It would make for good propaganda on how the country will rally behind the new leadership."

This option takes Ustinov aback. He thinks for a second, then speaks, "Comrade Kirilenko, thank you for your words. This is a good option, and indeed, we should do just that. I will meet with the General Staff as well, and this Politburo will present a united front, more united than ever."

Applause is heard in the room again, and then the emergency meeting is quickly adjourned. Andrei looks around as he is making his way out of the room, everyone with their own thoughts and worries. Not many people are sad about how quickly their former leader succumbed to the stress and pressure of leadership. Climbing into his car, his regular driver now. He sits in the back seat, pulling his collar up as the tiredness starts to get to him.

He tells the driver. "To the airport!" and quickly falls asleep.

Andrei walks into his office, greeting his secretary, Nadia, who springs up at the moment she sees him.

"Good morning, Nadia, get your pad and please can I have some coffee?"

Nadia nods. "Good morning, Comrade, anything else?"

Andrei responds, "My office, when the coffee is ready."

Nadia steps into the office after a minute, a cup of coffee in her hand. Andrei nods and gestures,

"Have a seat, Nadia."

After she sits down, Andrei glances for a second through the window, then continues. "Comrade Andropov suffered a heart attack yesterday. Unfortunately, the doctors were not able to save him."

Nadia gasps, "Comrade Kirilenko, this is such bad news, all our leaders, gone so quickly."

Andrei smiles sadly, "Maybe we're just too old, and our time has come."

Nadia shakes her head, "That's not true, Comrade, you would be a good Candidate for the General Secretary."

Andrei laughs, "Thank you, Nadia, but no, I was friends with Brezhnev, and part of his Troika, but with Andropov, I've never seen eye to eye. If anything, they would have asked me to retire soon. I'm too brash and I speak my mind too loudly, but that's not the case anymore, Ustinov will be the new General Secretary."

Nadia thinks for a second. "Marshal Ustinov, the army will rule the party now?"

Andrei nods, "Yes, this is not common, the army and the party under one hand, this is not a good option. However, I don't believe Ustinov is a politician."

Nadia nods, "What can we do, Comrade? How do we support the party from here?"

Andrei looks at Nadia with a piercing look. "That's what you think we should do, Nadia?"

Nadia looks puzzled, "Well, Comrade, that's what we always have to do."

Andrei replies, "Indeed, but our duty is to the people first. We should not forget that, but let's move on from ideology. Could you please call for my car? I need to go to the History Museum, also put a call to Pelše, and call for General Radzievsky, arrange a meeting after noon, thank you Nadia."

Nadia steps out of the office, and a few moments later, the phone rings. Andrei picks up and hears on the other end of the line. "Comrade Pelše on line two!"

Andrei pushes the line 2 button, hears the switch, and then a voice from the other end of the line. "Good morning, Comrade Kirilenko. I was also planning to call you. Such terrible news."

Andrei responded. "Good morning, terrible news indeed, Comrade Pelše."

Pelše continues, "But you did exemplary, how you managed to put the voice of the party and its people back into this. That was very well thought out."

Andrei replies. "People have to come first, always!"

Pelše responds, "I couldn't agree more, Comrade Kirilenko."

Andrei takes a deep breath. "Remember those kids sent out to camp? I would like to expand on that. The day after the State Funeral, I would like us to take action. Do you think there will be other ..... camps in other parts of the country?"

Pelše takes a moment. "Comrade Kirilenko, we could do that in all the Baltic countries, in Bessarabia, in Georgia, even in Belarus."

Andrei thinks for a second. "Then I will ask for a meeting with all the representatives, and we shall see." Pelše replies,

"And we should all have a voice at the same time." Andrei responds, "Goodbye, Comrade Pelše, I do hope we will not fail." Pelše replies, "Goodbye, Comrade Kirilenko, and if we do, at least we tried."

Andrei runs his hands over his face, the gesture he always does when he is tired and lost in his thoughts. Picks up the phone and calls Nadia, "Is the car ready?"

Nadia responds, "Yes, Comrade, waiting in front." Andrei thanks her and puts the phone down.

As the car gets closer to the museum, Andrei taps the driver on the shoulder.

"Drive around the back. I want to speak with the Museum Director." The driver nods and drives around the museum.

Andrei gets inside the museum through the administrative door. Knocks once and enters the Director's office.

"Good afternoon, Comrade Director." Andrei greets him.

The Director gets up from his chair, surprised by this unexpected visit. "Such a surprise, Comrade Kirilenko, this is unexpected, on a day like this. What is the occasion?"

Andrei looks at the Museum Director, trying to gauge what kind of person he is. A true historian, balding head, glasses with a thick black frame, on his desk, some old documents, a pair of tweezers, a magnifying glass, and a cleaning brush. The Director was reading an old document.

"Comrade, I wonder, what is stored in the archives of the museum?"

The Director looks puzzled. Andrei smiles and thinks for a second, realizing that the office may be bugged. "I always wanted to see the archives. Maybe there are new collections there. And some old items from Brezhnev, and when Andropov was young. It would be good on a day like this."

The Director nods, "Of course, we can go down and show you."

They walk together to the Museum archives, going down a few flights of stairs.

Andrei continues, "Actually, I was wondering what collections you may have from, let's say, 1917, 1918, before the Soviets and the Bolsheviks, maybe from January 1918."

The Director gasps, realizing what Andrei is asking. In January 1918, Ukraine declared its independence from Russia, before the Bolsheviks conquered Ukraine again.

"Comrade Kirilenko, is that what you are trying to find here?"

Andrei's face turns to stone, not showing a single feeling or thought. "Yes, is there anything we can find in here?"

The Museum Director opens his eyes wide. "Many years ago, we were asked to destroy items like this. I was a junior working in restoration back then. I couldn't. It seemed important for us not to lose a part of what makes us Ukrainians. So, I kept them. Maybe it was wrong, but as a historian, I couldn't get rid of part of our heritage."

Andrei asks, "What is that you kept?"

The Director draws himself up. "The flags, Comrade Kirilenko, the first three flags from Ukraine in 1918, I thought that maybe one day, we will get to display them again, maybe here in the museum, or one would hope, up there, on the flagpole."

Andrei places his hands on the Director's shoulders, looks into his eyes, and pulls him closer in the old Ukrainian fashion, kissing him on both cheeks.

"Comrade Director, thank you for this. Could I have them ready in a few days?"

The Director asks, "Ready for what?"

Andrei laughs, "Ready to be displayed, and not in the museum, up there on the flagpole."

Taking the Director arm, walking out whispering, "This is just between you and me, now please come up with something to be displayed, if your office is bugged, we have to have had a reason for this walk in the archives, bring the flags to me as soon as they are ready, talk just with Nadia, my secretary, and when you call, tell her you found one of Andropov, old tank hat."

Andrei gets back to the office, greets Nadia, then says, "Nadia, the Director of the History Museum will call you in a few days, with some old artefacts. When he calls, send a car for him right away, and clear my schedule right away for him."

Nadia nods, "Yes, Comrade, the General is here waiting for you."

Andrei replies, "Thank you, Nadia."

Stepping into his office and shaking the General's hand. "Thank you for coming, Comrade General. Please have a seat."

The General sits, and Andrei goes back to his massive chair on the other side of his desk. "So, General, it is a sad time for the Soviet Union. What do you think about our new General Secretary?"

The General clears his throat, then speaks, "Comrade Kirilenko, Marshall Ustinov is not a politician. He is a good soldier, a bit too impetuous, but he never struck me as a politician."

Andrei listens intently, "But it seems that he is, and now, the army and the party have a single leader, and that is worrisome for some."

General nods, "This can be a big burden indeed, and the KGB leader is new as well. Are we looking at someone who will have that immense power in his hands?"

Andrei thinks for a second. "To be honest, General, I don't think this is the case, but I fear that Marshall Ustinov wants to lead with a much stronger hand, and he will think about the military actions. I believe he will focus more on that."

Andrei looks concerned, "This could escalate, all the way to a nuclear conflict?"

The General replies, "The nuclear option is always a political option, even when applied at a tactical level."

Andrei becomes worried. "This should not be an option in any way."

The General nods, "This is true. It is impossible to predict how this could escalate."

Andrei responds, "This is where I think you are mistaken, escalation is always bad, and there will be escalation."

Andrei takes a few seconds' pause, then continues, "You are Ukrainian, aren't you, General?"

The General responds, "Yes, I am."

Andrei continues, "What if at some point we will have to decide between Ukrainians and the rest of the Union?"

The General becomes very aware of where this conversation is leading. "Comrade Kirilenko, this is treason!"

Andrei was unfazed at this point. "No, it is not, we are responsible for all the people, but we are here in this part of our Union, and we have responsibilities here, and from what you are telling me, we could face a lot of challenges."

The General considers it for a second. "You are right, if it gets there, I trust we will make the right decision, Comrade Kirilenko." Andrei nods, "Thank you, General."

Andrei walks the general out of his office and gets back to his desk and sits down, starting to look at the list of the Party representatives, thinking to himself, *"This is the moment, I can ask them to decide, are we going to have the strength to do what we did in the past? Are we strong enough to be free? For the first time in 1000 years, we could be free and decide for ourselves. Andrei, in a few days from now, you will probably be dead, but at least you stand out to what mattered."*

8

Chapter 8: The Break

KYIV, USSR
August 12th, 1978

Andrei reviews the papers he prepared for his speech to the Party representatives from Ukraine. He is tired and weary. Sleep has not come easily over the past few nights. He makes a fist a few times with his empty hand in an effort to regain his composure. The General in the room with him, looking at him, Andrei finds his composure, looks up at the General,

"You know what I'm about to do?"

The General nods, Andrei continues." When you figured it out?"

The General continues, "I had my doubts after the meeting we had a few months ago, when you told me about our readiness, that was a general mobilization, without anyone giving the order. Our last meeting solidified my suspicion."

Andrei looks into the General's eyes. "You could stop me right now, you would be Ustinov's right hand, a Marshall, before this day is over."

The General nods. "Yes, I could."

Andrei looks at him with an inquisitive look on his face. "Then, why not?"

The General remains unfazed, "Because I agree with you, and I think you are doing the right thing."

Andrei clasps his shoulder. "You have no idea what this means to me. There will be trouble."

The General smiles, "I have ten APCs and four tanks to surround the building if needed, but I don't think we will need them."

Andrei smiles, "I wish I were as optimistic as you."

The General pumps Andrei's hand. "Comrade Kirilenko, it's been an honor. I wish you the best of luck."

Andrei steps into the large room, where 350 representatives of the Communist Party are seated, staring at the empty podium. The podium was ornate with the Soviet Union flag, and the drapes behind the curtain were all red. Andrei walks toward the podium, holding his papers in hand, a speech prepared in advance. The Party members are quiet, and Andrei surveys the room. Looking at his watch. 12:00 o'clock, a bit too late, but knowing that he had to account for the 1-hour time difference between the Baltic countries and Ukraine, the Baltic countries, Bessarabia, Georgia, and Belarus had similar meetings.

"Dear Comrades, we have gathered here after a moment of sadness. The Soviet Union has gone through multiple leadership changes, and unfortunately, we must go through one more change. The party leadership is proposing Marshall Ustinov as the Secretary General."

Andrei makes a sign to the members to quiet any applause. "At the same time, Comrade from other parts of the Soviet

Union are having the same talks, in Riga, Vilnius, Kishinev, Minsk, Comrades all over the Soviet Union are deciding their future, however, Comrades, I would like us to think thoroughly at the next steps, and where this country is leading and where our people are being lead to. The party is not perfect, our communist society is not yet built, and it will take years and years to get there. And in the past, we have made mistakes. For far too long, we have tried to rule the world while forgetting about our own people! For years and years, we were one, but we were also divided. We had to share all good that came from Ukraine, but we had little support. For all this, we lost traditions and identity. This may be the time we can decide our future. Our future may be bleak. The Ukrainian future was bleak before, but that doesn't mean it has to be, and here and now in this crucial moment, we can change that!"

Andrei takes a moment to let what he said sink in. Looking around the room, people glance at each other, trying to see what the ones sitting next to them will say.

Andrei reaches from behind the podium, picks up one of the flags from the museum, unfurls it, and lets it fall over the podium, covering the Soviet Union flag with the old blue and yellow flag of the old Ukraine. The flag that was up in 1918. Waiting for a moment and looking in the room.

"Comrades, this is the day we can decide, as our ancestors wanted, if we want to have our country free to decide for itself, to carve its own path in the same way our ancestors wanted during the Czars times, during the Bolsheviks times, and how many of us wanted it throughout these years. Today we can decide this! Today, we can display this old flag here on this podium, along with the other two flags, the old flags of 1918, which some of our ancestors died for, flying high on the

Government building and the Monastery of Caves. Comrades, this is up to us, right now, it is for us to decide!"

Andrei throws his papers on the floor, realizing that he had not read a single word from them and that he had not used a single phrase from what he had carefully prepared. Looking in the big room. Hands on the side of the podium, glancing into the room as the representatives rise and start to applaud, a few people sit down but eventually get up and join in the applause. Voices from the crowd yell "Slava Ukraine," the old battle cry from 1918. Andrei was on the verge of collapse under the stress, allowing the crowd to soak in the moment. Knowing that the first hurdle has been passed, I also realize that there may be many other hurdles that will need to be cleared in the next hours and days.

Andrei begins to address the crowd, discussing the following steps, including the need for a referendum to determine Ukraine's fate, and how the existing local Government will continue to operate until the referendum is held. At the same time, as he continues to talk and tries to respond to the crowd's questions, a growing sound seems to be getting closer and closer, strong and powerful. As the sound gets closer, Andrei recognizes thousands of voices singing "Ukraine's glory has not yet died." The old Ukrainian anthem that was written in 1862, the one that he barely remembers the words, as he looks around the room.

"Comrades, here the voices outside, we spoke tonight to the Ukrainians, and now they are speaking to us."

Andrei walks out. As he walks out, the General shakes his hand and tells him that the flags are up. Andrei thanks him and walks up the stairs towards the balcony, where he will have to give another speech.

WASHINGTON, USA
August 12th, 1978

It is 5:00 AM in Washington, and President Jimmy Carter steps into the Oval Office, not fully awake, as he is confused by the amount of information coming at him. Two aides are with him, working through the telexes that are coming from news agencies, embassies, and consulates.

President Carter picks up the phone and selects the line labeled for Vice-President Mondale. "Walter, such a morning, I trust you are getting the news."

......President Carter listens, "Walter, I would like you to go to Cheyene Mountain NORAD site and use the alternate command center. We don't know what the next few hours will hold, and we should be prepared for the worst. I'll have the cabinet here, and we will sort it out. As soon as you are there, we'll link up."

President Carter listens for Walter Mondale to confirm, then hangs up the phone.

Looking at his aides, "When will Vance and Brown be here?"

One of the aides responds, "In 10 minutes."

President Carter continues to review the telexes arriving from various news agencies, which are filled with ambiguous information and contradictory details, offering little certainty. A few minutes passed, then Secretary of State Cyrus Vance stepped into the Oval Office, and a few seconds after, Secretary of Defence Harold Brown stepped in.

President Carter motions the two members of his cabinet to be seated,

"I've instructed the Vice President to relocate to Cheyenne Mountain, just in case, once he is set up in the Command Center, he will join if needed. What do we know so far?"

Vance the Secretary of State starts first, "Tonight, at 11:00 Moscow time, Lithuania, Latvia, Estonia, Ukraine, Georgia, and a few others all declared their independence from the Soviet Union, this seem to be related with the death of Andropov, and with Marshall Ustinov becoming the Secretary General of the Communist party, from what we are gathering, this move has not been received all that well by the rest of the Party, probably Ustinov was not able to gain a lot of support from senior member, and no-one else raised to the task."

President Carter nods and asks. "What is the ambassador saying?"

Vance replies, "Absolutely nothing, I contacted him before I got here, and he said that he is still waiting for instructions from Moscow."

President Carter thinks for a few seconds, "What about their readiness? Do we see anything out of the ordinary?"

Secretary of Defence Brown responds, "There was no change in the past few days, their posture was the same, there are training exercises far East, we think that they had plans to go in Afghanistan, and even Iran, but nothing that was confirmed, in Ukraine and Georgia, their supply level increased over the last few months, but the same nothing that should trigger any worries."

Secretary of Defence takes a sip of coffee and continues, "SIGINT from the Baltic States is showing that they moved some troops on their Eastern border, away from us. And that makes sense with declaring independence from the Soviet Union,"

President Carter answers, "How about the nukes?"

The Secretary of Defence continues, "We're trailing their nuke subs to the best of our abilities, and I believe we know where all are and none of them are close to a launch basket, of course, that could always change. No other indications that this could escalate into a nuclear strike, not against us anyway."

President Carter runs a hand over his face, "So, what do we do? This new... countries, their leaders? Still communist?"

The Secretary of State responds, "It looks like they are senior Party Leaders, so yes, for now, they are still communist, but I'm assuming that this could change, eventually."

President Carter asks another question, "Do we know who these people are? Do we contact them? What is our next step?"

Secretary Vance responds, "Mister President, I suggest that right now, we will try to contact them through unofficial channels, let's see what they have to say, our official posture right now would be to wait, I would highly recommend to see what other countries will react to, and if we want to legitimize these countries, let's not be the first one to start. I would rather see the European Countries react first. However, this could mean the end of the Cold War and a big step towards peace, so we will have to support them at some point."

President Carter nods, "I believe you are right. I can go out on the air today with a message that we are worried and want to maintain peace, and this will buy us a bit more time. Secretary of Defence? What's your take on our next steps?"

The Secretary of Defence responds, "We have the Rapid Deploying Force in Europe and the USA. The first thing to do is to increase their readiness, nothing too escalatory, but just to get them ready. Also, we will coordinate with NATO commanders to do that at the borders. It is normal, and it will not be seen as an escalation. We need to organize supplies, so we will temporarily halt tankers and transport vessels in port to maintain our transport capacity. If anything starts, we will need supplies. It is crucial."

President Carter nods, "Thank you, gentlemen. I suggest we meet again with the rest of the cabinet in a few hours, and from now on, we will remain around here until we will know more."

9

Chapter 9: The Unknown

Krasnodar, Krasnodar Krai, USSR
August 13th, 1978

Katya, Tanya's mom, is listening to the radio in the kitchen. Her husband and Tanya are at the kitchen table, listening to Radio Free Europe. The volume is turned low, and the news of the breakup of the Soviet Union is almost too difficult to comprehend. Katya has her mouth covered with her hand, listening with a worried look on her face, her eyes almost on the verge of tears.

"But how come all these people, why did they want to break apart like this, when we were brothers and friends, and we fought together, one nation?" Katya shakes her head.

Nikolay continues, keeping the same tone, "Katya, I don't know, I can see it though, you know, even us, we laugh about the other nations, we make jokes, we look at them differently, we laugh about Armenians, we don't trust Georgians, and we make jokes about Ukrainians, in the end, not like brothers would do."

Katya replies, "But these are jokes. Nothing serious."

Tanya joins the conversation, "But they are not, we always treated other people differently, even within Russia, we're not treated the same as the people in Moscow, or the ones in Leningrad, there was always division between the Soviet Union."

Nikolay replies, "You don't know how it was, and how we got to stick together during the Great Patriotic War. It was the only way to succeed."

Tanya replies, "Back then, yes, but before, we learn some things during history, but other people tell different stories of what happened back then during the Bolshevik revolution, and how people died, and how many people died during the famine. Dad, you know, history is written by the victors."

Katya replies, "You, young lady, will have to be careful, make sure that you come home early, and don't get into any trouble! The KGB and the Militia will be even more dangerous these days until everything is sorted out."

Tanya nods, "I know, Mom, who knows how this will be sorted out?"

Nikolay replies, "It will get sorted out, if worst comes to worst, we move to the countryside for a bit until it all clears up. I'm scared that here, where we are, caught in between Ukraine and Georgia, things may be getting heated."

SOCHI, Krasnodar Krai, USSR
August 13th, 1978

The Colonel steps into the room, and all the pilots and the rest of the officers from the 982nd Fighter Regiment are gathered in the unit's big ceremony room.

"Be seated!" barks the Colonel. "As of now, for the next week, nobody leaves the base! We are at the highest alert status."

The Colonel stops for a few seconds and surveys the room. "As you are aware, several States from the Union declared independence yesterday. It is not my place to engage in politics, but those who did this and support this move are considered traitors. I will have to remind you of your oath that you will defend the Soviet Union and its people at all costs, and without sparing any effort. We will not take any steps back to bring traitors to justice and to establish and maintain the peace and unity of the Soviet Union. If you have any questions, talk to the political officers in the Staff."

The Colonel stops for a few seconds and surveys the room. "This regiment is a Red Star regiment. I will expect you to uphold that honor, nothing less. If we will be deployed, against any target, we will execute our mission perfectly and inflict maximum damage. I will expect nothing less from you. Until then, the ground personnel will ensure that our state of readiness is at its highest. For the flight personnel, I require you to go through the simulators for all flight procedures and also study your weapons deployment. I will not hear about any technical failures or weapon malfunctions. From now on, the regiment is in a state of war."

The Colonel stops for a few seconds and looks in the room. His face set and his jaws clenched.

"When this will calm down, we will allow for the ones with families to visit their families, but for the next 7 days, expect this base to be locked. The only things going in and out are supplies. Any questions?"

The Colonel waits a few seconds, then continues. "Glory to

the Soviet Union, its workers and its soldiers."

All the officers respond in unison as the Colonel is leaving, "Glory to the Soviet Union!"

The Colonel is walking out, and Vanea leans over towards Piotr's shoulder and whispers, "I don't get it, we're going to bring back the people, but it seems like the people wanted out too, it's not like they are calling us back."

Piotr gives a quick chuckle, "Stop it, Vanea, you know how it is."

Vanea smiles, "I know how it is, it's just that when I drop bombs somewhere, I hope I will be helping someone, not punishing some other folks."

Piotr nods, "I know, I know, in the end we will do our duty."

Vanea nods back. "That we will, we will do our duty."

KYIV, UKRAINE
August 13th, 1978

Andrei is getting up from his desk, stretching his arms behind his back to loosen up, feeling tired and sore. Almost two days without sleep, a day after he gave the speech, a day full of unknowns, a day where so much happened, and yet, a day that was quiet, people still in the streets celebrating, the tanks surrounding Verkhovna Rada. This building was built to be the Supreme Soviet of the Ukrainian SSR and now symbolizes the place where the independence movement began. Surrounded by tanks and APCs, but the tanks have flowers in their muzzles, and they are draped with blue and yellow flags, Andrei looks at the square in front of the building. When the telephone in his office rings, the button labeled Moscow flashes white.

Andrei thinks, *"Well, here we go, it took some time, I was expecting this sooner."* Andrei picks up. "Kirilenko!"

A voice from the other end of the line. "That was crafty, Comrade Kirilenko. It was well done. We picked up on it too late. We figured out Pelše's move sooner, but not yours."

Andrei responds, "Who is this?"

The voice on the other end, "This is Cebrikov."

Andrei takes a few seconds. Cebrikov, the new KGB Chief, is supposed to support Marshal Ustinov.

Andrei answers, "What can I do for you, Comrade Cebrikov?"

Cebrikov continues without answering his question. "Ukraine has part of the Soviet Union nuclear missiles, but not the codes, that's with the KGB."

Andrei agrees, "Indeed, and no matter what, I would like those never to be used, against anyone, ever."

Cebrikov responds, "We can agree with that statement. However, the rest will not go easily, Comrade Kirilenko."

Andrei responds, "Nothing that is right is easy, and this was the decision of the people, and I intend to have a referendum, and this will make the voice of the people sound stronger and louder."

Cebrikov responds. "I agree with you."

Andrei is surprised, "Do you?"

Cebrikov answers, "Of course, how else do you think Pelše is still alive today?"

Andrei continues, "Viktor Mikhailovich, people should not suffer, in the end we are all Communists, and good ones, but people suffered enough, and we should work on them not suffering, either Ukrainians, or Russian, or Georgian or what else, and for our countries to survive, and maybe, if the people want to be together again in the future, we must not fight with each other."

Cebrikov takes a few seconds to respond, "This is another fact we can agree upon. One more thing, the KGB in Ukraine, the Chief there, Vitali Fedorchuk, will never work with you, but his second in command will. Until we speak again, I wish you well, Comrade Kirilenko."

The line clicks and gets quiet. Andrei puts the phone down, then lifts it again,

"Nadia, General Radzievsky, please."

Nadia responds, "Right away, Comrade Kirilenko!"

A few seconds pass, and on the other end of the line, Andrei hears the General's voice.

"Comrade Kirilenko, what can I do for you?"

Andrei responds quickly, "Go to the KGB with a complete group of officers and request a meeting with Comrade Mukha, together with him, arrest Comrade Fedorchuk, and allow Comrade Mukha to take the Directorate role. This must be discreet."

The General responds, "Right away, Comrade, I will contact you when it's done. It should be in about an hour."

The line clicks. Andrei clicks the secretary button. "Nadia, a coffee, please, the one that you make special with a few drops of vodka in it."

He puts the phone down and glances at the square again, wondering what he should do with Fedorchuk's fate, smiling as he thinks about how much easier it would be for Fedorchuk if the roles were reversed.

Nadia steps into the office, a coffee cup in one hand and a bottle of Stolichnaya in the other. "Comrade Kirilenko, your coffee, may I suggest, Comrade. You had not had anything to eat since yesterday."

Andrei smiles, "The appetite is not there, Nadia."

Nadia draws herself up. "Comrade Kirilenko, you may be the hero of the Ukrainian people now, but, if need be, I'll feed you."

Andrei bursts into laughter, all tension gone for a few seconds. "Nadia, I'm not a hero, and I truly believe that you will feed me with a spoon. I would say that we should both save ourselves from this embarrassment. The kitchens, if they could rustle up some sandwiches, would be good. And I promise I'll eat them. Also, see if they can do something for the folks in the square, at least for those who need anything. Those are the real heroes, and we need to take care of our heroes. If we have to feed the people in the square, let's do so!"

Nadia nods, her chin quivering a bit, walks towards the door, and takes a few steps, then comes quickly back and hugs Andrei and kisses both of his cheeks, looking down, embarrassed as she hurries out of the office, muttering, "Sorry, Comrade Kirilenko."

10

Chapter 10: Georgia

WASHINGTON, USA
August 14th, 1978

President Carter steps into the Oval Office, where Secretary of State Cyrus Vance, Secretary of Defence Harold Brown, and Director of the CIA Stansfield Turner are already waiting. Everyone greets the President, and after he takes his seat.

Cyrus Vance begins. "Mr. President, Poland and West Germany are officially recognizing the states of Ukraine, Belarus, Latvia, Lithuania, Estonia, and Moldova. Our channels are reporting that the rest of the European nations will follow within the hour, and the countries of the Warsaw Pact will also do the same."

President Carter nods and thinks for a few moments. "Well, we should do the same, within the hour."

Cyrus Vance agrees, "We're preparing a declaration as we speak, and we should be able to go out to the press soon. My advice is to wait a few more hours and re-evaluate."

President Carter concurs, "I agree. However, we should not look undecided on this matter."

Cyrus Vance continues, "Mr. President, you may have noticed that Georgia is missing from that list. Nine hours ago, Eduard Shevardnadze, the leader of Georgia, was arrested. It seems that the Georgian leader was unable to gain support from the local military forces, and the separatist movement in Georgia is, to put it bluntly. Georgia is being crushed. And Mr. President, it is bad."

President Carter is clenching his fist, his worst fears starting to come true. He asks, "How bad?"

The Director of the CIA, Stansfield Turner, intervenes, "SIG-INT operations are telling us that troops are moving from the Krasnodar Krai region down South towards Georgia, linking up with the existing forces there. We assume that military forces there are still trying to maintain the presence along the Southern border with Turkey, and they are using the Krasnodar Krai army group to secure the rest of the country."

President Carter asks, "Is this a violent reprisal?"

Cyrus Vance replies, "From what we know, and that is very little right now, yes, as violent as it can be. Tanks rolled into Tbilisi, rolled into the crowd, firing. Demonstrators and protestors have been killed. We have some footage from AFP, and it is bad. Bodies in the streets, casualties by the thousands. The tanks did not stop. The local militia, formed just a few days ago, is being dismantled by force, and any units that showed loyalty to the Georgian movement are also being dismantled by force. Mr. President, this is a blood bath."

President Carter's face is set, his jaws clenching repeatedly, pacing around the room and looking at the window outside, the sun rising over the White House lawn, a peaceful world. At the same time, on the other end, ordinary people are turned into mincemeat by tanks. "Damnit, this is what I was afraid of. Not on my watch. Not after Vietnam. What can we do? Where is our nearest carrier group?"

Secretary of Defence, Harold Brown, responds, "Mediterranean Sea, the group was positioned close to Cyprus. However, Mr. President, we cannot cross the Bosphorus Strait. The Montreux Convention does not allow the passage of ships that big. Of course, we could do it, but it would be a major violation of the treaty with a key NATO ally. From a military perspective, not much can be done, and I would advise against military action. This should be solved through diplomacy, and it should be a UN mandate."

President Carter nods, "I agree, however, diplomacy takes months, and people there, by the looks of it, are dying by the minute. How do we collect information?"

Stansfield Turner responds, "Reconnaissance flights from Turkey, SR-71s and U-2s scanning along the border and over the Black Sea, the SR-71s are taking photos, and we're able to recon the whole region without crossing the territorial waters, and the U-2s are used for sniffing."

President Carter asks, "Sniffing?"

Turner responds, "Yes, sniffing, this is something we did with the U-2s for the longest time, we collect air samples at high altitude for nuclear particles, any changes mean that there are either movements, or preparation of a strike, or accidents, with the wind condition, and other information from the physicists, we can understand quite well if there are any potential nuclear threats. Also, if I may continue, we're repositioning the KH-11 satellite over the area right now, and in 12 to 18 hours, we should be able to gain more intelligence from the area."

President Carter looks puzzled again, "KH-11?"

Turner smiles and responds, "The Keyhole satellite that we launched in '76, in theory, we can detect a Ping-Pong ball resting on an icefield, but that's the theory. We should be able to have good imagery soon. Of course, this is all dependent on interpreting the imagery."

President Carter absorbs the information. "It seems like we have to go through a world crisis for me to get to know what toys we have in our bag."

Turner smiles, "Mr. President, you asked for the information, and we provided it, but you don't always ask how."

President Carter continues, "We have intel, and we will have better intel soon, but this doesn't help them much. We have our hands tied when it comes to the Navy. Anything else?"

Harold Brown responds, "There is our Quick Reaction Force that could be deployed within a day's notice, but Mister President, this is a big logistic operation and could lead to escalating into a broader conflict."

President Carter paces around the Oval Office and nods. "What else do we know, their readiness, their nukes?"

Turner responds, "Mr. President, I had contact with Viktor Cebrikov through our channels. He is highly regarded in our community. He conveyed one message. That this should not escalate to a nuclear conflict, either tactical or strategic. To me, it appears that there is still conflict up top in Moscow, and Cebrikov holds the keys to the biggest threat to humanity. From what people who had contact with him in Germany in the past say, he is a man of his word, dedicated to his craft, but an honorable counterpart."

President Carter gives a forced smile. "At least the top spy is honorable, at least there's that. So, our actions, we go out to the press in the next few hours, we validate their independence, and we express our concern over the situation in Georgia, focusing on the loss of life."

Cyrus Vance nods, "I believe this is the most reasonable course of action for now."

President Carter continues, "One more thing, get our UN envoy, and get working with the UN. This must be ratified by the UN, and these countries must have a voice in the process. Also, work on getting some contact with all these ... new countries. Gentlemen, we have a lot of work ahead of us."

President Carter runs his hand through his hair and walks out of the Oval Office, his face set, facing so many unknowns and so many decisions. He bangs the side of his fist against the door frame as he walks out, muttering, "They are running over their people with tanks, damnit!"

Krasnodar, Krasnodar Krai, USSR
August 14th, 1978

Tanya is walking with the rest of the crowd towards Theater Square, the square where all the political rallies are being held in the city. Her arm wrapped around Mischa's arm.

Mischa, a young man, 19 years old, a student at the Mechanical University of Krasnodar, with his brown hair a little longer than the norm, a tall young man, quite scrawny, the typical kid who spends more time in the library, or listening to music, than on the playground in his youth.

Walking with all the locals. In the morning, announcements were made over the PAs, radios, and local Militia, informing everyone to go to a big rally to show their support for the party and their leaders. Her parents, most likely pulled from work, somewhere along the moving crowd, people carrying old placards with Lenin and Stalin's faces, with Marx and Engels, and a new one, that of Ustinov's, new placards done in the same design, with revolutionary quotes from old Leninist books, glory this and slava that.

Tanya looks around her, tired faces, worried faces, some folks smiling at some joke spoken in a whisper, some lost in thought over their lives. All were walking towards the square, none wanting to be there. As they approached the square, officials seconded by the Militia were organizing them into designated sectors. Factory workers are divided by factory, students are in their respective sectors, and pensioners are in the next ones. A grid is meticulously arranged to fill in the square.

Tanya leans over Mischa's shoulder. "Look how organized and happy we all are, Mischa."

Mischa hides his face and Tanya's hair and chuckles, "Yes, Tanya, everyone is so happy to be here."

At 1 o'clock sharp, a voice comes from the PA and keeps reading from a script, talking about the achievements of the Communist Party on the 5-year plan, and talking about the successes that have been achieved in agriculture. The speech has pauses for the people to cheer and applaud. However, the cheers are from the PA. Tanya looks around and sees that only the front two rows of people in the square are cheering and applauding with tremendous verve.

She whispers to Mischa, "Let's sneak out, what do you

think?"

Mischa squeezes her hand, "No, you know they have eyes everywhere, you will get in trouble when the school starts in a few days, you've got to hang in there, and we can't be the first ones to sneak out."

Tanya nods, "Alright, I'll stay here, I swear, I'll yawn so big the guy presiding there is going to think I'm going to eat him whole."

Mischa laughs. Tanya looks around. Everyone around her looks tired and disinterested. The placards are now hanging low, some dumped them against a tree in the Theater Square, Tanya shakes her head thinking to herself, *"This is pointless, it does not make any sense. Don't they see? The ones up there? Don't they see that none of us wants to be here? Are they that blind?"* At some point during a break in the speech, in that second before the prerecorded cheers and applause would have started, a loud and clear voice yells from the crowd. "Freeeeeedom!, Slava Georgia, Slava Ukraine!"

Tanya looks around, hearing the crowd gasping collectively, people moving away from that one singular voice in the crowd.

Mischa pulls Tanya away, "Come, come, this is not going to be good."

A few Militia men in uniform are making their way towards the man who's now in the middle of a circle made by the crowd, trying to reach the man who gave that one rebelling yell and arrest him. One Militia man is lifting his truncheon, coming down with it on someone's shoulder to make room for the rest of his troop. A collective yell starts from the crowd, and people begin to push away from it. In the crowd, one strong hand grabs the truncheon and pushes it down on the Militia man's hat. The hat flips in the air. The men in uniform falter for a second, not able to go through, while a single man, dressed in plain clothes, pushes from the crowd. Pushing into the small circle that was formed by the retreating crowd, tackling the man who yelled, trying to arrest him, as they struggled on the ground, the plain-clothed officer pinned him down, holding him down and trying to pin his hands back and put handcuffs on him. The man grunts and squirms on the ground under the pressure of the plain-clothed officer. That yell, just five words, five words enough to terrify everyone around him and everyone in the balcony where the speech was given. The plain-clothed KGB officer tackles the man who yelled, and they wrestle to the ground, while the crowd is gasping again.

Two men from the crowd, big burly men, dressed in their dirty work outfits, covered in soot, metallurgical workers by the looks of it, are lifting the plain-clothed officer and pushing him away, tossing him away like nothing, one of them grumbling, "*Chekist* bastard!"

Lifting a fist, a fist as big as a loaf of bread, and punching him square in the face. Turning around to the men who gave that loud yell, "Run, you idiot, run!"

Those five Militia men, truncheons up in their hands now, swatting left and right, carving a path, making their way towards the plain-clothed officer. One of them pulls out his gun and fires into the air. The crowd yells again in fear, everyone trying to move away, to make room for the Militia to go through, already trampling each other. Tanya feels a rumble in her chest and looks around. From the adjacent streets, firefighter trucks are making their way towards the square full of people, behind them, a few BTR APCs, their big eight wheels rolling slowly, on another street, a few T-72 tanks are making their way, rumbling slowly behind the firefighting trucks, one street left open, that's where everyone will have to go through, one choke point where Militia and KGB can pick any people from the crowd.

At one signal, the firefighting trucks start to spray water from their water cannons, spraying over the crowd, then lowering the jets of water onto the crowd, as everyone screams and tries to move away towards the only open street.

Voices from the crowd were louder now, "Chekist bastards! Chekist bastards!" and "Freeeedom!" echoing louder and louder in the Theater Square. Two short whistles can be heard from the Militia, and in the next seconds, tear gas canisters are launched into the crowd. The crowd erupts in screams, more coughing, and crying as they inhale the tear gas.

Mischa is cursing loudly, "Come, Tanya, come, we've got to make it to the edge of this trampling crowd".

Working his way through the coughing people, Mischa finds his way to the edge of the square, the edge of the crowd, coughing loudly and spitting, trying to clear his stinging eyes. Tanya, holding on tightly to him and coughing loudly, reaches the street blockade with Mischa and slides between a tank and a building wall. "Just a bit more, Tanya, just a bit more."

Tanya squeezes his hand, "I'm right behind you."

The moment she passes through, an arm reaches out and a Militia man grabs Tanya's arm. "Where do you think you two are going?"

Tanya screams and pulls, but the man grabs her arm tightly. Mischa turns around, moving around Tanya, and punches the man square in the face. The man stumbles and lets go of Tanya's arm. Mischa yells, "Run, Tanya, run!"

Tanya runs, runs as she never ran before, in all her years of track running in high school, she takes a few more steps. She turns her head, seeing a truncheon up high in the air, swung by the punched officer, the truncheon blow landing right into Mischa's face, his brow split, nose broken, blood pouring from his face, as the Militia officer hits and hits again.

Tanya yells "Miiiisssschaaaa!" and keeps running away, turning sideways on a small street, running more, then as she sees some other folks that have made it out of the square, she slows down and fixes her shirt, her shirt torn in a few places, where the officer grabbed her so tightly. Biting her lower lip to stop her crying as she thinks, *"Oh, poor Mischa, he's going to end up in jail all bloodied like that. What can I do? Why did they do that? It was one voice, that's all. Are they that afraid of one voice? What if we all yelled, all at once, would they have killed us all?"*

Tanya finally reaches home, where her parents are already waiting, safe and sound, their clothes crumpled, wet, and dusty from the water sprayed by the firetrucks. She hugs them and bursts into tears,

"Mom, they got Mischa, they got Mischa, and they beat him hard, his face was all bloody and broken."

Her mom hugs her even tighter, "Oh, Tanushka, what did you kids do?"

Tanya keeps holding her tight, her head buried in her mom's shoulder, "Nothing, Mom, I swear, nothing, we were 10 or 20 meters away from that guy that yelled Freedom. That's all, and we tried to stay out of the way. We slipped past some tanks, and some bastard tried to grab me. Mischa punched him, and I ran, and they beat him up badly. I don't know where he is, Mom, I don't know where he is."

Nikolay wraps his arms around Katia and Tanya and holds them tight, kissing the back of Tanya's head. "It's okay, you're alright, and Mischa, they arrested a lot of people, he's hurt, but he is going to be alright. What they did was wrong. So wrong. Don't worry, Tanya, he's going to be alright."

Nikolay lets go of them and goes into the hallway in the entrance, looking at his crumpled beret, grumbling something as he slaps his beret against his thigh to clean up the dust from it.

"Katia, I'm going back to the factory. I will talk with the union leaders. This is not right. I will come back later, you two lock the door and keep the lights off, and don't open the door to anyone."

Nikolay steps out, and Katya covers her mouth with her hand. Not wanting to say anything, worried about what might happen next.

11

Chapter 11: Krasnodar

Krasnodar, Krasnodar Krai, USSR
August 15th, 1978

It's late at night in Krasnodar. The city is quiet, on a warm summer night, where nothing is heard, no sound, no sirens, just a distant humming sound from the refineries and factories on the South side of the city. Katia is holding Tanya in her arms, both sitting on the couch, not able to sleep, Katia not knowing anything about her husband, Nikolay, and Tanya worried that Mischa, her friend, her boyfriend now, since that kiss after one of their teas, worried that Mischa is arrested and beaten more.

Katia talks, "I'm sure Dad is alright, he went to the plant with the rest of the union members, and they will talk and talk about how they have been mistreated, and he is going to come home later and all will be good again."

Tanya sobs, "What about Mischa, Mom? What will happen with him?"

Katia holds her tight, "Mischa is just a kid, they will rough him up a bit more, make him make a declaration and criticize his actions, and then they will let him go, and that's that."

A few minutes after that, a noise starts to grow in the city of Krasnodar, a rumbling sound of thousands of people marching towards the Theater Square, with yells of "Freedom!" and "Down with the bastards!!" growing louder and louder. Tanya pulls away from her mother's arms and looks through the window in the street, people walking towards the square, no longer beaten, no longer bored, going down there where they have been hurt during the day.

Katia takes Tanya's arm. "No, Tanya, don't go out, not tonight, it may end badly."

Tanya responds, "But Mom, I want to be there, I want to go! Please! I must go there!"

Katia is placing herself between the door and Tanya, "And who am I going to stay with? What happens if you and your dad are getting hurt, or worse, killed? What am I going to do?"

Tanya sighs deeply. "Oh, Mom, am I going to stay here like a coward and not do anything?"

Katia puts her hands on her shoulders. "Yes, please, for now, there will be time to help, and we will know soon what's going on."

Tanya goes back to the window, "We know what's going on, Mom, they are going over to the soldiers, and going to the Party headquarters, and they will storm it and kick them out. That's what's going to happen."

Tanya goes to her bedroom and slams the door behind her. Katia is trying to follow, opening her mouth to admonish her, but she sighs and stops, then goes back to the couch, cradling a blanket and waiting there, alone on the couch, waiting.

Around 6 o'clock in the morning, Katia opens her eyes. She fell asleep there on the couch, waiting for Nikolay. She blinks a few times, looking at the sun rising through the window. The city is calm now, and she listens outside, but hears nothing out of the ordinary. After a few minutes, she hears footsteps coming up the stairs of her apartment building, accompanied by a familiar voice. She hears the keys in the lock, and she bolts upright, her eyes glued to the entrance.

The door opens, and Nikolay steps in, tired, dirty, but with a big smile on his face, "Good morning! Where are my girls?"

Katia gasps and runs towards Nikolay and hugs him, "Nikolay! What happened? Where have you been?"

Tanya bursts out of her bedroom, her eyes red from crying, her hair a mess, running towards her dad to hug him.

Nikolay stops them, "Girls, look what I found. Come on, Mischa, get in!"

Nikolay lets Mischa get into the small vestibule of their apartment. Tanya gasps when she sees Mischa, his head bandaged, his nose covered with a big plaster, blood dried under his nose, two big shiners turning darker under his eyes, but underneath all that, smiling big.

Tanya yells. "Miiischa!" she says, getting closer to him and taking him in her arms. She looks at his face, leans over, and tries to kiss him, but not quite finding the right spot that isn't bruised. After looking into his eyes for a few moments, she plants a kiss on his lips.

"Mischa, what happened? Where did they take you?"

Turning towards her dad, her cheeks flushed at the realization that her dad saw her kissing a guy, "Dad, how? Where did you find him?"

Nikolay laughs and puts his beret up on the hook in the

vestibule. "I'll let Mischa tell his story. Let's sit down in the kitchen, maybe we can have some tea or coffee."

They all cram in the small kitchen, Katia turning on the stove and boiling some water.

Mischa looks at Tanya, "God, I'm glad you are alright." He smiles and continues. "After I punched that officer, have you seen that punch? It was magnificent."

Tanya nods, "Mischa, you haven't been in a fight in your entire life, what were you thinking?"

Mischa smiles again, "I wasn't! After I threw that punch and saw you run away, wherever that guy was swinging his truncheon, I kept parrying with my head. I kept on parrying like that three or four times until I passed out. Tanya, you won't believe the stars I saw."

Tanya puts his hand on his face, "Oh, you poor guy, you parried so well. Didn't miss a single blow."

Misha smiles and kisses Tanya's palm. "Not a single one. I woke up a few minutes after, I was dragged in some paddy wagon, along with other folks, all bloodied and hurt, then they took us to the Militia station in the center of the town and put us into their holding cells to be processed. They dragged a few guys out for interrogation. Those guys never return."

Mischa looks down, a shade of sadness and fear in his eyes, "We heard their screams. What kind of interrogation was that? All they could do was scream. Sometimes, the screams went silent. Those bastards!"

Nikolay pats Mischa's back and grabs his shoulder, and, squeezing it tight, says, "It's alright, sonny, they paid for that."

Mischa nods and sniffles a bit, trying to breathe through his broken nose. "We heard noises on the street and screaming and shouting, and grunting, a few shots were fired, then your dad showed up, with other workers, and got us all out."

Katia gasps, "Nikolai, what happened? What did you?"

Nikolai blows into his cup of tea. "Katia darling, after a night like this, wouldn't you think that maybe a splash of something stronger would be good in this tea?"

Tania smiles, realizing that her dad is scared of how his wife will react when she hears his story. Even more afraid than he was when facing the Militia guards. She quickly goes to the counter, grabs a bottle of vodka, and pours generously into her dad's cup.

"Thank you, Tanushka." Said her dad. He clears his throat, "Well, I went to the plant, we all got together, union members, party members, workers, just us, the workers, and we talked, what had happened was not right. To be beaten like this, by our people, ordered by the ones who should lead us. Where is the fraternity, where's the equality of all the workers? There were workers, students, pensioners, and people who may have fought against the Germans. To be treated like this? Like livestock?!"

Nikolay sighed. Nobody spoke of the true realization of what had happened. Nikolay takes another sip from his cup and continues. "We sounded three short blasts from sirens, and other blasts responded, so we got out and started marching towards the square just like that, some with wrenches, some with spades and shovels. One Militiaman tried to stop us. He took a shovel on his back."

Katia gasped and Nikolay continued, we silently approached the soldiers left in the tanks and pulled them out, what happened with them after that, I don't know, we marched in the square and some got into the party headquarters, some got into the Militia station in the center of the city, I went for that, I was hoping to find Mischa, and I did, we stormed the place. They didn't fight much. Most of them ran away, some of them joined us, some officers tried to stop us, but they didn't stand a chance."

Nikolay stops and puts his head down. "We found the interrogation rooms, bloody slaughter, maybe one of them will live, but I don't know."

Nikolay shakes his head, as if trying to wipe a bad dream from his mind. "I took this mighty fighter with me." Nikolay pats Mischa on the shoulder again. "And we went to the party headquarters, it was all done by the time we got there, all the council members were bound, they looked better than Mischa, but not by much. Now they were writing a proclamation."

Katia looks puzzled. "What are they proclaiming?"

Nikolay lifts his shoulders, "It doesn't make much sense to me, but we had enough of Moscow and the party and all the leaders from there, so now, maybe the nation of Krasnodar Krai is rising, we're Russians, but maybe it's better this way. I don't know."

Katia looks unbelieving. "But, Nikolay, they are going to roll over us. They will crush every last one of us."

Nikolay thinks for a moment, "Yes, they will, but they'd better be willing to fight, because I'm tired of getting beaten up."

Nikolay takes a deep breath. "Now, we all had a rough night. I want to sleep, Mischa. Your parents must be worried sick."

Mischa lifts his shoulders. "Dad is working on the Oil fields in Kazakhstan. He comes home once every three months, and Mom is with Grandma in a village next to Pshada. I'm sure they are worried, but not that much."

Nikolay nods, "That's why all the teas are done at your place, I understand. You can crash here on the couch. Not there!" Nikolay points towards Tanya's bedroom door, "Not there, Tanya will take care of you. You need to clean those cuts. I'm afraid your nose will be crooked from now on, but wear it with pride. You did well, sonny. "

Drained of all energy, Nikolay walks towards his bedroom, followed by Katia, all quiet, all trying to process what happened that night and how their lives had been changed in a few hours.

KYIV, UKRAINE
August 15th ,1978

Andrei walks into his office at 8 o'clock, followed by General Radzievsky, who sits behind his desk and motions for the General to have a seat.

Andrei starts the conversation. "So, tell me, General, what happened in Krasnodar?"

The General riffles through some of his papers, "After the situation in Georgia...."

Andrei shakes his head, interrupting the General. "Poor Eduard, do we know anything about him?"

The General responds, "We think he was executed, but we don't have a confirmation."

Both men hang their heads low in a moment of silence. The General continues after a moment,

"After the situation in Georgia, the Communist Party leaders in Krasnodar Krai organized a rally to show support for the Soviet Union and Chairman Ustinov. Fearing that there may be a popular reaction, they had an army contingent mixed with the KGB and the Militia. The people reacted, and the forces on the ground counter-reacted. There were multiple wounded, and four or five people died in the struggle, and when people trampled around."

Andrei clenches his fists, "Are they completely stupid? Why would they do that?"

The General shakes his head, "Comrade Kirilenko, how many communist leaders grow up to be completely unaware of the people's needs? Can you name a few?"

Andrei nods, "Yes, unfortunately, I can name too many."

The General continues, "From the little information we have on the ground, it looks like the union leaders got together in the night and decided that was too much, and workers from all the plants and refineries rallied in the night and stormed the Party Headquarters, the Militia station, and the TV and Radio station. And this morning, they proclaimed that the Krasnodar Krai will be an independent country and an independent nation, free of Moscow's influence. This is all we know."

Andrei shakes his head, "They will all be dead by tomorrow."

The General responds, "Not by tomorrow, most of the armed forces in Krasnodar are further down South, trying to link up with the troops in Georgia, there's not much opposition South, we have a border with them now, that flank is safe. But, they will be crushed, in a week or two or a month maximum."

Andrei gets up and walks around his office for a few moments, looking at the window, then turns towards the General, "What can we do to help them?"

The General thinks for a moment, "Comrade Kirilenko, in my opinion, not much. We are already in a perilous situation. This would be a blatant act of war against Russia if we do anything. So, we cannot do much."

Andrei asks, "Do you know who's their leader?"

The General continues, "His name is Ruslan Chernogorov, he is an engineer at the metallurgical plant in Krasnodar. And he proclaimed his movement under the name of the Communist Front of Liberation."

Andrei lets out a forced laugh, "Communist this, communist that, soon there will be none of that."

Andrei continues. "First, we must establish some contact, get a line going with these folks. they have to know they are not alone. Second, we must press the UN. I'll work on that. Third, how is Mukha? Could he work out some contacts there, on his line of work?"

The General is taking some notes. "Yes, I'll get going on that, and the UN is a good idea. There's enough information out there to be able to make a strong claim that there is a need for external help in maintaining the peace. I believe, Comrade Kirilenko, that Krasnodar is becoming a key factor in this. If it fails quickly, it may be the turning point for all of us to fail just as quickly."

Andrei thinks for a moment, contemplating the hard truth in the General's opinion, shakes the General's hand, and walks him out of his office. "Nadia, please get Comrade Pelše on the phone for me."

A few moments later, the phone rings on Andrei's desk. He picks up and hears Pelše's voice from the other side. "Comrade Pelše, I'm glad you are still alive. I'm truly glad of that. How are you holding up?"

Pelše answers from the other side, "Comrade Kirilenko, the same goes for me. And for now, we are holding up. It seems that our movement is getting external support, but so far these are just words of encouragement, and nothing else, but it is still better than facing tanks."

Andrei agrees, and he gets up from his desk, stretching to release some of the tension from the past week. "Indeed, it is way better than facing an open war, Comrade Pelše. We must present a united voice at the UN next week. We all have to show that we want our new nations to continue to live independently and without external interference."

Andrei pauses for a few seconds, taking a sip from his cup of coffee, then speaks again, "And by doing this, we will legitimize our movement not just by popular rallies but by holding referendums and having them supervised by neutral nations, or even, with supervisors from Russia."

Pelše responds, "I agree with you, Comrade Kirilenko. However, supervisors from Russia are like inviting the wolf to dine with the sheep."

Andrei laughs on the phone. "That is true, Arvid Yanovich, but it also shows that we are bold and believe in what we do. I'm sure that the observers they will send will be KGB people, but we know those too, as I am sure that observers coming here from Western countries will be CIA and MI6, and other names that I don't recall."

Pelše responds, "Andrei Pavlovich, I like your resolve in this, and I agree with you, we were bold and we must continue to be bold, this is the only way we can support our friends in Georgia, and the folks in Krasnodar. This latter one was a surprise."

Andrei nods slightly, "Yes, that was a surprise, and I'm sorry for those folks there, they will be the ones to suffer."

Andrei says goodbye to Pelše, hangs up the phone, and leaves his office, talking to Nadia about his upcoming visit to the UN in New York. Plans over plans slowly coming together, one step at a time, each step taken unravelling a future problem.

Tyndall AFB, Florida, USA

August 15th, 1978

James is taxiing his F-5 on the apron of Tyndall AFB, following closely the hand signals for the Ground Marshall. Seeing the Marshall holding his hands over his head, the signal to sit on the brakes so the ground crew to put the chocks under the wheels. Watching the ground crew running under the plane and feeling the jolt of his F-5 when the chocks are pressed against the tires. The Marshall gives him the cut signal, and James shuts down the engines, flicking the switches in the cabin to turn the plane off. He opens the canopy, and the warm air in Florida makes him sweat almost immediately. He unstraps his helmet, and with the help of the ground crew, he unstraps from his plane, jumping out from the cockpit.

Taking the logbook from the Crew Chief, he signs and tells the Chief, "The plane is Code One, chief, no snags, no problems, and not over G'd. Thank you."

He shakes the Chief's hand and walks towards the other F-5, where Ronald is finishing his talk with his Crew Chief. James yells, "Baaaanjooo!"

Ronald lifts his head and grins at James, exchanging a quick handshake. They walk together to the building where they will remove their flight suits and have their debrief. It was a 2v2 flight against a flight of Turkish F-4Es, part of the Turkish Air Force training curriculum. Both start to talk animatedly, already shooting their watches. James mimics his plane sliding behind another plane.

"When I get there in lag pursuit, you have to go up quicker and cover me from up high. With our Tigers, we lack the energy the Phantoms have, and this way we could control the engagement better."

Ronald replies, "I know, I hesitated for a second, I was sure that the number two plane would try and split their formation and try to shake you, so I stayed there to cover you. I lost 2 or 3 seconds."

James nods, "Yeah, I had them all the way, they are still learning, they are not using the Phantom to its full potential."

Ronald laughs, "If they would, you wouldn't be so cocky now."

James laughs, "That's a bunch of bullcrap. I can tangle with them. I'm small and nimble. I'm not saying it would be easy, but it can be done. One day, it would be nice to jump an element of the Navy or Marines and have a little fun with them."

Ronald nods, "Soon, when we go to Red Flag, that's going to be fun." They walk together in the locker room and start to take off their flight suits, zipper by zipper.

Ronald continues the conversation. "Man, you've seen the crap over there in Georgia and Ukraine, and what else did they say? Something with K?"

James nods, "Yeah, Krasnodar, man, when Russians start to do something, they do it right, no kidding, they went to dismantle their whole country and dismantle they did."

Ronald shakes his head. "And run it over too...."

James nods, "That's messed up. Who does that to their people?"

Ronald sighs, "Hey man, remember Chicago in '68? We were not much better."

James responds quickly, "Come on, we didn't use tanks."

Ronald gets back to him, "You are right, but it's the same, it's just crazy how one day there's peace and the other day the whole world turns to crap."

James nods again, slamming the door of his locker. "Do you think they will send us there?"

Ronald shakes his head, "No way, to do what? Fight with the Russians, or against, 'cause no one could tell, and anyway, not us, we're training and such."

James looks a bit worried, "I don't know, you were saying that we're the best-trained squadron, Diane is worried sick."

Ronald sighs, "Jayne too, but they are used to it. They have been through that before, in the end, Badger, we have to worry about the things we can control, and right about now, after we have our debrief, I worry that my beer will not be cold enough."

James slaps his shoulder, "Man, I can't have Diane worry too much, she's pregnant, I think I'm getting more worried than her, it's tough, you know, growing a person, turning him into a good human being."

Ronald laughs, "You big softie, before you know it, you will be old and grandkids will tug on your mustache, and you will tell big fat lies with airplanes and battles. Come on, let's go, if we have to go there, we will, we'll kick ass and come back, and that's it!"

12

Chapter 12: U.N.

U.N. Headquarters, USA
August 25th, 1978

Andrei is tired, 5th hour into this UN meeting, tired of listening to the translators. *"I should've studied more English,"* Andrei thinks, trying to get back into focusing on yet another delegate expressing his concerns about the instability in the area. The six former Soviet Union regions are being admitted, together, as observers for now, not yet as full members. *"It's better than nothing for now, but at least everyone got to hear us and our stories."*

A U.S. Delegate walks around the General Assembly Hall, making his way towards the table of the Chinese delegation. Upon reaching there, he greets and shakes hands with a few of the other delegates, then leans towards the leading Chinese representative.

"Good afternoon, Mr. Xi."

The Chinese representative pulls his headset down and nods

at the US representative. "Good afternoon, Mr. Young, how can I help you?"

The US representative leans even closer, "Mr. Xi, if China will not exercise its veto right, I have guarantees that we will have a very good agricultural deal for the next years to come, also, those new helicopters, the UH-60, we can secure that deal and also licensing rights."

The Chinese representative nods and puts his headset back on, listening intently to the speech from the Polish representative. Watching as the US representative moves back to the US table and leans towards one of his colleagues, he says, "I believe we just kicked Russia out of the Security Council."

The next representative, Alex Jackson Young, comes to the podium and arranges his stack of papers. He presents Resolution 423, which revokes the USSR's veto rights and removes the USSR from the UN Security Council for a period of two years. There is shock and awe across the floor. All the representatives are talking with each other, consulting with their advisors.

Andrei turns around towards his newly appointed External Affairs Minister, Borys Klymenko, "If this passes through, it removes the veto right from Russia. This would be a huge victory. Also, it can be seen as a declaration of war. However, they structured it well. It's just two years. Two years where we can consolidate."

Andrei turns the other way, towards Pelše, nodding slightly at him, as Pelše glances back and returns the nod. *"Two years, would that be enough? And even so, they could attack us tomorrow, or next week, this does not change a single thing."*

The United Kingdom representative sustains the resolution proposed by the US representative, and a vote is taking place.

The resolution passes by a narrow margin, and as of tomorrow, the former USSR will no longer have veto rights in the UN Security Council. This right will be reinstated after a two-year period.

The session is stopped and will resume tomorrow. As Andrei is walking out of the hall, he is greeted by various representatives. Andrei keeps thanking them all, trying to be as cordial as possible.

Eventually, the US Representative is making his way towards him. "It is finally nice to meet you, Mr. Kirilenko."

Alex Young is pumping his hand as he speaks. Andrei listens to the interpreter and turns back to Alex Young, replying, "It is my pleasure as well, and thank you for all your support today."

Young continues, "It takes a man of extraordinary courage to do what you and others have done."

Andrei laughs. "Or incredibly stupid, Mr. Young, or a little bit of both, but history will decide."

Alex Young pats Andrei on his back as he walks away. Turning around and telling him. "History is being done today, Mr. Kirilenko."

Andrei nods and keeps walking, thinking about what Alex Young had said. *"History was being done, history was done on the streets of Krasnodar, on the bloody streets of Tbilisi, and on the streets of Kyiv, and so many other streets. What's being done today is just that you dared to admit it, and you try to steal all the glory by admitting that you dared to do something right."*

As he continues to walk out of the Assembly Hall, Andrei notices the Russian delegation holding an impromptu press conference. Mikhail Sytenko, the newly appointed UN representative, is speaking in perfect English about the risks of removing the veto rights and how this decision could increase instability in the region. He acknowledges the Soviet Union is facing struggles but expresses confidence in the Soviet people's resolve.

Andrei, trying to understand all that, without a translator, shakes his head, disgusted by the whole speech.

"Yeah... running people over with tanks, sending them away to gulags, keeping them hungry. Good resolve, that one. Very good resolve."

U.N. Headquarters, USA
August 26th, 1978

The next day's session, after the official roll call and a review of the agenda for this emergency session, the UN President-Elect, Indalecio Liévano, opens the floor. The first to take the podium is Alex Young. Andrei watches him with curiosity, wondering what the US is planning today. Alex Young starts his speech by presenting the violent events that happened in Tbilisi, presenting the crowd almost minute by minute how the independent movement was crushed there, how Eduard Shevardnadze was captured and executed. He addresses the situation in Krasnodar, highlighting the quick and violent movement there.

Andrei shakes his head in awe, *"Damn, this is one good orator, he's playing all of them like a violin, I wouldn't want to be at the receiving end of this resolution."*

Alex Young continues his speech, presenting how the new countries, now observers, are making every effort to listen to the voice of the people organizing referendums and relying on public opinion. Showing that this is above democracy, but just fundamental human rights. He continues to emphasize that people in Krasnodar have the same rights and should receive the same support. He points out that the other member nations in the room have also gone through similar struggles. He presents the struggle of the South American countries and their fight for independence, then moves on to Algeria and Tunisia, and even mentions Vietnam and its fight.

Andrei smiles. *"Mr. Young is openly accepting that America was the oppressor there. That is profound and very crafty, Mr. Young, way to open towards everyone in the room."*

Alex Young continues in his speech and tells the General Assembly that the mission of the UN in this case is to protect and maintain the peace in the Krasnodar region. He is proposing Resolution 424. A Peacekeeping mission in the Region of Krasnodar, until an agreement is reached between the Soviet Union, or Russia, and the leaders of Krasnodar.

The room erupts, with some applauding and others leaning over to talk with their representatives and advisors. Loud voices from the Russian table protest vehemently. Andrei continues to observe the room, showing no emotion. *"Again, crafty, the region of Krasnodar, not a country yet, but there are distinct leaders in Krasnodar, thus giving it legitimacy, diplomats, always walking the tightest rope, and this one is a good one."*

The Russian delegation continues to speak, all of them at once, with the microphones off, and Andrei hears a swear word spoken in Russian. The Russian delegate, Mikhail Sytenko, throws papers, then turns around and calms his delegation.

Leaning over his microphone and addressing the President of the General Assembly. The President responds, "Yes, the Soviet Union delegation will have the opportunity to take the floor now, and no, the Soviet Union delegation does not have the veto right. I can read you the Resolution 423 if you would like, Mr. Sytenko."

The Russian delegation is speaking for a few seconds, trying to quickly formulate a response to this proposed resolution.

Then, Mikhail Sytenko walks towards the podium, clears his voice, and starts, "Unfortunately, unlike my eloquent predecessor, I did not have the luxury to prepare a speech, but I will speak from the heart. Yes, it is true, the Soviet Union is going through some struggles. However, this resolution, although layered in all the right ideologies, if put into practice, will be nothing but a blatant invasion by imperialist countries. We're talking here about peace and human rights. I will have to remind you, distinguished colleagues, that the Soviet Union's resolve will be strong, sustained, and complete. However, for the time being, the Soviet Union will respect the decisions of this General Assembly, but also, the Soviet Union will scrutinize every development of this so-called peacekeeping resolution. And I warn this assembly. This has been tried before. Great Britain and France have opposed the Bolsheviks and failed. Great Britain and France have divided Russia before and failed to do so. This is how this feeble effort will fail. This is my warning, my distinguished colleagues." Sytenko steps off the podium and sits down at this table, looking defiantly at the rest of the assembly.

The assembly room remains silent. Andrei runs his hands through his hair. Looking at Pelše's table, he remains quiet, his face like stone, not showing any emotions. *"I think this is the moment I realize I may have been stupid and not heroic, or probably both. When Pelše said about inviting the wolves to the table, it looks like we're inviting the whole pack now."*

The President of the General Assembly asks if there are any other requests to take the floor and notes that countries with

"Observer" status are not permitted to do so. He then proposes holding a vote, as this Resolution will not be unanimous and is contested. The hall becomes agitated again, with the rustling of papers and hushed voices as representatives and advisors confer. From time to time, Andrei notices that buttons on the voting machine are being pressed.

A few minutes later, the results of the vote are in, and Resolution 424 is passed with a majority. China abstains again and does not exercise its veto rights. Applause coming from various countries in the hall. Andrei noticed that the US delegates are maintaining their composure, and they are not as flamboyant as he would be. The President is closing the session, thanking everyone in the room and reminding all the representatives that the UN's role is to maintain international peace and security, as well as to protect human rights. The Assembly is dismissed, and everyone gathers their papers and slowly exits the General Assembly Hall.

Andrei shakes hands with his External Affairs Minister, and together they walk towards the exit. Alex Young is stopping them.

Andrei shakes his hand, "Congratulations on your speech, Mr. Young. Those were powerful words."

Young responds, "Thank you, Mr. Kirilenko, as I was saying, sometimes, we make history in this hall. However, the words of my Russian counterpart had some weight as well."

Andrei nods, "Indeed, Mr. Young. I appreciate your support."

Young continues, "Mr. Kirilenko, from my understanding, your plane leaves tomorrow. I want to extend an invitation to Camp David today. The President would like to meet you for an unofficial visit. We will make sure you get back on time for your flight."

Andrei thinks for a second. "Mr. Young, it would be an honor, and I gladly accept your invitation, but I want to emphasize the unofficial part, and maybe I would like this to be discreet."

Young smiles, "Mr. Kirilenko, we feel the same way. There is a helicopter waiting on top of your hotel. It would be the easiest way to take the limo designated for you to your hotel. Press the elevator button for the top-floor heliport, and we will take it from there. And in about an hour and a half, we will meet at Camp David."

Andrei nods, "In this case, M. Young, we will meet at Camp David. Goodbye." Andrei walks out, maintaining the same pace, knowing well that someone must have seen that conversation, but from afar, it didn't look like more than just regular chitchat.

Andrei is watching the American scenery from the window of the Bell 206 helicopter, a small and quiet helicopter, rushing at 500 feet of altitude, getting closer to Camp David. Andrei reflects on his first trip into the United States, *"Indeed, everything is bigger here, buildings, cities, farms, cars, God, cars here are big. But I'm sure it's not all fun and games, just like everywhere, the grass is greener on the other side, but damn, this grass is green."* Andrei chuckles, *"Andrei, you old man, you can't have capitalist dreams now, you are too old for this."* The helicopter slows to land on the lawn in front of Camp David, gracefully descending and lowering, touching down gently. The pilot turns his head and gives Andrei a quick salute, and Andrei responds with a salute of his own. Andrei sees President Carter walking out and coming to open the helicopter door. Quickly getting out of the helicopter and meeting the president, both shaking hands, and walking bent over so they don't hit the spinning propeller.

Carter is the first one to speak. "President Kirilenko, nice to meet you. I hope the helicopter ride here was pleasant."

Andrei nods, "President Carter, nice to meet you as well, it was indeed, thank you for the invitation."

They both step in, and President Carter is inviting Andrei and his translator to have a seat. As the President sits in an armchair in front of him, Andrei quickly scans the room and sees Turner and Vance seated across the room.

President Carter starts to talk first, "President Kirilenko, anything to drink? We will have dinner later. If it pleases you, you can spend the night here at Camp David, and we will make sure you return in time for your scheduled flight."

Andrei responds, "Thank you, Mr. President. First, according to the protocol, I don't even know my title yet. You see, we're still working on our constitution in Ukraine, and to be honest, Andrei is just fine. Second, I would like to try your favorite whiskey. As for staying here for the night, thank you for the invitation, but I would like to return to New York tonight. I believe it will be better for me to be seen leaving the hotel on my way to the airport."

President Carter smiles and nods. "I agree, Andrei, and I think this is a wise choice. Also, I'm more of a wine drinker myself, but I'd like to toast with you over a glass of Woodford Reserve. This is excellent bourbon made here in the United States. Also, the hell with protocol, I'm James Carter."

In a few seconds, an aide serves a tray of glasses, and they lift their glasses. President Carter toasts first. "To your health, Andrei, cheers!"

Andrei goes second, "*Nazdrovia,* James. Cheers!"

They clink their glasses and drink at the same time, President Carter huffing a bit, not used to it, and Andrei showing no strain from the burn of the bourbon.

Andrei smiles, "This is a delicious drink, James. I see why the cowboys in the movies loved this."

President Carter puts the glass down and takes a sip of water. "Andrei, what do you think about what happened today?"

Andrei thinks for a second, then replies, "It was a courageous thing to do. People there need support. It is also very risky, indeed, the Russians will see that as a threat. It also shows the rest of us that we are not forgotten and that we will not be ignored. For this, I thank you, from me, from the Ukrainian people, and the ones in Krasnodar and Georgia."

The President nods, "What do you think about what is happening in Moscow? You, of all people, must know, and you must know better than any of us."

Andrei smiles, realizing that this is the purpose of the meeting, assessing the power struggle in Moscow. "James, Soviet political structure is entirely different than what it is here in the United States. The General Secretary is the leader of the Party, and as such, he is also the leader of the country. However, the Politburo is the one that makes decisions in theory. In practice, it is a bit different. Each General Secretary must have a troika, which consists of three, four, or five senior Politburo members who will support the General Secretary's decisions. To answer your question. I don't believe Ustinov has a troika. He has some support, and since he controls the army, he carries considerable weight. However, I don't think he has that system in place yet, so every action is delayed now."

President Carter nods and glances at Vance, "This is what we believe as well."

Andrei continues, "I also believe that Viktor Chebrikov, the new Chief at KGB, is the voice of reason there in the Politburo, although new in his position, he is held in high regard by his peers and carries a lot of weight."

President Carter responds, "Thank you for this assessment, Andrei. What can we do to help you?"

Andrei takes a second to think. "James, right now we are learning, we're learning what we forgot for 60 years or so, the Soviet Union was a centralized system, and now, we must learn how to survive on our own. And I'm sure we will make mistakes. We can sustain it for now, but these next few months, we must learn on our own, without upsetting our neighbor anymore. Every move we would make towards the West, even towards other countries in the East, could be seen as a form of aggression for now. We must learn to navigate that."

President Carter thinks about what Andrei just said. "I must agree with you, it is a tough position you are in right now, and I appreciate your honesty and how cautious you are."

Andrei laughs, "James, we are like in that joke, I don't know if you know it. A guy falls from the 20th floor of a building, and he screams while plummeting towards the ground. Another guy pops his head out from his balcony on the 10th floor and asks, 'How is it?' And the falling guy responds, So far, so good! That's how we are! So far, so good."

President Carter bursts into laughter, slapping his thigh as he laughs, "Oh God, this is a good one, Andrei, can I steal this?"

Andrei laughs, "Absolutely, James, it would be my honor."

President Carter continues, "I think you and I could be good friends. How about we have some dinner, and we will talk more there."

Andrei smiles and gets up. "James, I hope we will be good friends, and yes, dinner would be just fine now."

All of them are walking towards the dining room at Camp

David, two people from two different worlds, finding that there are so many things they have in common.

Brecon Beacons, Wales, UK
August 27th, 1978

Two officers are standing on top of a mountain in the Brecon Beacons range, supervising the re-qual tests for Special Air Service officers and NCOs. Looking through their clipboards and scanning the range in front of them, trying to stay warm in the cold climate of the mountains in Wales, one of the officers asks, "What do we have?"

The other one responds, "Well, two failed, one injured, broken ankle."

The officer nods, "So three disqualified, oh well, and one late, isn't it?" The other officer confirms, "Yeah, Angus. He's 3 hours late."

They look at each other, "Should we send a search party?" The officer lifts his shoulders, "It's Angus, so I'm assuming he's dead. He was never late before, in any of his tests, and he is an old head. I'd give him more time. It will be dark soon, so no matter what, we won't be able to do much."

Minutes are passing by, when one of the officers feels something grabbing his leg, pulling him down with a sudden move. "Aaaarrrgghhh bloody hell!"

A burst of laughter comes from a green mound behind the officers, a mound that wasn't there a few minutes ago.

The mound moves, and a face emerges. "I could have killed both of you. You old farts are losing it."

One of the officers is clutching his heart. "Bloody hell,

Angus, you almost gave me a heart attack."

Angus laughs, his laughter echoing in the mountains. He's tall, 6.4, and almost as wide. His short-cropped red hair and long red beard looked wild in his camo suit. Angus starts to take off his camo suit, and one of the officers speaks again.

"You are late, though."

Angus grins and responds, "Bollocks. Flip your fancy clipboard, check the back. I signed in four hours ago, when you were off having a piss and chomping your sandwich. I was here 4 hours ago. It just took me 4 hours to move behind you two blokes and scare you."

The officer turns his clipboard and looks in disbelief. "You are nuts, you know that, totally nuts, ready to be institutionalized."

Angus laughs again, "And what's that institution that is going to be able to keep me there?"

The officer lifts his shoulders. "He's right. Bloody perfect soldier, you are. Forty miles in under twenty-two hours. In this weather. That's a record."

The other officer speaks, "We got words on the radio that we will have to go through a brief, it looks like we will do a little trip in Russia. Somewhere picturesque, I'm guessing."

Angus nods, "I figured, probably in the mountains somewhere in Georgia or Krasnodar, get that radio and call the chopper, let's pack all this and go, I'm thirsty."

One of the officers speaks, "We have water."

Angus laughs again, "You can wash your face with that. I want a beer."

WASHINGTON, USA

August 14th, 1978

In the Oval Office, President Carter is having another meeting with members of his cabinet. Vice President Walter Mondale is back. With the imminent danger gone, the cabinet should work together. Secretary of State Cyrus Vance and Secretary of Defense Harold Brown are present, along with Alex Young, Zbigniew Brzezinski from the National Security Advisor's office, and Stansfield Turner from the Central Intelligence Agency. The topic of today's meeting is the Peacekeeping mission in Krasnodar.

President Carter is greeting everyone and surveys the Oval Office, where a map of the region is already on display, along with pins and markers.

President Carter starts the meeting. "Good morning, everyone, now that we have a UN resolution about this mess in Krasnodar, thanks to Mr. Young. That was a brilliant speech, by the way. And after a short meeting with Andrei Kirilenko, it is time to start to sort this out."

Turner is asking, "How was Kirilenko, by the way?"

President Carter responds, "He was a down-to-earth fellow, a bit overwhelmed and tired, but in all honesty, he seems to be a nice guy."

Turner replies, "Indeed, but in the end, he is a true communist."

President Carter nods, "That may be, but he is also a true patriot, and he had enough guts to pull this move. We may not share the same ideology, but we see eye to eye on human rights, at least that's what I gathered from him. "

Turner nods, and President Carter continues. "Mr. Brown, how do we start this. I can't stress enough." President Carter starts to punctuate every word, tapping his index finger on the Resolute Desk. "I do not want another Vietnam, I do not want a prolonged war, especially with Russia!"

Harold Brown opens his notebook, which he has already prepared. "Mr. President, let's talk about our constraints first. Logistics: This will be a long supply route, with supplies primarily transported by ships. We can stage in Mediterranean ports, allowing us to consider the days at sea through the Dardanelles, the Bosphorus, and then across the Black Sea. Even by plane, assuming we can secure one or two airports, that means we will have to fly over the airspace of Eastern European countries, which will raise difficulties."

Secretary of State Cyrus Vance joins the conversation. "We are talking with Romania, Bulgaria, and Poland, and we are trying to resolve this as we speak. Bulgaria is reluctant to offer any support, as Turkey has declared neutrality in this whole affair. It seems like Bulgarians are doing the same. However, the Romanian and Polish governments are willing to listen. Romanians have extended port facilities in Constanta, and it appears they are willing to allow us to use an airport as a refueling base, specifically the airport in Timisoara, which is one of their MiG-21 bases and is well-equipped."

President Carter listens, then asks. "Can we trust them?"

Vance replies, "We were enemies until 2 months ago. However, Ceaușescu, the Secretary General in Romania, opposed the Soviet invasion in 1968 in Czechoslovakia, so among all of them, he is the most pro-Western. However, the country is not doing well economically, so they will look for various concessions, and that's fine in my books."

President Carter thinks for a moment, "Alright, so, it seems like we have some options when it comes to logistics, that's good, what were the other problems, Mr. Brown?"

Harold Brown continues, "The other one is the involvement on the ground, my suggestion would be to secure two airports, the one at Krimsk and the one in Krasnodar, which seem suitable, the Krasnodar airport is a training base and it has the proper facilities. However, it is within the range of the aviation units based in Sochi and Maykop. The airport at Krimsk is probably the best one to use. We can start organizing the 1st Marine Division and the 9th Infantry Division, supported by the 1st Cavalry Air Brigade, for now. Germany, France, and Great Britain are willing to collaborate in this effort."

President Carter smiles, "Well, I suggest transiting the German tanks through Poland, then Ukraine, all the way into the heart of Russia. I'm sure nobody thought about this plan."

Everyone in the room starts laughing. President Carter quiets them, "Now, gentlemen, I want to emphasize another point. This involvement is for the people of Krasnodar and those in Georgia. I demand that all briefings, notices, and rules of engagement be inclusive. Civilians' lives must be protected! Villages, cities, property, infrastructure, this must be protected at all costs. We will not save this country by bombing it to hell. I believe that in this case, we have most of the civilians on our side, but we know from experience how quickly this can change. I know! The expression hearts and minds has been used before in this office. I hope we learn from those mistakes. Mr. Turner, no more Phoenix projects, and Mr. Brown, if we can avoid napalm, it would be great. I will not do this like LBJ. We will not select targets here. The commander on the scene will make this decision. By the way, we will have to name one."

Harold Brown speaks, "Mr. President, I have two names

that come to mind, Gen. Henry 'Hank' Emerson or Gen. Fred Franks Jr., both are experienced commanders, and both are sharp, and have extensive knowledge of operating in a combined arms environment."

President Carter paces around the office for a few seconds. "Those are good options. Give me a day or so, and I will tell you my recommendation."

Harold Brown continues. "The Chief of Staff suggests that first, we should set up a camp base, right about here." Harold Brown points to a specific location on the map. "Between Krimsk and Krasnodar, we can set up a camp, with a helicopter pad and all the logistics necessary to conduct operations. This way, we show presence in the region, make it easily defensible, and avoid interfering with the local population. However, with helicopter support, we can conduct operations throughout the entire region. This will give us time to secure the port at Novorossiysk, secure the Krimsk airport, and build our presence in the region, and depending on the Russian response, we can either escalate or de-escalate with ease."

President Carter replies, "This is a good idea, and I can get behind that, Mr. Vance. Please work with our counterparts in Krasnodar and Ukraine to ensure they are aware of this plan. Of course, avoid mentioning the exact location and so on, just in case there are other ears there. Mr. Brown, what do you think the Russian response will be?"

Harold Brown flips through his notepad. "Mr. President, from a logistical standpoint, the Russians are even worse than we. The route to support the troops in Georgia is even more complicated than ours. Of course, they could use air support, but eventually, we will be able to negate that. Based on all the intel we have, and considering the calendar, it's now the end of August, and the rains and cold will soon start there. Just like us, they are not keen on major operations during the winter. I believe that we will have a slowdown until March, which will give us time to consolidate. I am confident that we can have our camp set up by the end of this year, with the necessary assets already in place. 1st Cav for helicopters and transport, and SOG assets, Green Berets, SEAL, SAS, CIA, and Australians are willing to help."

President Carter looks confused, "Australians?"

Harold Brown nods, "Yes, SARS, also known as The Sneak Eaters."

President Carter smiles, "Well, it figures, Australians, are they good?"

Harold Brown replies, "Yes, they are, and they have worked together before in training during NATO exercises and also in operations in Laos."

President Carter looks at the man for a few seconds, "This seems to be a good approach, at least for a start. Let's make sure that this is public and transparent, at least what we can offer to the media."

President Carter looks at the map once more, arranging the papers on his desk, thinking to himself, *"Here we go again, and I hoped to be one of the presidents without wars, and here we are, deploying troops in Russia."*

13

Chapter 13: Camp London

30 miles West of Novorossiysk, KRASNODAR KRAI
January 14th, 1979

Aboard USS Austin, an amphibious transport dock vessel that's carrying elements of the 1st Cavalry Combat Aviation Brigade, 1st Battalion, is approaching the port of Novorossiysk. The 1MC comes to life. A loud whistle sounds, followed by a voice blaring.

"On the flight deck, all personnel are ready for launch! All loose gear must be stowed, helmets on and buckled, sleeves rolled down, and be aware of spinning propellers. Stand by for launch!"

The 1MC clicks and becomes quiet, and on the flight deck at the back of the ship, sailors are starting to prepare the deck for launch. The hangar door opens, and a tow cart is pushing out a UH-1 Huey helicopter. The crew follows. The two pilots, a crew chief, and a gunner. One of the pilots jumps into the right seat, the first pilot's spot. Richard Miller, a seven-year veteran with time in Vietnam, nods when he sees the other pilot, Daniel Williams, a much younger aviator with three years of service as a Huey pilot, being deployed for the first time.

Richard starts to organize his seat and prepare the checklists. "Hey, Daniel, no sweat on this one. We took off from ships before, so it's no sweat."

Daniel nods, "Yep, no sweat, it's just so damn cold, man. On the water, it just gets in your bones, you know?"

Richard nods, "We'll get it warm soon. Hey chief!? Preflight is done?"

The Crew Chief, Mark Moore, one of the old heads with many years of service and two tours in Vietnam, yells back from outside. "Yes, preflight done, I'm just going to go out one more time and check the Jesus nut."

The Jesus nut, the nut that transfers the entire weight of the helicopter to the main rotor, was the most critical single point of failure in the UH-1 Huey, and it was the component that was checked the most by any Crew Chief in the Army. It was called the Jesus nut because if it fails in flight, all that is left is to pray to Jesus. Richard and Daniel go through the pre-start checklist and then mark it as complete.

Mark Moore, the Crew Chief, gets back inside and closes the big sideways door of the Huey, muttering. "Damn cold this place", Daniel turns back, "Winter in Russia, man, what were you expecting? Florida's heat and humidity?"

Richard smiles and leans over, looking at the deck signal. The deck is RED, not ready for takeoff. They feel the ship's vibration as the engines increase power, and the captain turns the boat around, giving them 10 knots of wind, enough to help them take off with a full load of fuel. Richard puts his helmet on and signals the crew to do the same.

Turning the intercom on, "Crew check!" The rest of the crew checks back, now connected on their headsets. Richard continues, "Let's crank it!"

He goes over the startup procedure of the Huey. The helicopter comes to life quickly. The turbine starts to whine as its RPM increases. The main rotor begins to turn slowly, the inertia in the large, wide blades causes it to jolt sideways, the familiar jolt of a starting Huey. RPM and torque are increasing, and the turbine's temperatures are all looking good as the rotor starts to spin up. Richard and Daniel are doing the final checks, checking the controls.

Daniel looks sideways now towards the deck and sees a spray of water coming from the sides of the ship as it goes faster, "We won't make it more than 3 minutes in this water, guys. If we must ditch, remember your training, get out of the water in your raft as soon as possible. Out in the air, no matter how cold, you will make it......for a while longer."

A silhouette comes running towards the helicopter, bent over to avoid the rotor wash, but even so, quite a big fellow. He bangs on the helicopter door and yells! "Hey, lads, you got room for one more? All the way to London?"

Richard turns his head and sees a big guy, over six feet tall and about as wide, with his face almost completely covered in a red beard, dressed in an unfamiliar camouflage uniform. Richard asks the Crew Chief, "Can we take him?"

The Crew Chief measures Angus for a fraction of a second, "This is one big fellow. She's a good bird, this one. It will make it with the extra load."

Richard motions him inside and yells. "Alright, hop in! Have a seat, strap in!" He taps his head and motions toward an extra headset on the side of the helicopter. Angus puts it in.

Richard looks again at the flight deck light as it turns green. He motions with his hands towards the sailors on the deck, indicating that he will take off. Then, he flicks his landing lights on and off, which is the signal to the deck controller that he will proceed. They operate in EMCOM conditions, with no radio transmitted from the ship. Richard's fingers are wrapped around the cyclic and collective, his toes on the pedals. He looks at Daniel, who is doing the same, nodding slightly and rechecking the engine parameters while speaking on the intercom. "Chief says you are too heavy, and we might not be able to take off with you."

Angus laughs, "Aye! I'll go down and push!"

Richard pulls up the collective, and the Huey gets light on the skids. Then he pulls more, settling the helicopter a few inches from the deck. Turning it upwind, he gains a bit of speed and slides sideways off the deck. The moment the deck is clear, he puts the nose down, gaining speed and altitude, and turns away from the ship.

Daniel comes on the intercom, "Alright, let's head for the harbor. Heading 342."

Richard responds, "Rog! 342, gotta love the weather here."

With all the heating in the Huey, the windows have a film of ice from the moisture and the spray of the ship. Richard turns the helicopter on heading 342, climbs to 500 ft, trims the helicopter to fly straight and level, and holds the cyclic with his fingertips. Leaned forward a bit, the classic helicopter pilot position when you can't see well outside. At 8:15 in January, it is still quite dark outside.

Richard talks again on his intercom, "Welcome to ... how do you say it? Krasnodar Airlines. I hope you're enjoying the flight so far. We'll be starting cabin service soon. May we ask?

Who the hell are you?"

Angus smiles and taps Richard's shoulder. "Thanks, boys. My name is Angus. Angus MacGavin, and I'm a captain in the SAS."

Richard responds, "How did you end up here?"

Angus replies, "Same as you boys, I got ordered. When this whole mess started with the United Nations and the Soviets, some guys got ordered here to set up Camp London, and also to help these guys get some troops trained and put into shape. There are some of us from the SAS, some of your lot from SEALS and the Green Berets, and believe it or not, some Aussies, they call themselves "The Sneak Eaters" and bloody right of a name. That lot is mad."

Richard pauses for a bit, taking it all in. "And you guys are training some paramilitary of some sort, some Militia?"

Angus continues. "Aye! Now, keep in mind that all the Russian boys went to military service for two years. So, they have the basics, and they know from what end to hold the AK-47 and how to clean it like a shiny coin. They can parade like clockwork, but other than that, they don't know a whole lot. So, we're here to train them up a little bit. Remember the Great Patriotic War? They were more scared of the *politruk's* than the enemy, and now, there's no more *politruk's.*"

Richard slightly adjusts the heading of the Huey as the wind changes, ensuring he stays on course and speaks back. "Yeah, just like they tried in Vietnam. These boys. Are they willing to fight when push comes to shove?"

Angus runs a hand over his beard. "Lad, a lot of them suffered from the joy of communism, but you are asking for a guy to go against his brother or cousin. Who can tell?"

Richard looks a bit worried, "Are they still fighting now?

This should be a cease-fire of some sort."

Angus smiles, seeing that Richard is completely unfamiliar with the situation in Krasnodar. "Aye, it's too cold for everyone to fight, but it won't stay cold for much longer, and the Russians are already sending small units over the mountains and through the passes, like skirmishes. Good lads, a lot of them trained well. They smell like Spetsnaz. They go to villages and either kill the new mayor or the old party member and blame each other."

Richard responds, "Sounds like they read the project Phoenix."

Angus grins. "That did a lot of good, didn't it?"

Richard continues to fly on the same heading. Far in the distance, he sees the port lights, and further in the distance, the city lights. He turns his head slightly towards Angus, "We will work with you?"

Angus responds, "We'll see, lad. Depends on what the brass wants to do with us. I keep saying that we have to show these people that we can give them some support. We need to win some. Otherwise, they will lose whatever little hope they have. These people have been used to being led with a lot of stick and not much carrot. Now we're showing them just carrots. Bloody sods have no clue what to do with them."

Richard smiles, "I had no idea they make good philosophers in the SAS, Angus."

Angus shakes his head. "The don't, lad. As you see, I'm behind a rifle instead of writing a book."

Daniel flips through his kneeboard. "The harbor is coming up ahead. I'll switch to their frequency and contact them when we are a bit closer."

Angus looks at Daniel, "Are you guys going to sling two tons of ammo underneath? From the port? I should've picked a different ride."

Richard laughs, "Hey, don't be scared, we made it this far. Not bad for our first flight. We read about flying this crate in a book during our passage."

Angus grunts. "Damn comedian, and you look like one kid, you might have shaven once or twice, but there's no way you did it three times."

Daniel turns around and asks. "Are you always that scared in helicopters, Captain?"

Angus continues with the banter, "Only when they are flying, on the ground, I'm fine. I got spilled out of one, some years ago, during a training in the mountains. He tumbled over and spat me out. I was in the door. The only one that survived."

Nobody talks after that, like all aviators, keeping a moment of silence for a fallen pilot, and knowing that it could happen to any of them.

Daniel contacts the tower over the radio. "Novo harbor, Huey 1-1 ready for sling load."

The radio response is two clicks of the microphone, serving as confirmation. A soldier comes from a shack with two red glow markers, pointing at one of the loads lined up on the pier.

Richard quickly tells the Crew Chief. "Get the sling ready, Chief."

Richard slows down to a hover, 30 feet over the load, holding the helicopter steady and listening to the Crew Chief's commands: "Left 2, Forward 5." Richard is maneuvering the helicopter in hover position. Amazing, how a helicopter appears to be holding still in the air while the pilot's hands and feet move so much.

The Crew Chief speaks, "Good sling, take it away!"

Richard pulls on the collective and takes altitude, increasing his speed. Daniel calls the new heading, "Heading 037, keep climbing, we have some mountains up ahead, 1500 feet."

Richard confirms." I got it, she's heavy and swinging."

He comments about the swing of the 2-ton load, swinging back and forth from the belly of the Huey.

Angus shakes his head. "Never liked how it feels with that load under you guys. How the bloody hell you guys are doing it, I don't know."

Richard replies, "You get used to it after a while, Angus, after doing it 20 times a day in Saigon, you don't think about it."

Angus raises his eyebrows, "Oh, you've been to Saigon?"

Richard nods, "Just at the end, buddy, just at the end. You? Have you ever been to Southeast Asia?"

Angus nods, "I might have seen Laos once or twice, made some good friends with some Green Berets there."

Richard continues, "Are they here as well?" Angus nods, "Some of them, yes, they are."

Richard smiles, "Small world, eh?"

Angus adjusts his headset a bit, "Neah lad, it's just that there aren't too many idiots willing to go to any God forsaken place on this planet when ordered. So, whenever there's a God forsaken place, we tend to go together."

Another moment of pause as they clear the mountain range, and they settle over the plains around Krimsk. Angus talks again, "So, you've seen some action in Vietnam?"

Richard responds, "I was there at the tail end of it, I got shot at, but mostly were just tailing out of there."

Angus listens and nods. "That was some nasty work there. The whole deal."

Richard replies, "Yes, sir, it was. And yet, here we are, once again."

Angus has a faint smile on his lips, "This is different, lad."

Richard turns his head. "How so?"

Angus almost can't keep his laughter in. "It's colder up here in case you haven't noticed."

Everyone in the helicopter starts to laugh. As the meaning of Angus's words sinks in.

A few minutes later, Richard asks, "Hey, Chief, are we looking good there?"

The Crew chief responds. "I feel it under us. I really don't want to open the door and peek out."

Richard replies, "Roger that, Chief. I'll tell you if we get light, and you can tell me how the fireworks are."

The Chief tries to look out through the window, "Those things never set off like this."

Richard lifts his shoulders. "Not even in this cold?"

The Chief seems concerned, realizing that fuses are behaving differently in freezing temperatures. "Well, just keep her steady, and keep in mind, you may be hurting for fuel soon."

Angus joins in the conversation. "Lads, one more thing, Never drink any booze if you don't see the bottle being open and if it is without the seal and label, Stolichnaya is the vodka to go, and on the country side some villagers make good booze, but I've seen folks going for antifreeze of brake fluid, they filter it or refine it, either way you will go blind,"

Richard replies. "Thanks for the tip, Angus. We have a stock of our own for now."

Angus grins, "And how much do you think that will last with me around, eh?"

Daniel talks with the Camp London tower, then turns to Richard. "As you approach, watch out for that comms tower in the middle of the camp. The cargo drop zone is on the North Side of the camp, marked with old tires. Put the load there, they will pop smoke once we get close. The crew views the camp from above. A big square, almost a quarter of a mile. The sides are made from stacked shipping containers. There are tents, buildings, and two secure gates, all within a fully contained operation.

As they approach the drop zone, Angus talks again. "After you get your bearings here, in a couple of days, I'll take you on a recce run down South, towards the mountains and the passes. You will learn the lay of the land before it gets too nasty."

Richard replies as he slows down for the drop zone and loses altitude, ensuring the sling load remains completely balanced and prevents it from swinging underneath. "What are we reconning for?"

Angus explains, "See, there are no cars or trucks around here. There isn't a lot of gas available, and there's a curfew. So, we look for anything that moves on the road. More often than not, Soviet forces are patrolling. We respect the Rules of Engagement. We buzz them. If they fire at us, we fire back."

Richard groans, "Just like always, gotta wait to get my ass shot at before I can do something. What happened with us shooting first?"

Angus pats his back. "You know how it is, lad, we are the good guys. Gotta play by the rules."

Daniel and the Chief are surveying the drop zone. "You've got to put this down gently, after that comment of yours with frozen fuses, I'm not thrilled now with this thing."

Richard nods, "Roggo, I got it." He inches down the loaded Huey, slowly lowering down while the chief gives him the altitude of the sling load, 10 feet, 5, come left a bit, steady,

3 feet now, 1. Load is down."

Waiting for the soldiers down below to release the sling after they are done. The Chief signals Richard. "Done! Sling is clear."

Richard turns the Huey towards a landing pad and slides through the air gracefully. Landing the helicopter slowly.

The moment the skids touch the ground. Angus takes his headset off, pats Richard's shoulder, and yells, "That was smooth! I'll see you guys at the mess tent. Chief, open the door for me. Cheerio, guys!"

Richard is shutting the Huey down, the rotor starting to slow down, he looks around at his crew, "What's the name of this village close by? Welcome to .... How do you say it? Il'skiy? I can't do that many vowels at once."

Daniel smiles, "Welcome to London! Sounds a bit better, doesn't it?"

The crew looks around. The Chief speaks, "Well, it ain't much, but I guess it's home for now."

14

Chapter 14: Between Promises.

Tyndall AFB, Florida, USA
January 15th, 1979

James parks his car in front of the garage. He takes a deep breath, gets up, and straightens his flight suit, reaching into the back and getting the big bucket of roses he brought for Diane.

Taking another deep breath, he walks to the front door and steps in. "Honey! I'm home!"

Diane comes to the vestibule of their house and sees James with a bucket of flowers. "Oh, darling! They are beautiful!"

Wrapping his arms around James's neck, he kisses him sweetly. She takes a quick glance at his face and goes. "What happened? What have you done? These are apologies, roses!"

James has a sad smile on his face. "You know me so well, dear. I did not do anything, but we're getting deployed."

Diane takes a step back and covers her mouth. "No! But James, I'm due in a month and a half. Where?"

James looks down, "In Russia, where do you think?"

Diane looks at him, trying to hold back her tears. "You picked this squadron, and you said it's just training and other stuff, and now you tell me you're going to war, God knows where? When I'm just about to give birth?"

James wraps her in his arms, "Darling, I can ask to stay behind, I can ask for a transfer, that would be the end of my career in the Air Force, but if you want to, I'll do it. But for the guys that are flying with me, I want to go."

Diane replies with her head on James's shoulder. "Of course you want to go. I married a fighter pilot, always with your hair on fire. I hate this! When?"

James "I don't know, in a few weeks, we got the orange poop suits today."

Diane draws back. "The orange what?"

James smiles, "The orange suits we must wear for ocean crossing, survival suits, but, since you can't open them if something happens, and it takes about 2 hours to put them on, we call them poop suits. Also, we have to wear diapers."

Diane laughs, "Before our child was born. One way to test the process, Major Boyd."

James picks her up in his arms again. "You know I can't promise anything. I'm not going to tell you not to worry because everything will be fine. I've never done that, and I'm not doing it now. But all I can say is that I'll do my best to come back the way I'm leaving,"

Diane nods, "When it was me, it was easier. Now, I can't even think about it."

James continues, "Darling, we still have a bit of time. I have nursery to finish, and maybe this will blow over before we even get there."

Diane asks, "Can it blow over?"

James shakes his head, "I don't think so, but if we are sent there, it means it will get serious. And this is unknown to us. The intel we get on our weekly briefings is mixed."

Diane turns towards the living room, moving away from James and trying to hide her face. Tears were already filling her eyes. She takes a quick deep breath and rubs her eyes quickly. That quick gesture is only something a woman can do when she's trying not to show how much she's suffering. She picks up a vase from the counter and puts the roses in the water. "Come on here and tell me all about it."

James follows her, sits down on an armchair, watches Diane, and then continues. "There are troops there, and quite a lot of them. Their morale and the willingness to fight are unknown. They are not doing very well managing to put their country back together, their supply lines are even more messed up than those of the folks in Krasnodar, you know, guys from the 1st Cav are there, the helicopter guys that used to fly here."

Diane nods, "I know, if it's like that, it should be okay, the ladies in our support group are getting letters and such, all they are doing is transport."

James smiles, "Remember, we're trained a lot like them, and we study how they operate. So, we're the best ones for this."

Diane keeps fiddling with the roses. "Well, in times like this, I would have wished you were some mediocre pilot that nobody wants to go to war with."

James smiles, "No, you wouldn't!"

Diane snaps, "Major Boyd! You know damn well I wouldn't, and I'm proud of you. But damnit, I hate it! You're going there fighting someone's war."

James smiles, knowing well that this will not go easily.

"Yeah, darling, but it doesn't look like there's anyone willing to fight for them."

James gets up and helps her with the roses, pouring water into the vase as Diane finishes clipping the last ones. "What about you, darling? How are we going to do this?"

Diane sighs, "I'll have my parents over. Mom can't wait to see her granddaughter."

James interjects, "Excuse me! Grandson!"

Diane sticks her tongue at him. "Daughter! Anyway, my folks will be here. Dad knows the drill. He was in the Navy, you know how we had to follow him around. So, gruff as he is, probably the baby will make his heart melt. And I intend to be the Wonder Woman with a stroller. I'll visit everyone, help everyone, and keep this community of women tight. No one will have to cope with this alone. There won't be a meeting I won't attend, I will help anyone who needs anything, and Jayne and I have a plan already."

She takes a quick pause, looking at James, and he listens with intent. "You guys are always focused on your planes and your missions and all that, and that's the job, but this is our community, and it takes a village, and I intend to be that village. Otherwise...." She looks down, "Otherwise, I'll die of worry."

James pulls her in his arms, holds her tight, and guides her to the couch. "I think that's a brilliant idea, darling. And you are right, we're all a big family here."

James puts a hand on her belly, feeling a kick in return, smiling big. "You, young one, listen to your dad. You'd better behave and not cause any trouble, and before you know it, I'll be back, and we can play catch and build model airplanes."

Diane smiles and strokes James's hair, "Honey, she's going to be a girl."

James smiles and kisses Diane's belly. "So what? As long as she's healthy, I don't see a problem. And too bad for her, she's still going to play catch and build model airplanes after we play princess and have our tea. I'll even put my pinky out, in a proper fashion."

Diane laughs, "Can't wait to see Major 'Badger' Boyd drinking tea with his daughter, while having his nails polished with red color."

James bursts into laughter, "Just imagine how the Colonel would burst if I showed up one day with pink nails or something."

A few hours later, James gets up from the bed, unable to sleep. He looks at Diane sleeping peacefully next to him, kisses her forehead, smiles, and then she grumbles something in her sleep as he turns around. He gets up, goes to the fridge, grabs a can of Coke, lifts the tab, and opens it. James walks to the nursery. All finished now. The crib and mobile are in place, wrapping blankets and diapers are ready, and everything is arranged neatly. James smiles, thinking to himself. *"Almost in military fashion. You'd better come back, buddy. You must come back when this is filled with laughter, giggles, and late-night crying. You owe it to this little person that's not in this world yet."*

Krasnodar, Krasnodar Krai
January 16th, 1979

Andrei looks through the window of the AN-24 he used to fly from Kyiv to Krasnodar, where he meets for the first time with the leader of Krasnodar's independence movement, accompanied by a few aides and General Radzievsky on the plane. Andrei cranks his head, trying to see the activity at the airport, as the plane approaches the runway. A lineup of L-39 planes, some Yak-52s, and a few AN-24s, like the one he is flying, are visible. After the landing, as the airplane pulls onto the apron, Andrei gets up and straightens his suit, making his way to the door, which is already waiting for him to open. As soon as the door opens and the stairway is attached to the plane, he begins to go down the few steps, looking around. A small delegation is waiting for him.

A man comes to the last step with his hand up. "Comrade Kirilenko, nice to finally meet you. I'm Ruslan. We spoke on the phone a few times."

Andrei shakes his hand. "Nice to finally meet you, Comrade Chernogorov."

Ruslan is guiding Andrei towards the main airport building, "I figure, Comrade Kirilenko, that it is better to talk here in the airport building in a meeting room, than traveling to Krasnodar. I'm afraid for your safety."

Andrei looks at some men in uniform, using a camo pattern that is unfamiliar to him. These military personnel are placed in strategic places around the airport's main building. Andrei speaks with Ruslan. "Is it this bad? And who are those folks?"

Ruslan responds, "It's more of a precaution, you see, it wouldn't be difficult for someone to attempt something. Our Independence Forces are young and not experienced and not well equipped. What you see are the UN peacekeeping forces. They are tough soldiers, but it's just a handful of them. They advised us that this would be easier to protect."

Ruslan, Andrei, and General Radzievsky are walking past a few young soldiers dressed in Soviet uniforms, each with a purple, wide brassard on their left arm. Some parade guard, not correctly lined up, and not properly presenting arms,

General Radzievsky salutes them as they walk by, and Andrei sees with the corner of his eye a helmet that is way too big, the uniform on a frame that is way too small, and a set of blond curls popping from under the helmet.

He suddenly stops and turns around, facing the girl, "...and who are you?"

Tanya draws herself up, trying her best to present arms. "Corporal Petrov, Tanya, reporting for duty, Comrade Kirilenko!"

Andrei smiles. "The uniform is not too tight for you, Corporal? And the helmet? Maybe you need a bigger one."

Tanya realizes that she's being mocked, "Comrade Kirilenko, I would rather be in the field, drilling and on the range firing than finding a tailor, and if it gets too bad, I can hide inside my helmet. Comrade!"

Andrei starts to laugh. "Corporal, if that's the spirit of the whole troops, I pity the soldier that will stand in your way, but shouldn't you be in school?"

Tanya responds, "I'm a student at the Polytechnical University, Comrade, but with all this, classes have not started in September, and anyway, we need more than just engineers these days."

Andrei smiles, "Let's make a deal, when this is all over, and you graduate, I'll be there, celebrating with your graduation class. This, of course, if Comrade Chernogorov will allow it."

Ruslan smiles, "Of course, that class will be special, that's for sure, half of them are here, and the other half would like to join, we just don't have enough gear for everyone."

Andrei steps into the meeting room in the airport, followed by Ruslan and The General. In the room, two people are already coming to attention in the instant the door opens. These two individuals, dressed in the camo Andrei saw around the airport, are introduced by Ruslan.

"Comrade Kirilenko, these are some of the UN peacekeepers: Major Henry Anderson from the United States, and Captain Angus MacGavin from Great Britain. These are some of the soldiers who advise us and help us with our training."

Andrei walks to them and shakes their hands, "Thank you, gentlemen, for all the support provided."

They both respond in Russian, and Andrei is surprised at how good their Russian is. They all sit around the table, and Andrei starts the conversation. "Thanks for having us here, Comrade Chernogorov. I realized that with the whole madness of the last months, I don't know anything about you."

Ruslan looks down, suddenly getting shy. "Comrade Kirilenko, thank you for coming. I know it's a big risk for you. Truth to be told, there's not much to know about me. I was a lead hand at the metallurgical plant here. I worked the line for 25 years and paid my dues, attended meetings, and helped the people in the union. But when I saw that poor bloke, yelling what we all wanted to shout, being tackled on the ground, I picked that *checkist* bastard and punched him and threw him 5 meters, after that we've been beaten and chased out of that square, and for what? For standing up to one of ours? I then gathered all my mates in the plant, and it wasn't just me, and we said that enough is enough. Somehow, people agreed with what I was saying, and I kept saying it, and it all led to this. Truth to be told, I'm no politician, and no statesman, and I'm afraid that I'm in it way over my head. And I'm convinced that I'm not going to make it alive out of this, but then, you see those young kids, they came, they wanted to help, they had the same voice as ours. So, I'm thinking, it must be right, what we're doing, it must be right. But at the end of this, I don't want any of this. I want to get back to my factory, and maybe I'll retire."

Andrei claps his shoulder, "Ruslan, you did what's right, and your story is no different than mine. During the Great Patriotic War, I realized that I was good at organizing and making things happen. I continued to do so, and once it worked, people kept asking me to do more, which is what I did. And a few months ago, I had enough. And here we are now."

Andrei takes a sip of water and continues, "But what you did here is great, and like it or not, you are a leader, and people look up to you, so now, this becomes your duty, until you can't do it anymore or there is someone better, and that's your burden, and you will have to carry it, and I'm sure you will carry it until the end, whatever that end may be."

Ruslan nods. "Thank you, Andrei."

Andrei takes another sip of water, and he looks around the room. "But we're here now, and there's more work and worries ahead of us. How are things here, Ruslan?"

Ruslan clears his voice and responds, "We will survive this winter, lucky for us, it wasn't too cold, and we have enough resources to keep everyone relatively warm, for the big cities, we have enough food until April, and by then, we're hoping that we will have more food from the villages, fuel is short, but I think we'll manage, so, the people will live, better term would be that they will survive. On the military side, that's a bigger problem. Maykop base is a fortress. Everything south of the three big lakes that divide our country is within the reach of Soviet forces, and they are now encamped around Sochi, Tuapse, Labinsk, and... Nalchik. Reports from the field and intelligence from our friends indicate that elements are already moving north, breaching the UN resolution. However, how can this be enforced when there are only a handful of peacekeeping forces? These are better designed to maintain security in the cities, but not to fight a war. We have our Freedom Militia, but you saw how well-equipped they are. I don't want to send them to die, and they will if nothing changes."

Major Henry "Hawk" Anderson joins the conversation, speaking in Russian, with a distinct accent, "Gentlemen, I have reassurance from the General Staff that as of next week, we will see the first elements of ground forces here, offloaded from the port of Novorossiysk. These will be significant forces that could counter a Soviet advance. We hope they will be enough to act as a deterrent. However, if need be, they will be more than just a deterrent. Gen. Henry 'Hank' Emerson is now in Berlin, making the final preparations, and he is expected to arrive at Camp London as of next week."

General Radzievsky joins the conversation. "This is good news indeed. I can almost guarantee that the moment the weather permits, this is mid-March or April, you will have a three pronged attack, if these officers will follow my teachings at Frunze academy, you will have forces somewhere along the coast, I would say amassed around Pshada, that would be the last river to cross before reaching open ground, you will have another contingent of forces in the mountains, trying to exploit one of the passes around Guamka, and another push on the Maykop axis. They will strive to find a breakthrough, and once a breakthrough is established, it will be challenging for any opposing force to counter it. You can expect advances of over 80 kilometers each day. All these attacks will be heavily supported by aviation and helicopters. The bases in Georgia and Southern Krasnodar are well-equipped. You are looking here at forces that are comparable to what you would expect on an attack on the Fulda Gap. This is a grim situation, and I am not confident that you will be able to muster enough resistance here."

Angus and Henry are exchanging a quick glance. Hawk responds. "General, although I'm not a strategist like you, I'm confident we will be able to contain this threat. We've been training for 30 years for this."

The General smiles, "So did we, Major. I'm just giving you my honest opinion."

Hawk responds, "And thank you for that. It is a great insight, and I will relay these as soon as possible. The elements that will arrive next week are combined armed forces, self-sustaining units that should be able to counter this. To me, the most important thing on this is exactly our mission, peace-keeping, and not just avoiding battle, if we have to fight, be sure we will, but also, preserving civilian lives and civilian assets, and from what we have seen so far, this is a one sided battle, it looks like the troops that are doing incursions here are not concerned with that."

The General lifts his shoulders, "Unfortunately, this was not the soviet doctrine, and I'm convinced that the high command of the Soviet forces will not spend a single thought on that aspect."

Hawk continues, "Then we have to do more on this side, and Mr. Chernogorov, we must find a way to notify the population in the villages and cities when troops are getting closer, so they can evacuate. Additionally, from our end, starting tomorrow, we will start to "prosecute" any incursions and skirmishes that we encounter. Of course, respecting our Rules of Engagement, but soviet forces must realize that this will not be easy."

Andrei joins the conversation. "Ruslan, you know we can't do much, but when it comes to evacuation, when it comes to helping out people thrown away from their homes, we will help with that in the best way we can. We're Ukrainians, but we will help our brothers. You can be sure of that."

Ruslan smiles, "Thank you, Andrei, this is what I'm most afraid of, that this will cause more hurt and suffering than just bowing our heads."

An hour and a half later, after the meeting is over, Andrei is back on the plane, looking out the window as Krasnodar Airport disappears beneath him. "General, those two soldiers, what do you think of them?"

The General thinks for a second, "You saw the look in their eyes, those are highly trained special forces, highly trained killers."

Andrei nods his head. "I have not heard of a killer being concerned to preserve life."

The General tilts his head and thinks for a second. "Maybe I'm getting too old, you are right, and maybe I was too trained to hate them, and it's hard to admit that they are better than me."

Andrei smiles, "You got one thing right, we're getting too old, and yes, this is new, we were trained to hate them, and yet, these two soldiers come and teach the young ones how to fight and how to survive."

The General smiles, "It turns out, old as I am, I still have a lot to learn."

15

Chapter 15: Target Lock.

Sochi, Krasnodar Krai
January 16th, 1979

The Colonel steps into the briefing room where Vanea, Piotr, and two other pilots are plotting their course for their new mission. The moment he steps in, all pilots are coming to attention.

The Colonel waves them off, "At ease! Carry on. What are we planning today?"

Vanea responds. "Comrade Colonel, as we start to relocate the squadron to Maykop, we'll take advantage of our relocation flight and work with the pilots from the 455th Bomber Aviation Squadron on an escort flight. Additionally, before reaching Maykop, we will conduct a live ammunition exercise on the Slavianskii range. The range will feature both elements, the MiG-21 and the Su-24, operating within the same range. We believe that it is good for cooperation between the elements."

The Colonel nods, "That is a good use of resources, Major Gureevich. Your MiG-21 will have enough range to execute this mission, with the escort flight?"

Vanea nods, "Comrade Colonel, by looking at the map, and having to plan for operations around Krimsk, Krasnodar, and the port of Novorossiysk, operating from either Sochi or Maykop, we will be at the limits of our operational range, however, we must understand better what real capabilities we have and this exercise will give us a lot of knowledge. I believe that we have the capability to operate with great efficiency in this theatre."

The Colonel looks at the map, checking their flight plan and altitudes, speeds, and timings. "This is good, it seems well within our capabilities. I have another ask for you. On the second plane of the Su-24 flight, instead of your co-pilot, I'd like you to take a passenger, an official photographer from Pravda. With the good weather in the forecast, and with a mix of planes, we could get some great shots, and they will serve as a good propaganda tool. You boys will have to work a tighter formation on your transit, but it's nothing that you can't manage."

All pilots come to attention and nod in agreement. Vanea replies. "It is an excellent idea, Comrade Colonel. Of course, on an escort flight, we will not be flying this tight of a formation, but those shots will be a good way to show our work."

The Colonel replies. "What ammo will you carry? Vanea responds, "We will have our standard ground attack loadout. Two hundred fifty kilo bombs on the inner pilons and unguided rockets on the outer pilons, and the Su-24 will have its standard load of two hundred fifty kilo bombs."

The Colonel gives them a quick nod. "Carry on. Can't wait to see those pictures."

He does a quick about-face and walks out of the briefing

room. Vanea gets back over to the briefing table, looks at the map, pointing at an area over the mountains, "Around here, after we join up with those snow-covered peaks in the background, we can have those shots. We'll burn more fuel to stay in tight formation, but I think we will manage. We'll have to scrap the proper escort flight. We won't be able to push forward and sweep in front of you loaded with bombs like this. But I guess there's value in those photos."

Four hours later, Vanea is in the MiG-21 cockpit, all strapped, holding short before entering the runway, adjusting the rear periscopic mirror on top of his canopy, glancing at Piotr's MiG lined up behind him. Turning his head and trying to spot the two Su-24s coming towards the base, he finally spots them up in the distance, 7000 meters high. Vanea glances at the clock in the cockpit. "*Two minutes late.*"

Shaking his head, he clicks on the microphone button. "Sochi tower, 110 flight, ready for takeoff."

The tower replies. "Clear for takeoff 110!"

Vanea lines up on the runway, taking the left side, letting the plane roll forward so Piotr on the second Mig can take the right side. Holding the brakes and looking to see Piotr lined up on his side, he moved his hand forward, signaling to Piotr that they would take off. Counting to two, then pushing the throttles all the way to military power, holding the brakes, glancing at Piotr again, and seeing his plane ready for takeoff. Throttle into afterburner, releasing the brakes as the Mig accelerates down the runway, feeling that lovely sensation on his backside as the afterburner thuds and accelerates him even further. Lifting the nose, the plane was heavy and sluggish with a full load of fuel and ammo, finally lifting into the air, accelerating past 450 km per hour. Gear up, flaps up, cleaning the plane, letting it build speed. Now, 700 km per hour. Glancing to his right, he sees Piotr already in formation, tucked in on his right wing. Pulling the throttle back and trimming the plane to climb at 700 km per hour, aiming for the invisible point in the sky where he should meet the Su-24 formation.

The tower comes on the radio, "110 flight, Sochi Tower, switch to Sochi control on channel 10."

Vanea replies, "Sochi Control 110!"

He wags his wings side to side to signal Piotr and then makes the motion of switching channels with his right hand.

Looking at Piotr and seeing the nod of his helmet. "Sochi Control, 110 with you, 2000 meters."

Sochi control responds. "Identified! Continue as fragged."

A few minutes later, the two formations join in the sky, Vanea and Piotr pulling closer, from underneath, getting on the wing of the second Su-24.

Vanea comes on the radio. "204, 110 in formation with you."

The Su-24 pilot replies. "204 confirms, we will turn towards waypoint two and go to cruise speed."

Vanea maintains the formation as the Su-24s accelerate, the variable geometry wings pulling back to match the increased airspeed. Vanea grins under his oxygen mask, *"These planes, they are fat and full of bombs, but they look pretty like this."*

A voice comes on the radio. "Can you get closer? I'll start taking pictures now."

Vanea clicks his microphone button twice and inches in even closer to the wing of the Sukhoi, about 12 inches from the wing of the other airplane.

Vanea thinks, *"If you sneeze now, we're all dead."* The voice of the photographer comes on the radio again. "Smile for the camera!"

Vanea gets back on the radio quickly, and he admonishes the photographer. "Masks on, everybody, masks on. If you have a leak in the pressurized cabin, you'll go hypoxic in two minutes. Masks on!"

They continue to execute this tight dance for the next fifteen minutes, shifting from one formation to another, flying in a close formation of fingertips, with four airplanes loaded with ground ordinance.

As they approach Maykop, they switch the channel to Maykop control, and then the radio crackles again. "This is Maykop control, 110 switch to channel 20, for live range control."

Vanea responds, "Channel 20, live range control."

Motioning Piotr to switch the frequencies. "Range control, 110 with you, we're two MiG-21 armed with bombs and rockets. What work do you have for us?"

The range control responds, "110, I have two targets for you, ready for my mark?"

Vanea sets up his cockpit for a ground attack, selecting the bombs, setting up his reticle, fuzing the bombs, and preparing his Mig. "110 flight! Trail formation!"

He instructs Piotr to drop back behind him. "110, ready for your mark."

The range control gives him instructions. "Target is marked with white smoke. Wind 175 for 6, clear to engage from South to North, fly heading 300 after your pass."

Vanea confirms, "Engaging the white smoke. South to North, turning 300 after drop." Vanea lines up his target, turning the Mig around, diving towards the target, speed building up, monitoring his radar range indicator to compute a solution, keeping the target lined up, as the pipper moves towards the smoke, once it's lined up, Vanea keeps it there for a fraction of a second, he mashes with his thumb the release button on the stick. He feels the thud and slight shudder of the plane releasing the two 250-kilogram bombs. Gently pulling up, making sure he is not exceeding 5 G's, that's how much the rocket's pilons could take. Extending upward, gaining altitude, Vanea turns on the heading he received from the ground controller, cranking his head and looking at the smoke to spot the impact of his bombs. Vanea grins as he sees two explosions in quick succession. The shockwave on the ground expands rapidly, dispersing the white smoke in the middle of the target. He then spots another two explosions, close to his bombs. Piotr puts his bombs right on target.

Vanea transmits on the radio, "110 flight is off target!"

The range control replies. "Confirm! Good hits! Good hits! You put the bombs right on the smoke."

Vanea checks the sky around him and sees, in the distance, the two Su-24s on their bomb run, flying straight and level at 7,000 meters, dropping all 18 bombs they carry. Watching the impact of the bombs on the ground, a quick succession of explosions that are creating a destructive trail of shockwaves, fire, and debris. "*Whatever these guys would hit, won't stand a chance, a trail almost half a kilometer long of pain and misery for whoever might be on the ground.*" Vanea shakes his head. Suddenly, this is becoming real. He realizes that soon, this may not be a live ammo range, but a column of enemies, or a village, or a bridge somewhere.

The ground controller's voice crackles on the radio again. "110, Range control, I have a target for you, a column of vehicles, 500 meters East of the white smoke, work the target with rockets, single pass, clear in range!"

Vanea flicks the stick on the left, turning the plane around, cranking his head to spot the target, "110 received. Vehicle column, working with rockets, single pass. 111 trail formation, single pass!"

Piotr responds, his voice straining under the 5 G load of their turn. "111 confirm, target in sight!"

Vanea selects the outer pilons for the rockets, selecting to shoot all of them in a single pass. Diving towards the target, allowing his aiming reticle to converge on the tip of the column, gyroscopes finally stabilizing after the turn. The MiG-21 with the old gyroscopes always makes you lose a fraction of a second before they catch up. Letting the Mig dive on the target, speed is building up. The range indicator is coming alive and is almost in range now. Vanea is looking at the charred trucks that have been hit so many times during all the trainings. Finally in range, he mashes the trigger with his thumb and hears the hissing sound of the rockets flying away one by one in quick succession, moving the pipper up, letting the rockets cover all the trucks in the column, Vanea starts to see the impact points of each rocket covering the truck column, and as soon as the last rocket is gone, he pulls up and turns the plane to the left, in a tight turn. Turning his head to watch Piotr's pass. Piotr, a few seconds behind him, was finishing his pass and pulling away to join him.

"110 flight, off target!"

The controller responds, "110 flight, good hits, good results, turn left 270, you are clear off range, contact Mayko Control on channel 14."

Vanea confirms, "110 flight is clear off range, Maykop Control, turning 270."

A few minutes later, the two Migs are approaching Maykop airport, setting up for landing, when the controller's voice comes into the radio. "110 report fuel state!"

Vanea turns his head and looks at Piotr, his hand showing four fingers, then five. Vanea responds to the controller, "110 is at 900 liters."

Maykop control responds, "Confirm, 110 extend your flight on heading 3 0 0, this is where we see a lot of helicopters, report any findings, return when you reach your fuel limit."

Vanea confirms and turns the plane around on the requested heading, signaling Piotr to take a spread formation so they can better survey the area. He turns his radar on and stays right under the cloud ceiling, allowing him to see the ground. Watching his fuel closely, Vanea is preparing to turn around, with nothing to report. At that moment, his RWR radar indicator begins to chirp, indicating a radar emission directly in front of him.

The radar operator at the Hawk SAM site, which was just deployed at the Krimsk airport, reports, "I have contacts, 1 6 0, around 6000 ft, they are pretty fast and hot."

The captain supervising the radar crew orders, "Energize guiding radar!"

The radar operator replies. "Guidance radar coming up, 30 seconds!"

The captain looks at the screens and sees the guidance radar indicators coming green. "Weapons cold!!"

The operators report that the Hawk SAM missiles are safe and will not launch. The captain orders again, "Lock targets!"

The operator responds. "Target locked, tracking, and guidance! Good lock on target! Aspect unchanged!"

Vanea freezes for a second as he sees the RWR turning solid, accompanied by a warning beep on his helmet, indicating that a guidance radar is actively locking him. "Maykop Control! 110 flight is being locked by guidance. Locked by guidance radar!"

Turning his plane away from the radar threat, putting some distance between him and where he thinks the radar is. Vanea scans the horizon for a sign of a missile launch.

Back on the radar trailer, the captain is watching the radar screens, "Hold the lock, hold it as long as you can, it's a good practice for us. Start a tape, let's record their radar profiles."

Vanea turns away from the threat, accelerating as quickly as he can, keeping a close eye on his fuel. This is not yet becoming critical. "*If they launch, I can't run away from it and make it back to base.*"

Vanea gets on the radio, "Maykop control, 110 returning to base, we're still locked, no sign of launch."

The controller replies, "Confirm, return to base, direct landing, runway is open." The radar lock on Vanea's airplane drops, just the little chirps and blips on his RWR from the tracking radar.

After landing, Vanea gets on a telephone call with the Colonel. "Yes, Comrade Colonel, we've got locked, 30 kilometers from Maykop. I don't think we were in the missile range, but 30 kilometers is very close to us. It will hamper operations from here if the Americans are bringing SAM missiles in."

Vanea listens on the other side, nodding occasionally. "No, I don't know what kind of SAM it was. The radar operators at Maykop are stating that the signal resembles a Hawk surface-to-air missile. These are medium-range, and depending on the version, they have a reasonable rate of success."

Vanea continues to listen to the Colonel on the other end.

"Yes, Comrade Colonel, as soon as the rest of the squadron arrives, we'll get our readiness quick and start the readiness schedule here."

Vanea puts the phone down, ruffling his hair, still matted from the helmet. Turning towards Piotr, "Hey, this was good, until it wasn't."

Piotr smiles, "Yeah, I thought the instruments got broken when it lit up like that. I froze for a moment there."

Vanea nods, "Me too, that's okay, at least now we're used to it and know what to expect. It's better this way. Let's find our rooms and unwind a bit."

Moscow, USSR
January 16th, 1979

Chairman Ustinov is at the General Staff council. "So, they have a SAM site at Krimsk already, which means that they will consolidate there. And they will come with airplanes. How are we going to counter this threat, Comrade Kutakhov?"

Pavel Kutakhov, the Chief Marshall of the Soviet Air Force, responds, "Comrade Ustinov, we are setting up our SAMs as we speak, the weather is still bad over the mountains, but we will have a net of S-125 Neva SAMs, we will have five sites lined up, creating a barrier for anyone trying to come South towards Maykop and Sochi, also, we're interlining with 2K12 Kub, these are mobile so we can move them around and close any gaps, we have about eight operational sites, but, as I was saying with the weather it is still difficult with the terrain."

Ustinov walks around the room, "Why wasn't this done in the fall? We gave these separatists time to set up, and I warned you about it!"

The Marshall looks down, keeping calm. "Comrade Ustinov, with all the delicate electronics, in the cold, we will not be operational too long. As long as we have no air threats, it doesn't make any sense to camp in the snow. However, now that we are deploying, it will take a maximum of 5 days to be operational, with contingency, possibly 10 days to have all the pieces in place."

Ustinov looks around the room. "This will be dealt with soon. Comrades! We now have foreign forces operating uninterrupted on the territory of the Soviet Union. How can we let this happen? This is a slap on the face of the Soviet Union, and this will be dealt with soon."

Ustinov bangs his hands on the table. "We're talking about bad weather, supplies, and all that. Have we forgotten Stalingrad? Have we forgotten Leningrad? Are we not men to fight anywhere and in all kinds of weather? This is not our strength anymore!? Comrades, you have three weeks to prepare your troops. In three weeks' time, I will declare all foreign troops on the territory of the Soviet Union, UN resolution or not, I will declare them enemies and order them to be dealt with accordingly."

Ustinov turns around and walks out of the presidium room, slamming the door behind him.

No one moved in the room, knowing that this was it, the moment when the metal met the meat would soon come, and they were the ones responsible for ordering soldiers and ordering someone's son to go and die for his country.

Krasnodar, Krasnodar Krai,
January 16th, 1979

Nikolay looks through the window at another column of APCs

thundering down the streets. The boxy M-113 APC is followed by one equipped with a Vulcan gun for anti-air protection, and at the end of the column, a few brand-new M-2 Bradleys are visible, with their TOW missile launchers extended sideways. The Bradley engine coughs, grinds its gears, and pulls over. A soldier jumps out and opens a hatch. Yelling at someone inside. "Tommy, you were all thrilled about using the new toys, but this hunk of junk is half finished. It died three times on us, and the war didn't even start. But rest assured. We'll never make it to the battle with this piece of junk."

Nikolay turns around, "That's it. Katya, Tanya, let's pack a few things, we're leaving."

Katia looks at him, "Nikolay, where? Where do you want to leave?"

Nikolay moves towards the closet and pulls out a suitcase. "Let's go to the countryside for a bit, to your mom and dad, we'll live with them for a few weeks."

Tanya comes out of her bedroom. "But Dad, I'm on guard duty tomorrow at the water treatment plant."

Nikolay shakes his head. "No, you are not, you are not a soldier, and this is enough. There are American and German tanks on the streets, moving in a hurry. That means something. It's brewing, Tanya, they will bomb, they will shell, here, we are not safe."

Katia realizes what Nikolay said, and she starts packing. Tanya is protesting, "But Dad, it's my duty, Mischa is here, and I want to do my duty, and people are relying on me."

Nikolay shakes his head, "No, it is not, you swore an oath to someone, to some flag? No! Your duty? Your duty is with your parents, and your duty is to grow and to live your life, not to guard and fight. Go pack! Now! I'll take your uniform and your rifle to the militia headquarters and tell them that daughters should not fight. Tanya, we will not argue on this one. We're going! And Mischa can come too. But I'm sure he won't."

Tanya starts to cry and slams the door to her bedroom.

Nikolay lifts his shoulders. "Katia, I'll go take that rifle and the helmet. Someone else may need it. Finish here, please. I'll be back in 20 minutes."

Katia looks at him, "I know you are right, but you won't be able to protect her forever. Eventually, you will have to let her go."

Nikolay grumbles, "I'm doing this for all of us, you, her, and me. I have a feeling that this will turn bad. There in that small village, nothing will happen to us, we're going to be peasants for a few weeks, and that's that."

Nikolay picks out Tanya's AK-47, checks the magazines, makes sure that the safety is on and there's no bullet in the chamber, takes the helmet, and puts Tanya's green military coat over his arm and walks out in a hurry.

16

Chapter 16: No Place Is Safe

Camp London, Krasnodar Krai,
January 26th, 1979

Richard Miller takes one quick look at his crew, the UH-1 Huey all set up for startup. "All is ready there in the back, Chief?"

The Crew Chief, Mark Moore, nods, "Yessir!"

Richard replies on the intercom, "Let's crank 'er up!"

Starting to go through the startup procedure of his helicopter, power, fuel, the turbine starting to whine as it begins to spin, from the side of the landing pad Angus walks towards the helicopter and steps in, slapping Richard shoulder then Daniels's, shaking the Crew Chief hand, grabbing a helmet with a headset and putting it on, neatly storing his camo bush hat in one of his vest pockets.

The Huey comes to life, the rotor gaining speed, Richard and Daniel doing the final checks, Richard comes on the radio.

"London Camp, Pontiac 1, ready for takeoff."

The tower replies quickly, "Clear for takeoff, Pontiac 1, wind

0 6 0 for 3 knots, QNH 1013."

Richard pulls the power and lifts the helicopter up, one or two feet off the ground. Holding the Huey into a hover, and pointing the nose into the wind, a quick control check, sliding the helicopter forward, backward, then side to side, moving the nose left and right with the pedals. Happy with the quick check, Richard puts the nose down, and the Huey starts to gain speed quickly, holding the helicopter in ground effect until it transitions into horizontal flight, then climbs gently into the morning sky. Daniel keeps surveying the sky, cloud cover around 500 feet, and a few flurries of snow in the air.

Daniel says on the intercom. "The weather is stinko, heading 1 6 0 to Krepotsnaya."

Richard responds, "1 6 0, Roger, Chief, all good back there?"

The Crew Chief responds, "Yessir, all good, just so damn cold this morning."

Richard nods, "We won't be opening the side doors unless we must."

Angus joins in, "Let's hope we won't have to open the doors. How do you like it so far?"

Richard smiles, "I'd rather not say, buddy."

Angus replies, "Come on, lads, the club is fun."

A few seconds pass as Richard tunes the NDB receiver to the Camp London radio, giving him a way to track back towards the base if needed.

Richard then responds to Angus, "It ain't bad, man. It's just that for the last three days, we've been doing ass and trash flights for eight hours straight. Truck drivers have it easier than us."

Angus laughs. "Aye! Have you seen the trucks around here? Careful what you wish for."

Richard nods, "What are we up to today? This is the first time we've been in a gunship since we got here."

Angus turns around and sits between the two pilots, laying his hands on both of their shoulders. "Like I told you last time we flew together. Let's fly around and see what trouble we can run into. You guys know the lay of the land around the base and the port. Let's go down Soth and see how the people are doing. There have been some propaganda pamphlets that are popping up in these villages and some of the clearings. Maybe we will spot a trail in the snow."

Richard thinks for a moment. "Maybe they are dropped from the air?"

Angus shakes his head, "Neah, we would have heard them. Anyway, you guys keep your eyes open. We fly as briefed, and we'll check some clearings and villages. Maybe we will spot something."

As they fly towards their first waypoint, Richard looks at Daniel, "Take it for a bit, I need to adjust my helmet."

Daniel confirms, "Roger, my bird."

Richard responds, "Your bird."

Richard adjusts his helmet, tightening the strap slightly, then stretches his arms, turns his head, and looks at the skids. He then turns his head backwards to glance at the flex guns hanging from the pilon, then at the rocket pods slung under the main pilon, the little Huey armed to the teeth.

Richard puts his hands back on the controls, "My bird."

Daniel nods, "Your bird."

A few minutes passed by, and the Huey approached the first village.

Angus comes on the intercom, "Let's follow the river and the road Southwest. Stay low for now."

Richard confirms, "Roger that."

Turning the helicopter left and descending, 150 feet over the river and the road that follows the river.

Angus moves from one side window to the other, scanning the road and the clearings in the thick forest that surrounds the village. "See that clearing? There are some truck tracks in there."

Richard looks where Angus is pointing, "You want to have a closer look?"

Angus shakes his head, "No, keep going!"

Angus examines another clearing mumbling on the intercom, "This one is clean, nothing went through there."

The Huey continues its way following the river. Richard pulls up and gains more altitude, 250 feet above the ground, as Krepotsnaya village now comes into view in the distance. A little glint of light, probably from a mirror, catches his attention.

Richard focuses on where that light was shining and spots something. "Hey, Angus, up ahead, where the road turns! Two trucks?"

Angus looks there, "Good eyes, lad, like you are a pilot. Look at those bastards. Those are not civilian trucks."

Two green trucks covered with a camo tarp in the Soviet army pattern. A few feet ahead of them, a small UAZ 4x4 is leading the small convoy.

Richard asks, "Okay, what do we do? We have our ROE."

Angus looks at the village, surveys the surrounding mountains for a moment, "Don't get close yet, stay close to the ceiling and keep your distance, let's see if we can track what they are doing."

Richard confirms, "Roger, but they will hear us."

Angus tilts his head, "Those trucks are quite noisy, let's see. Chief, open doors and arm your peashooters. Go hot!"

In the next second, the Huey's side doors slide backward and are secured in place. The Crew Chief and the door gunner are setting up their M-60 machine guns. Richard pulls his reticle down and adjusts the mill depression for rockets. Daniel pulls his reticle down and gets the handles for the flex guns, all happening in a quick choreography learned after so many years of training and combat. Angus's face is set, no more smiling. He's all business now, his senses attuned to what will come next. Richards keeps the helicopter high, 500 feet above the ground, close to the cloud layer, circling the trucks on a wide circle, almost a mile away from the trucks, trying not to lose track of them between the trees and the houses in the village. At a fork on the road, Angus curses,

"Damnit, they are splitting!"

The small 4x4 turns left, and the trucks proceed onto the field, driving through a snowy field towards the river.

Daniel mumbles in the intercom, "If these guys are the postal workers, I'll eat my kneeboard."

Angus grunts, "Stay with the trucks, we've been spotted, let's thump them."

Richard points the Huey towards the trucks, accelerating as they speed up and splash through the cold river waters, fording it at what appears to be a well-known spot, marked by tracks on the ground. Speeding up on the other side, towards the edge of the forest.

Angus speaks on the intercom, "We'll come back for that car later. Stay with them!"

Richard replies. "Roger, Roger, Daniel, I'll keep it moving. If I'm hit, you take it."

Keeping it moving means that from now on, Richard will keep the helicopter moving in all three axes, making himself a harder target to hit. He will vary speed, direction, and altitude every 2 seconds or so, while still gaining on the trucks. Richard zooms past the trucks as they reach the edge of the forest, pulling up and gaining altitude, then circling quickly above the trees.

Daniel yells on the intercom. "Infantry on the ground, those trucks were loaded with troops."

Soldiers are running away from the trucks, forming a line at the edge of the forest, and in the next second, the edge of the forest gets lit with muzzle flashes. Bullets are zipping by the Huey fast and low above the trees, hard to hit. However, two distinct "ting-ting" sounds come from the tail boom of the Huey. Those were hits.

Richard's hands are tightening on the controls, and he quickly checks all the controls, making the Huey sway sideways on its already erratic path.

Angus yells back, "Damnit, they opened on us. One whistled past! Okay boys! Let them have it!"

In the next instant, the Crew Chief opens fire with his M60, spraying the edge of the forest with bullets. Richard keeps turning until the nose of the Huey is facing the trucks. He lets out a volley of rockets, adjusting the aim slightly and firing again, aiming for one of the trucks. Daniel is working the flex guns, the two M134 miniguns, each firing at 4000 rounds a minute, making the sound of a large zipper being pulled across the sky, covering the edge of the forest with a shower of steel. Richard hits one of the trucks, it explodes with large fireball, probably filled with ammo and diesel fuel, swings the nose to the right and shoots at the other truck hitting it with another volley of rockets, then unloads the rest of them into the edge of the forest, as they zip past the carnage bellow, turning around again, keeping it fast and low, keeping it moving all the time. From the forest, nothing, no moves, no muzzle flash, just the two trucks burning with large columns of black smoke.

Richard slows down, bringing the helicopter into a hover, the Crew Chief and the other door gunner, swinging their M60's to cover forward as much as they can, Daniel with his flex guns, swinging them left to right, looking for any movement in the tree, Richard looking through the gunsight setup for rockets, letting the Huey slide left, still keeping it moving, "*You never know where one of them might be hiding.*"

Angus speaks first, "Good job, lads, looks like you got them all. Everyone okay?"

Richard nods, "Yeah, we're good, those bastards are aiming better than Vietcong."

Angus nods, "Aye! They do. I need you to land there, close to them, between the burning trucks. Chief, cover me! I must step out and see if I can get some intel off them."

Richard nods and replies, "Okay! I don't like you already. You must be one of those shit magnets that get into trouble all the time.

Angus grins, "I wonder about that all the time."

Richard comes to land between the trucks, swinging the helicopter around, sideways from the line of trees, so he can take off in a hurry if needed. Watches Angus jumping off the helicopter the moment the skids touch the ground. Angus is moving quickly, checking a few bodies.

The Crew Chief gasps on the intercom. "Damn, this guy is nuts! Geez, he just slit the throat of a guy that was still moving."

Angus sprints into the helicopter and yells. "Go! Go! Go!"

Richard takes off, and as soon as Angus puts his helmet back on, he asks. "Did you just slit a guy's throat?"

Angus looks at him, cleaning his knife on the inside of his elbow. "He wasn't going to make it anyway. Why waste a bullet? Easier to go this way. Had to be done."

A few moments of silence, as they fly back towards the village, Angus talks again, "Look for that little staff care we lost back when they split! Keep your eyes open. You still have ordinance left?"

Daniel smirks, "Like I would have the guts to lie to you. We've got plenty."

Krepotsnaya, Krasnodar Krai,
January 26th, 1979

Tanya opens the door of the chicken coop in her grandparents' backyard, letting the thirty or so chickens out into the small enclosure, and gives the rooster an angry glance. "*I wish I'll see you in soup one day, I'm sick of your annoying voice every morning at 5 o'clock.*" She checks the straw of the chicken coup for eggs, finding four eggs, "*Good enough for breakfast, but it's winter, Granda said they don't lay as many eggs during winter.*" She puts the eggs in a small basket, then reaches for the bucket that holds corn and grains for the chickens. She takes a handful and draws a line of corn and grains in the frozen muck that's in the chicken enclosure. The chickens follow her hand and start to eat, pecking at each other and flapping their wings. She puts some feed into the rusted bowl for later and sprinkles more on the ground for the chickens to dig around, just as her grandma taught her.

Tanya lifts her head, listening. She hears the grinding gears of a truck, the noise getting closer, still far away, on the main street of the village. She then hears the faint "chop-chop-chop" sound far away, a sound she had heard before at the airport in Krasnodar. "*Must be a helicopter far away.*"

Nikolay, her dad, yells from the shed behind the house. "Tanushka, don't forget to feed the piglets!"

Tanya smiles, "I will, Dad, in a moment."

Nadia, her mom, opens the kitchen window and yells, "I got the slop right here. It's all ready."

Tanya closes the chicken coop door and the enclosure after her and goes towards the kitchen. Thinking to herself, *"Two weeks ago I was guarding the airport, now I'm feeding the pigs. I became a peasant girl, and my fingernails are dirty and broken."*

She enters the kitchen, retrieves the bucket of food for the piglets, and then gives her mom the basket with the eggs. "Thanks, Mom. Where's grandma and grandpa?"

Katia kisses her forehead and responds, "They left this morning, there's a funeral in the nearby village, some folks they used to know, and they went there for the wake and to help out. They will be gone for a few days, you know how it is here. Whoever can help, they will."

Tanya nods. "I'll go feed those cute piglets."

Tanya gets into the pigsty, and the eight-week-old piglets dart towards her, knowing she brings food. She sits down on some clean straw, criss-cross, and starts scratching and petting the piglets. Both grunting around her, loving their pets and scratches, *"You two are the cutest things ever."* She keeps scratching them on that magic spot under their chins, the piglets grunting happily, then she gets up and picks the bucket, emptying it in their feed tray, crinkling her nose at the smell of the slop, leftover food, leftover borscht, some cabbage, some red beets, all mixed with corn and grains. She keeps patting their backs as they eat, their curled tails wagging fast as they dive into the slop, munching away. Tanya gets out of the pigsty, cleans the bucket, then fills it with water, and returns to the pigsty to fill the water tray for the pigs. She exits again and locks the pigsty door behind her. She hears the sound of the helicopter again, growing louder. The chopping sound of the blades cutting through the air seems faster, as if it's picking up speed. Some popping sounds in the background, the same sounds she had heard on the firing range when she fired the AK-47, but far, far away. Then, a sound like a zipper ripping through the sky, followed by a whooshing sound, and then explosions.

Nikolay gets out of the shed, a farrier's apron tied around his neck and waist, "What was that?"

The window to the kitchen opens again, and Katia's head pops out, looking towards the source of the noise. Far in the distance, two columns of black smoke are appearing.

Tanya replies, "Those first ones, where AK-47s, then a helicopter, I don't know what that was, some bombs? Artillery? Who's fighting?"

Nikolay gets nervous, "I'm sure it's nothing, we mind our own business, they won't come here."

Tanya looks at him. "Dad, you said...."

Nikolay snaps at her. "I know what I said, here in the middle of nowhere, nothing will come here!"

Nikolay turns around and returns to the shed, trying to appear unaffected by the explosions outside. Tanya stays outside, looking towards the columns of black smoke.

A few minutes after this, Nikolay gets out of the shed, "Katia, I'll go fix that corner of the fence, there where the rotten posts are."

As he walks towards the fence, Nikolay sees a speeding UAZ 4x4 on the street, rushing along. Nikolay hears the screech of the brakes and the tires skidding on the gravel on the road. He yells so loud that everyone can hear him. "Tanya, get in the shed and close the door! Katia, come up here!"

He's trying to locate the car, and to his horror, he sees the purple brassard that all the Freedom Militia members were wearing in Krasnodar. The one that Tanya put on the fence post right when they arrived ten days ago.

Nikolay hears the shed door and says again, "Stay there, Tanya, and don't make a sound!"

Nikolay sees two Senior Sergeants getting out of the staff car, followed by a soldier armed with an AK-47. Walking towards the gate, Nikolay walks to greet them. "Good morning, Comrade *Starshina,* how can we be of service?"

The gate door is kicked by one of the Sergeants, and all three of them step into the front yard.

One of them speaks. "That rag on your post, we know what that means. It means you are a traitor to the Soviet Union and a traitor to the party, and with traitors we deal with on the spot!"

Nikolay puts his hands up, "Comrades, I'm an old man, some kids put that there ages ago, we thought it looked cute."

The Sergeant replies, "Nice try, old man." He unholsters his handgun and pulls it up, aiming, and Nikolay and Katia start to sob already. The Sergeant squeezes the trigger of his gun, shooting once, then twice, shifting his aim towards Katia and shooting one more time.

Tanya hears the dialogue. Curled in a corner and crying. She hears the shots and lets out a blood-curdling scream. In a moment of madness, she gets up and busts the shed door, turning the corner and running towards her parents. "Noooooooooo!!!!!!" She turns the corner and sees her mom slumped against the wall, her dad lying down, curled in a puddle of blood, a black glinting object in front of her eyes, the butt stock of an AK-47 hitting her in the forehead, and all turns to black.

Up in the air, the crew of the Huey watches the scene unfolding before their eyes. The door busted, the shots, the bodies crumpled, Tanya being hit and falling, then being dragged inside, by the hair, by one of the Sergeants. Angus sits on the door of the helicopter, almost ready to jump out.

He turns around to Richard and points to a spot two hundred yards away from Tanya's house, "Land there, as quickly as you can."

Angus looks at the door gunner who's about to unstrap his M60 and take it with him. "Nobody follows me! Keep the bird running."

Richard is taking the helicopter down, almost dropping like a rock. He flares at the last moment and lands, skidding a bit on the frozen ground. Angus jumps out when the helicopter is still a foot off the ground. As he is running, he pulls his Browning High Power handgun out and chambers a round, running towards Tanya's house, jumping over a fence with the agility of a panther, and slowing down and getting behind the fence, where the post with the pink brassard is, peeking and clearing his corner, one of the Sergeants looking inside through the window. Angus picks up his knife and throws it, the knife hitting the Sergeant in the back of his neck. The Sergeant slumps down on the wall, not able to make a sound, because of the knife. Angus gets to him and pushes him against the wall. Pulling his knife out, he spots the soldier who is just getting out of the house and shoots twice. One in the chest, the other one right in the soldier's face. In two steps, Angus is at the door and bursts in. Another two shots are heard. A minute later, Angus gets out, holding Tanya in his arms, and she's covered with his coat. Her frame is so small that she appears to be wrapped in a large tarp. Angus runs with her towards the helicopter, just as quickly as he had run towards the house.

Daniel sees them and says, "Chief, go and help them."

The crew Chief gets out of the helicopter, and Angus grunts at him.

"Get back in, Chief!"

Angus gets in the Huey, Tanya still in his arms. He puts her down on the middle bench, signaling Richard, "Take off, let's go home! Quick! Don't go too high, if she has a head trauma, high altitude may hurt her more."

Richard pulls power, getting the Huey up in the air, and speeds at low altitude, while Daniel checks his map and gives Richard a heading. Pointing towards a valley between two hills where they could stay low.

Angus looks around for the Medical Kit and gets it. The Chief, close to him, said, "You need help, Angus?"

Angus nods, "Give me one of those thermal blankets, or maybe two, I want to wrap her up."

Angus covers her with the aluminum foil blankets, sliding his hand on Tanya's neck and checking her pulse.

Looking at the Crew Chief, "I think she's knocked out, bad!"

Richard comes on the intercom, "What happened there?"

Angus takes a deep breath, "You saw what happened from the air. I got there, I took one out with my knife, and another one I shot. I got inside, and the last of the bastards was tearing her clothes off. She was down to her boots, and that's all. He was unbuttoning his pants when I got in. You should see the surprise on his face when I put a bullet right in his face. Damn bastards, who in the bloody hell does that?"

Daniel looks back at Tanya. "At least you got her out alive."

Angus chews on his mustache. "I don't know, Daniel, she's alive on the outside, poor thing, what she saw.... She would wish..."

Angus is not finishing the phrase and turns around. How much longer? "

Richard responds, "Twenty minutes, maybe twenty-two."

Angus nods, "Don't land on the pad. Put it right there in front of the MASH tent, I'm afraid she's bleeding in her head."

Tanya jerks and Angus turns around, speaking with her in Russian, "It's okay, you are safe now, nothing happened, no, no, don't move, nothing happened, we're going to the hospital. Just one second."

Angus opens Tanya's eyelids and checks her pupils. "You are going to be alright, don't worry about a thing."

Angus rests his big hand on her cheek, holding her like this, his big warm hand as Tanya drifts away, a big hand on her face, just like her dad used to hold her face in his hands.

Nineteen minutes later, the Huey lands in front of the MASH at Camp London, orderlies waiting with a stretcher. Angus picks Tanya and goes with her in his arms straight into the tent, mumbling at the orderlies,

"Get lost, you bloody fools."

Making sure that Tanya is alright all the way, he will sit with her no matter how long it takes for her to wake up.

Camp London, Krasnodar Krai,
January 26th, 1979

It's nine o'clock at night in the O Club at Camp London, Richard and Daniel are sitting at a table drinking a beer, not much is said, after going over the mission that they flew in the morning a few times. Their usual debriefs, then a debrief with a Colonel and some guy from the CIA, wanting to know step by step what happened there, and how come they came with a young lady who was naked and wearing just a pair of old rubber boots. No one could get Angus to share his story, or, as Daniel pointed out, nobody had the guts to ask. Angus steps in, still dressed in his camo, wearing the same clothes, Richard notices the blood splattered on the side of his trousers. Angus gets to the bar and orders two glasses of scotch. He takes one and pours half of it on the floor, the libation for the dead, then dunks the rest into one gulp, chasing it with the other glass, then orders three more glasses. He takes them and comes to the table, where Daniel and Richard are sitting. He sits down between them and looks at the two pilots, a faint smile on his face,

"She's going to be alright. Bruised forehead and a big goose egg. How is her soul going to be? That remains to be seen."

Richard nods and stays silent.

Angus continues, "Drinks on me tonight, and drink, don't keep me waiting. You guys got shot at, and you came on top. I like you. Quick on the trigger and sharp."

Richard smiles, drinks his glass, and bangs the glass down on the table. "Angus, I gotta tell you, I don't know if you liking us is a good thing or not."

Angus smiles bigger now, "Well, if I keep you alive long enough, I guess you'll like me."

Richard shakes his head in disbelief. "I don't know if that's up to you, buddy."

Angus grins, "I made it this far, didnae?"

Richard starts to smile again, "Yeah, but it takes a bullet."

Angus keeps grinning, "Nonsense, tell that to the other five bullets that got me before. They are done, and I'm still here."

Daniel snorts with laughter, lifting his glass. "Can't argue with that logic, I guess we're safe now. Not bulletproof, but safe."

17

Chapter 17: A Hand to Hold

Camp London, Krasnodar Krai,
January 26th, 1979

The next morning, Angus sits there next to Tanya's bed. She has an IV attached to her hand. Angus sits on a chair next to her bed. His head in his hands, half asleep. Tanya opens her eyes and blinks a few times, the room coming into focus slowly, her thoughts moving very slowly in her head, groggy from the blow to her head and the sedatives. She looks around, the white room coming into focus, and sees the IV line attached to her hand. Following her eyes along the line, she notices the pole that holds the bag, where she sees Angus. Angus is aware of her movement, turning towards her and holding her hand.

Speaking in his heavy-accented Russian. "Don't move too much, no danger."

Angus takes a deep breath, finding his words. "You are alright, don't worry, you're not hurt, just a blow to the head, and you got knocked out."

Tanya's memories begin to return. Her parents, the blow to

the head, someone dragging her, her chin starts to tremble, she grips the bedsheet with her free hand, and Angus squeezes her other hand. "You saved me?"

Angus nods, Tanya asks more, "My parents? Are they alive?"

Angus looks down and closes his eyes. "I'm sorry, I was too late. I'm sorry, Miss."

Tanya starts to cry, turning her head away. "What happened? Why did those soldiers come in like that?"

Angus shakes his head. "I don't know, Miss, but they will not hurt anyone anymore,"

Tanya continues through the tears. "You... killed them?"

Angus nods, "Yes, I did."

Tanya continues and turns her head back, looking at Angus through her teary eyes. "But you were too late." Tanya tries to get up. "I must go back, my grandparents, they must be back by now, they will be hurt too. I must go back now. Where am I?"

Angus puts his hand on her shoulder and tries to keep it there on the bed. "You must stay here for a few days to get better. We had someone go back yesterday, and your grandparents are okay. The people in the village will take care of the rest."

Angus is not able to say that they will take care of the funeral of her parents. "Is there anyone we can try to find?"

Tanya is crying with full sobs now, realizing what Angus could not say. "How can I live? I've got nothing left, nothing to go back to? Nothing to live for."

Angus caresses her hand, "I know how you feel, you have your life, and you will find a reason to go past this. I know you are strong, and you will find that strength in you."

Tanya responds, "But how? I don't know what to do."

Angus nods, "I know it's hard, and you will find a way, and

I'll be there to support you however I can. And I'll make sure nobody will hurt you."

Tanya shakes her head, "You are just a soldier."

Angus nods, "Yes, I am, just a soldier, but I'll try my best."

Angus signals to one of the nurses that Tanya is awake.

Angus looks at her, "What's your name, young lady?"

Tanya is realizing that she doesn't know who the stranger is. "My name is Tanya, what's your name?"

Angus smiles, "My name is Angus, Angus MacGavin. The nurse and the doctor will be here. I'll come back later and see how you are doing. Don't try to run away."

Tanya nods, "I don't even know where I am and where to go."

WASHINGTON, USA

January 26th ,1979

In the Oval Office, President Carter is listening to the briefing that General Henry 'Hank' Emerson is giving, "Mr. President, as I was saying at the beginning of this brief, we're seeing an increase in the troop movement from Georgia and from the Krasnodar region. Troops are starting to amass in three areas. This shows us that within three to four weeks, they will be ready to engage. The areas are Pshada, Maykop, and Guamka, as the Ukrainian staff has warned us. The cruel reality is that, with the forces present in the region, we could stop one area. We have the rest of the Rapid deployment troops inbound. In the next two weeks, they will be deployed, but without proper aviation support, we will be unable to accomplish much. I cannot guarantee the safety of Krasnodar and Krimsk, the two biggest cities in the area. I am still waiting for your approval to transit the aviation units. My staff is certain that the two F-5 squadrons and the three F-4 squadrons that are currently preparing for transit will not be sufficient. Especially the F-5 units, although the pilots are certainly among the best-prepared in the US Air Force, the plane lacks the necessary capability. It is a small plane, with a limited number of weapons, and a limited number of guided munitions."

President Carter leans back into his chair, thinking about the briefing, "And we are fairly certain that they will push North once they are in position?"

The General nods, "Mr. President, you don't put your dance shoes just to look pretty, when you put your dance shoes and you dress for dancing, and you drive to the club, chances are you will do the boogie that night."

President Carter smiles, and General Emerson continues, "The weather will get better, and they will be in position to launch a massive attack on us and roll onto Krasnodar in less than 2 weeks."

President Carter gets up from his chair and studies the map for a few seconds. "Our mandate still stands! We are a peace-keeping force. I understand your concern. Continue to deploy the US, German, and Canadian forces that are allocated. Also, if needed, you can stage reinforcements in Germany and Italy. This way, we can use either the air or the navy to deploy them. You can do the same for aviation. However, I must emphasize that this is a peace-keeping mission, and I don't want to add another 4 or 5 aviation units, which could trigger even a bigger response from the Russians. This must be avoided."

General Emerson nods, "Just for once, Mr. President, I would like to go to war without having a hand tied behind my back. We're the best at fighting with one hand behind our back, but I wonder if the cost justifies it."

President Carter smiles, "I wonder the same thing, however, General, if this will avoid World War 3 or a nuclear conflagration, it is justified."

The General nods, "I agree with you, Mr. President, it is justified, with one condition, if we manage to win. If we don't, then all will be in vain."

President Carter smiles, "Well, that's your job, General."

General Emerson laughs, "I wonder if I should've called in sick that day, Mr. President. But maybe all is not lost, at least, from what I see on the ground, we have the support of the people, at least in the areas we are present."

President Carter turns towards Cyrus Vance, the Secretary of State, "How are we doing on that aspect, Mr. Vance?

Cyrus Vance takes a few seconds and looks through his papers. "Mr. President, indeed, from what we can gather from the ground, we have the support of the people, there are several factors that are working in our favor, the results from the referendums from the former Soviet republics that asked for independence have been in favor, with results in the 70 to 80 percent, and this has been made public and the people in Krasnodar Krai have seen those results, the TV and radio stations from Ukraine are available in the region. That is a huge factor. Additionally, Ukraine has navigated the winter well. Although it is not stellar, when it comes to improving people's lives, Andrei Kirilenko is taking the right steps, adopting a gradual approach to move the country in the direction he sees as beneficial. However, Kirilenko is a true communist, so I would not expect an emerging democratic country soon. And the same goes for the rest of the former Soviet countries."

President Carter interrupts, "You may be right, but I would rather have someone who puts the needs of his country first, even if we have a difference in ideology, than someone who shares the same ideology and puts his personal needs first."

Cyrus Vance nods. President Carter continues, "And in many ways, some of the people here should learn from people like Kirilenko and Pense and Ruslan. Now, changing the subject here, can we rely on any forces from Krasnodar's Freedom Militia?"

General Emerson shakes his head, "Unfortunately, no. They lack the proper training, equipment, and means to cooperate with the UN forces; however, some of my staff, from the special forces, are planning to use their local knowledge. This could prove to be a great help in the grand scheme of things. It will be the first step towards cooperation, but it poses a significant risk to the locals involved. If the Soviet forces ever caught them, this would mean the death penalty on the spot."

President Carter asks, "In what way will they cooperate?"

General Emerson responds, "With the language knowledge and the knowledge in geography, these troops, infiltrated behind the Soviets controlled areas, could provide target reconnaissance, Forward Air Control, and rescue capabilities for downed pilots. Although the job of a good Forward Air Control takes months to train, at least some basic form of target reconnaissance and acquisition can be provided by these troops. Achieving success with this program will open up other opportunities, utilizing guerrilla tactics similar to those employed by the French Resistance during World War II. The same way it was implemented in Vietnam and Laos, however, the success was debatable, but from the reports that I have on the ground, this could be better implemented."

President Carter thinks for a few seconds. "I agree with your approach. This will make them feel involved. I would advise ensuring that the feedback and communication work effectively between all parties, without jeopardizing the security of these individuals. But praise their success, hold them accountable, and make them feel heard."

General Emerson nods. "I'm glad you feel this way, Mr. President. My staff has exactly the same opinion!"

President Carter continues, "Thank you, General, I'm glad you did not call in sick that day."

President Carter shakes everyone's hand and walks out of the Oval Office. As he walks, he thinks, *'Well, the wheels are certainly in motion now, more like the tracks of Soviet tanks are in motion now. Time will tell.'*

Camp London, Krasnodar Krai,
January 27th, 1979

Angus enters the MASH hospital room, which was designed for 30 beds but now has only one patient. A green cover surrounds her bed for some privacy, with one side open to face the nurse's station. Angus looks at the bed and sees that Tanya is awake already.

Angus smiles, "Good morning, Miss Tanya, how are you feeling this morning?"

Tanya looks at him with a glint of hope in her red eyes. She's been crying the whole time she was awake. "Good morning, Mr. MacGavin. I am well, everyone is friendly to me, and they say I'll be up and ready in no time."

Angus pulls a chair and sits next to her, looking into her eyes, trying to read through the tears and sorrow that fill them.

"Miss Tanya, let's make a deal, you stop calling me Mister, and I won't feel so old, how does that sound?"

Tanya's lips are turning upwards a bit in a faint smile. "Since we are cutting deals, how about you call me Tanya, and I'll drop the Mister?"

Angus nods, "I think that's a fair deal, Tanya." She nods, "Thank you, Angus. Do you have any other news?"

Angus shakes his head, "I don't, I know your grandparents are okay, but that's all I know. Is there anyone else that we can try to contact? Maybe in Krasnodar?"

Tanya shakes her head, then thinks a bit, "There's this guy I was seeing, before I had to leave, Mischa is his name, you probably know him, he was guarding the airport with me, and we did some drill with the American officer, Hawk, or something like this."

Angus lifts his eyebrows. "Oh, I remember, a good kid, but very clumsy. I can ring them up, and we can get him here."

Tanya thinks for a second, "Who would want to be with me, like this, with no parents, beaten up, and shamed too?"

Her chin starts to quiver again, and tears start to roll down her face.

Angus takes her hand. "Tanya, nothing happened there. I took care of it before anything happened. And you, you are a brave girl, and that bruise will be gone in two days. Every boy should feel blessed to be close to you."

Angus pats her hand, "I tell you what, I'll ring him up, and if he doesn't like you anymore, I'll make him!"

Tanya smiles, "I'm sure you will, it doesn't work that way."

Angus mumbles, "You'd be surprised."

Angus continues, "Now, I know it's too early, but what would you like to do? We can arrange for you to go back to

Krasnodar."

Tanya shakes her head. "No, not there, I couldn't. I enjoyed serving in the Freedom Militia. I could join again, maybe here."

Angus thinks for a moment, "There's no Krasnodar forces here in this camp, but we have help here from the locals."

Tanya shakes her head, "No, I don't want to be in the kitchen, peeling potatoes and serving food."

Angus replies, "You would be safe. However, in a week or so, from Mischa's unit, a few volunteers will start to train with us for some work in the mountains."

Tanya's eyes became big, a shade of anger in them. "Teach me, train me! I'll join them."

Angus's eyes become steely. "Why? So you can make them pay? So you can get your revenge? So you can make them hurt just the way they hurt you?"

Tanya's face is set, and tears still roll from her eyes, "Yes, every one of them."

Angus's face becomes soft, and he chews his mustache while he thinks, "Take advice from an old soldier, Tanya. I've seen friends blown to bits right next to me, and I did not have a single scratch. I've seen people hurt that I could not save in time, and I've seen people hurt for doing stupid things that I couldn't save. And when you give in to hate like you, all that suffering you will cause will add to your pain, not make it better, but make it a bigger burden for you. And I won't allow it. If I can help it, I won't allow it."

Tanya looks at him, seeing him moved by what he said, "But, you are a soldier, you go there, and you kill, and ... you make them suffer, no?"

Angus shakes his head, "No! This, to me, is what I do, but I have to know that what I'm doing is the right thing, the honorable thing. If one of those bastards with a hat and stars on their shoulder orders me to do something that's not honorable, or to hurt the wrong people, I would tell them to..."

Angus smiles, "To ..... You know what. What I do is hard, but I know that each day, I can look in the mirror and not hate the face I'm seeing. And I can live with that. It is still hard sometimes, but I can live with it."

Tanya nods and, without realizing she's squeezing Angus's hand, says, "Then, maybe, teach me that."

Angus looks at her, "And if I tell you to do something, you will listen?"

Tanya nods. Angus continues, "And if I tell you to do something that you don't think is honorable, what will you do?"

Tanya smiles, realizing that she has found something to stand up against and a reason to keep going. "I'll stick my tongue out at you and tell you that you must be going crazy, because Angus MacGavin doesn't think that way."

Angus smiles, "Good, now the first lesson, and order of duty, I want you to rest, I want you to eat, I want you to talk with all the nurses and all the doctors here, work on your English, I know you know a bit, but talk to them and start learning. It will come in handy later. Understood?"

Tanya nods and salutes. Angus smiles, "Second lesson, out in the field, you never salute." Angus smiles. "Why do you think we have this rule?"

Tanya thinks for a bit, "Oh, if there's a bad guy, he would know who the officer is?"

Angus nods, "Exactly, now remember what I said, I'll be back later, if you can, and the doctors are okay with it, move about, get that strength back. I must go now, but I'll see you later."

Tanya looks at him as he walks away, "Angus, thank you, and be careful."

Angus turns around and grins. "Always!"

18

Chapter 18: Smoke and Steel

Camp London, Krasnodar Krai,
January 27th, 1979

Richard takes a quick look at the little OH-6 helicopter as it zooms past the camp wall made from old containers and speeds towards their meeting point. Richard is announcing his takeoff on the radio. He pulls power and gets the Huey in the air, keeping it hovering a few feet off the ground. After checking the controls and rechecking the engine parameters, he starts to accelerate. He moves forward, jumping over the walls of the camp and chasing the OH-6 helicopter. The Huey is always sluggish when loaded with miniguns and rockets, and with a full load of fuel.

The mission today, the two helicopters working in tandem, the small OH-6 as an Air Forward Air Controller, callsign Chevy, pretty much a flying bait, and the Huey, callsign Pontiac, trailing behind and engaging everything the OH-6 spots, or anything that will shoot at the little helicopter. This tactic had been tried and tested many times in Vietnam, a tactic that had taken the lives of a lot of brave OH-6 pilots.

Richard joins with the OH-6 Helicopter, and the second he is in formation, the radio crackles, "Nice of you to join me. Let's go! Follow me! Keep 500 yards behind me. If anyone is shooting at me, I want you guys to take them out in the next second. No questions asked!"

Richard confirms, "Roger Chevy! We'll cover your tail."

The helicopters turn towards their first waypoint, with Richard and his Huey dropping back to keep an eye on everything below the little OH-6, so close to base that nothing should be on the ground. However, he's getting into the habit of covering his "Loach". The flight continues like this, skimming over the trees, then going up when there's a hill. Slowing down and taking a quick look in the valley for any movement, peeking from over the trees, and then going down into the valley. This game of hide and seek has been going on for more than 20 minutes.

At some point, the radio comes to life again. "Pontiac, Chevy! You guys worked with that Scottish guy? That big and fat one?"

Richard and Daniel are grinning at each other, knowing that's some prank. Richard responds, "Yeah, we did Chevy. Quite a guy that one, don't land with him anywhere, he tends to like to use his knife."

Angus, sitting in the left seat of the OH-6, comes on the radio. "Oi! Lads! I'm on the left side of this little bird. Careful what you are saying. Some of you may wake up with a headache and a broken nose tomorrow!"

Richard laughs, then replies, "Chevy, Pontiac. Nice one! You thought we were gonna step into that trap? Can't miss that big one climbing on your bird, your skid is bent a bit after he got in."

Angus replies, "Oi! I'm not fat! It's all muscle! You rotten bastards!"

The flight continues for another 10 minutes or so, and Chevy comes on the radio again. "Pontiac! I'm going to slow down over this mountain and take a peek. Go weapons hot."

Richard responds, "Roge!"

Talking into the intercom, "Weapons hot!" and in that rehearsed choreography, the Huey becomes a lethal weapon again. The Crew Chief and the door gunner, with their M-60 machine guns, and Daniel, arming the flex guns and getting his sight ready. Richard is preparing his gun sight for the rockets. Richard is trailing closer to the OH-6, getting slightly above him, as he tries to see over the mountain.

Chevy comes on the radio, "Looks clear there."

Angus replies, "Oi! Wait a moment, look there!"

Richard is trying to understand what they are looking at. In the next second, trails of red tracers are coming towards them, as always when you are shot at. At first, the tracers seem slow, but then they start zooming past you at an incredible speed, big red tracers, like flying flaming apples. Chevy comes on the radio, his voice an octave higher, "Pontiac, Chevy, taking fire from the clearing in front. Holly shit! Big balls of fire! ZSU-23 on trucks. Fry them if you can, I'll mark them with Willy Pete!"

The little OH-6 peels right, gaining speed, then turns towards the triple-A guns mounted on flatbed trucks, and shoots two White Phosphorus Rockets. The Willy Pete will mark the target with white smoke. At the same time, Richard lowers the nose of the Huey to gain speed, checks the smoke to ensure he is looking at the same target, and growls on the radio. "I have your mark! In! Hot!"

Aiming for the two guns and the transport trucks parked behind them, Richard fires a volley of rockets, releasing half of the rockets loaded in his Huey. At the same time, Daniel fires his flex guns, moving them left to right, covering the forest clearing with a shower of bullets. Smaller tracers are converging on them now, AK-47s joining in the ZSU-guns, a second and a half for the rockets to reach their target, a second and a half that feels like an eternity. And finally, Richard is seeing the explosions of the rockets, trucks being hit and exploding, while the ammo and the gas tanks are erupting, soldiers dressed in green uniforms running away from the explosions. Ammunition cooking off in the trucks and exploding everywhere, tracers and sparks flying all around.

Richard is turning the Huey away in a fast right turn, talking on the radio, "Hits! Hits! Secondaries!" Richard sees with the corner of his eye another stream of tracers, those big red ones coming towards him from the other side of the mountain.

Chevy comes on the radio in the next moment. "Holy crap! There are more of them on the other side of the mountain!"

Angus joins in, "This is a bloody trap, mate. Get the hell out of there!"

Both helicopters are now caught in the crossfire between the ZSU guns and the soldiers who are still firing from the first flak site.

Chevy comes on the radio again. "London, Chevy, do you have any units in the area?"

The voice from the London Camp is calm and collected, like nothing is happening. "Stand by one Chevy!"

Richard grunts, trying to thread the Huey between the bullet streams as it flies fast, keeping it moving. Another stream of tracers is flying towards the Huey. Richard is trying to dip the nose down a bit. The rounds' air bursts right before they reach the Huey, creating a cloud of shrapnel. Richard hears the ting-ting of the shrapnel hitting the Huey, then the plexiglass canopy on Daniels' side shatters into pieces, and

Daniel groans in the intercom. Richard looks at the instrument console on Daniel's side and sees it splattered with blood. Daniel comes on the intercom, "I'm hit in the face! Keep going! Keep going!"

Richard sees the opportunity to launch another volley of rockets at the exact location where the first target was hit. And then turns away again, avoiding more fire.

The radio comes alive again. "Chevy, London, I have some help coming your way, ETA 1 minute."

Chevy responds, "Targets marked with Willy Pete! Clear to engage! We're taking fire!"

A few seconds later, two Cobras are popping up from behind a mountain, rockets firing, hitting the second flak site, guns from the chin turret blazing and working the target, swooping over the site, then turning towards the first one and shooting some more. Richard looks down at the carnage, trucks burning, bodies sprawled on the ground, then looks at Richard, his face covered in blood, his helmet busted around the ear, "Are you okay, man?"

Daniel grunts and lets out a swear word, "I caught some splinters in the face and ear, I'm good, not deep, just stings and bleeds like mad."

A new voice comes on the radio, the Cobra flight, "Hey guys, it looks clear for now. You guys need any more help? We're hurting for gas."

Chevy replies, "Cobra flight, Chevy, I think we're good.

Thanks a bunch. What flight is that? You weren't posted on the board!"

Cobra flight replies, "That's on a need-to-know basis, buddy. Cobra flight is out!"

Richard shakes his head. *Usually, that's some CIA stuff when they go like this, oh well, they were here at the right time."* He locates the OH-6 and comes in close formation, surveying the Little Bird and checking for damage. He notices a few holes in the tail boom, but there is no smoke or fluid leaking.

Chevy talks on the radio, "Pontiac, Chevy, I'm gonna have one more look around. Cover me!"

Richard replies and drops back in his trail position, "Don't let that one out! He's gonna make a mess in your bird."

Angus replies, "Don't worry, lad, I'm dumb and fat, but not that stupid."

The OH-6 swings around the two clearings, all quiet now, then he comes on the radio, "Alright, we've had enough fun for a day. Let's go home!"

Richard smiles and replies, "Yeah, so much fun, I should've put on my brown pants. I forgot how big those 23 millimeters look when they zoom past you."

Richard comes closer to the OH-6, and then he looks at Daniel. The Crew Chief assisted him in removing his helmet and applying a bandage to his cuts. Daniel gives him the thumbs up to let him know he is okay. Richard lifts his shoulders, then looks at the OH-6, Angus sitting on the back seat on the left side, with one foot nonchalantly dangling in the air, but the tip of his rifle is moving slightly as he aims from small clearing to small clearing, still alert to everything that goes on below. Richard settles down on his flight home. *Damn, this thing, being shot at, never gets old.* Flexing his fingers over the cyclic stick. *I was squeezing the black out of the stick. I hope I still have the strength to go through it all.*

Tyndall AFB, Florida, USA
January 27th, 1979

James is lying in the bed next to Diane. He managed to get a few hours of sleep before the departure this morning. Now, fully awake and unable to go back to sleep, thoughts are rushing through his mind. With his hand resting on Diane's belly, the baby kicking and pushing on it, James smiles. *Oh, you little thing, can't wait to see you when I'm back, and see what troubles you are going to get into when you are growing up. I really want to see you growing up.* Diane turns around, and James remains deep in his thoughts. *You don't have to do this. You don't have to go. You can say "enough" at any time.* James groans and fluffs his pillow, trying to get some more sleep. *You wouldn't be able to look at yourself, you wouldn't be able to look at your friends, and all the other pilots who are going. Major James Boyd, not so brave, what happened with compartmentalization? What happened with one step at a time? You worry like an old man.*

Diane turns around and pulls him into a hug, kissing him, "I know, James, I can't sleep either. You will go there and do your duty, making me proud. If not you, then who? Who's going to go and help those people who can't help themselves? Without you and the rest of the guys, they will have it rough, and from what you told me, this isn't Vietnam. I don't think you will get the same reaction as when you came back from your tours."

Diane kisses him again. "So put your worries away, you will do well and come back to us, I know it."

James smiles. "This thing you do, when you read my mind

like this, it's half cute and half scary."

Diane smiles, "It's called being a woman, James. And you have the emotional capability of a teacup most of the time. It's not that hard."

James pulls her in his arms and finally manages to fall asleep.

Two hours later, James quickly silences his alarm clock, not wanting to wake her up. He's trying to slide off the bed quietly, the moment he starts to move.

Diane's hand grips his chest and pulls him in for a kiss. "I don't have the strength to walk you to the door, darling. I wouldn't be able to keep it together. Please be safe out there."

James nods and kisses her back, walking out of their bedroom, hitting the shower, and getting himself ready. Knowing well the pain Diane is going through, *I marvel at how strong she is.* James wonders if the roles would be reversed, if he could have the same strength. Looking in the mirror, he grins at the realization that he would not have the same strength and composure. *So much for the strong and brave pilot, eh?*

Camp London, Krasnodar Krai,
January 27th, 1979

Daniel sits up on the bed in the MASH hospital ward at Camp London. "Come on, Doc, it was just two stitches. Do I need a tetanus shot? What's next, anti-rabies?"

The doctor smiles, "Did the bullets bark? Were they foaming at the mouth? Well, you know what? Since you brought it up, it's better to be safe. Nurse, can you please prep an anti-rabies shot? The one that goes in the belly."

Daniel gasps, "You must be bored in here, no, no, no, the bullets didn't bark, and do that tetanus shot and spare the rabies, please! Jesus, you're gonna poke more holes in me than the Soviet army."

The nurse comes grinning and turns Daniel on his side and pokes him with the tetanus shot in his butt cheek."

We're more than capable of that, Lieutenant." The nurse, a Captain, outranked Daniel.

Daniel groans, then looks at the nurse, "I'm sure you are very capable, Captain ma'am."

The Doctor looks at his chart one more time. "I can have you out of here in an hour, or you can spend the night."

Daniel looks at him, then at the nurse, "Doctor, I love the establishment, but I don't want to spend more time than needed here."

The Doctor nods and leaves. As he is going, he turns around and says, "Then, maybe don't get shot next time."

Daniel lifts his shoulder, "It's not like I'm not trying, Doc, but they get lucky sometimes."

Tanya comes closer to Daniel's bed, looking at him, then speaking in her heavily accented English, "Hello, you were in helicopter that day, when you saved me."

Daniel looks at her and smiles. "Yes, I was. My name is Daniel. Nice to meet you." Daniel gets up, then pulls the blanket up, realizing he is wearing a hospital gown. He shakes Tanya's hand, "You must be Tanya, right?"

Tanya smiles and shakes his hand. "Yes, my name is Tanya, and thanks you for saving me."

She corrects herself quickly. "Thank you. English is hard."

Daniel smiles, "Hey, your English is way better than my Russian."

Tanya looks at his face, "What happened to you? Angus was with you. Is he okay?"

Daniel responds, "The helicopter got shot, and shrapnel cut my face, just a few minor cuts, it's nothing. And Agnus was in another helicopter. Don't worry, he is good."

Tanya looks at him, "And you could still fly after you got hit?"

Daniel shakes his head, "I wasn't, Richard, the other pilot had the controls, but I could've if needed."

Tanya smiles, "You are very brave. Thank you again for saving me."

Daniel smiles and looks at the door. Angus is walking in. "Hey, you two have met. How is it, Daniel?"

Daniel shrugs, "It's nothing, just two stitches."

Angus examines his face, "Aye, I cut myself worse when I was shaving."

Daniel laughs, "You shave your ears, man? And what kind of shaving gear do you have in Scotland?"

Angus grins, "I shave with me knife, lad, that's how sharp it is."

Angus turns to Tanya, "I have news, Mischa and a few other guys will be here tomorrow. We need to provide you with some gear. I don't want to see any of you with those blasted green Soviet garbs. Can you help me out? You know how tall those guys are."

Tanya nods quickly, "Yes, I can help. After that, what will we do next?"

"We'll train you and the rest of the team a little bit, then I'll see how well you do. Can you run 2 miles?"

Tanya looks at him and blinks a few times, "How much is that in kilometers? I don't know about miles, but in high school, I used to run track. Five and ten kilometers was my specialty."

Angus laughs, "Good God, you are a runner, you'll run circles around an old guy like me."

Tanya grins, feeling more capable all of a sudden. Angus turns towards Daniel. "You'll be at the O Club later! No reason to sulk about in the bed here."

Daniel nods, "Man, believe me, I'll get out of here as soon as I can. The folks here are trigger-happy. They jabbed me with a needle already."

Angus turns to Tanya, "You should join us too, get to meet the rest of the guys that saved you. What is the drinking age in Russia?"

Tanya looks puzzled, not understanding what Angus was asking, "I don't know... twelve?"

Angus laughs, "And, you are older than that?"

Tanya draws herself up, looking defiant, "Mister Angus, I'm almost twenty years old."

Angus smiles, "Aye, you're all looking like kids to me."

19

Chapter 19: Lessons in the Snow

Camp London, Krasnodar Krai,
February 1st, 1979

Angus is leading his troop of new trainees through the snowy trails in the forest, a fifteen-mile ride on a Marine's M-113, then a seven-mile quick march through the snowy trails in the forests near Karskii, keeping a quick pace, all in full gear, backpacks and rations, equipped to spend a few days in the snow. His troop consisted of six people. Tanya, Mischa, and four other guys from the Freedom Militia had volunteered for this task. Angus looks around and finds a small clearing, making a sign to stop. Quick marching through a snowy forest is not an easy task, and it takes a toll on everyone. Angus takes a few deep breaths, feeling the effort as well. Mischa and a few guys are bent over, catching their breaths, and one of them is dunking his canteen. Tanya, hands on her hips, stood up to her full height, taking big gulps of air, not showing how tired she was, not reaching for her canteen, just her head tilted up, looking through the trees, and taking deep breaths, somehow looking better than the rest of the guys.

Angus looks at her, "How's your kit? What did you pack?"

Tanya responds, "The standard, like you told us. Ammo, five grenades, the radio, rations, water, socks, and tarp."

Angus asks, "And you are not tired?"

Tanya smiles, "I am, I don't want to show it. The guys were grumbling about having a girl with them and slowing them down. I won't show them. Shall we go further, maybe another kilometer?"

Angus smiles, "Aye, you are showing me. Keep it like this. Never show them any weakness."

Angus turns towards the rest of the troop, "Gather round, let's camp here for a bit. Get your canteens and stay hydrated. Keep your coats on, I know you are hot now, but don't lose body heat."

Angus turns facing them, "Now that we warmed up a bit, and you worked out all the tension and the nerves, you are ready to listen, what we will have to do, in the future, is to be the eyes and ears for the troops, we find something, we radio back, and if needed they will put a bomb or a rocket on it. For this, we don't need to be heroes, we need to be hunters, but remember, and remember it well, you are a hunter, but you will be hunted too."

Angus looks at them, then looks at Mischa, "Mischa, tell me, what would you do if you spot a column of tanks traveling down a road?"

Mischa answers quickly, "I'll report it on the radio: how many, what kind of equipment, if they have any anti-air, direction of travel, and speed."

Mischa looks at Angus, trying to see if Angus is happy with his answer, then he continues, "Then I'll try to maintain contact and evaluate if there is a strike."

Angus nods, "That's a textbook answer, it's good, but I'm afraid you will be dead."

Mischa has a puzzled look, trying to think of what he could have said better. Angus continues. "Listen, lads, you see them, and you mark all that on a map or in your head. You know from the radio traffic or the controller what kind of support we have in the air. So, if there are planes, they could be hitting those tanks within 2-3 minutes, so you must think, could the bad guys reach me within 2-3 minutes? If the answer is yes, then you must pull away and get yourself some room."

Angus starts to draw in the snow, the shape of a road, a few blobs resembling tanks or trucks, and where a FAC would be, showing them what he meant. "The tanks will travel, you know their speed and where they are going, the planes will see them anyway. This way, you increase your chances of staying alive. Anytime you send something on the radio, it can be pinpointed to you. When you pull away, you move in a different direction, increasing the spacing between your position and where you will be when they search for you. Understood?"

The guys are nodding their heads. Mischa talks first, "Well, yes, that makes sense."

Angus smiles, "Common sense and war don't go together well, lad. What seems like common sense now, when the rush of the battle comes, it will go out the window, so you must be the hunter. You don't see a cat flapping about when stalking a bird."

Tanya is asking, "What if they are further away? 10-15 minutes? Or, are there only helicopters in the area? Those are slower, no?"

Angus nods, "Aye, remember, I want you to stay alive, when we are doing this, this is the first rule, to stay alive, if we ever get into a firefight, then that's a different story, but for this, staying alive is the most important, so, work that problem, get that space, make sure you are well hidden, make sure no one can see you or hear you, then you call them in. It's the same. If they know the general area to look for something, the guys in the air will spot them. Also, remember never to rush back immediately to get a battle damage assessment. Whatever they hit will be there hours after. Right after an attack, they will be the most alert."

Angus looks at them, seeing their reaction. Mischa is thoughtful, as are the other guys, who are trying to remember it all, while Tanya is fully immersed in this lesson.

"Now, don't you worry, we're not going to send you all alone, you guys will be with me for quite some time, until I'm sure you can do well and stay out of trouble. I don't want to rescue you, or even worse, write to your parents. My Cyrillic Russian writing is terrible."

Angus clenches his cheeks, realizing that he made a mistake. Tanya is already sad, her eyes almost in tears, thinking about who Angus will write to if her number comes up. Wringing her hands together and looking away so nobody could see her eyes. Angus clears his voice with a short cough, then looks at Tanya, shakes his head, and puts his hands together, his expression sad. He looks at Tanya with his sad eyes, nodding slightly, apologizing with just one glance.

"Alright, folks, listen up, let's play a game of hide and seek, over there, 500 yards or so, that's about as many meters, there's another small opening, I'm going to rush quickly to it, and you should space out and come there as quiet and as hidden as you can, remember, if you can't see me, I can't see you. However, also remember that our human eye is designed by Mother Nature to capture motion, so if I stay still, I'll see you before you see me."

Mischa smiles, "Not really fair, Angus."

Angus smiles, "Kind of like life, Mischa." Angus slaps his shoulder. "That's how you learn, from your mistakes, and do all of them here with me."

Angus gathers them again. "Remember, if you look towards something that moves." Angus opens his eyes wide and stares at each one of them with a comical look on his face, eyes as wide as they can open. "Like this, you won't be seeing anything. That's another quirk that Mother Nature did on us. Our eyes capture movement with our peripheral vision, so we can protect ourselves from being the hunted. So, to observe better, move your head slowly from side to side and let your eyes and your brain catch everything."

Angus checks everyone's gear, admonishing one of the guys. "Don't keep a magazine in your rifle, you'll catch your safety on something and shoot your toes off. We won't be going to war just yet. Also, when you move, stay out of the light, keep in the shadow, don't silhouette yourself over anything high, a ridge, or even go over a tree trunk. You go underneath it or around it."

Angus smiles, "I'll go first, see how long you can spot me, and when you hear me whistle Scotland the Brave, you space out and come to me."

Tanya asks, "Scotland, what?" Angus starts to whistle the tune for a few measures. "This one, okay? I'm going."

Angus dashes into the forest, running low for a few steps,

dashing behind a tree, then behind a fallen tree trunk, and in thirty meters, he vanished. Mischa grumbles, "My God, this man is the devil. He is gone."

Tanya grins, "I'm glad he is our guardian devil."

A few minutes later, they hear the loud whistle of "Scotland the Brave," probably the first time this tune has ever been sung in the forests around Karskii. The troops spread out, and everyone began to move towards the clearing, slowly, each trying to find the best path.

After a few minutes, Angus, well hidden, just his eyes showing, gave out a loud whistle, "Vasea! Vasea! Turn the other way, you will get lost, you are going the wrong way, and I can still see you, follow my voice."

Angus laughs, "That's a good lad, no need to walk hunched now, my grandma could see you before her eye surgery!"

Angus shakes his head, "*This one is the one that's always getting lost. I need to keep an eye on him.*"

Angus keeps looking. A few minutes after this, he grins. "Ivan, I see you, lad, you can't go under the snow, you are not a mole, and a moving snow mound is a dead giveaway, and eventually you have to breathe. But you had a good idea overall. You didn't plan ahead. That area was exposed."

Igor gets up and huffs and puffs, out of breath after trying to move under the snow. Another guy was a spotter after he tried to peek around a tree. Then, a minute later, Mischa is spotted.

"Look how he flopped in the snow, jumping over a tree trunk." Angus laughs loudly, "That was spectacular, Mischa."

Mischa curses loudly. "This is tiring. Who knew moving slowly could be this tiring? I'd rather have the quick march."

Angus grins, still hidden. "I told you that was the warmup."

Angus keeps looking after Tanya, shifting around a bit,

thinking that she may have taken a different route, or maybe gotten lost. A sound of a boot scraping against a root is heard in the forest, accompanied by a grunting sound from Tanya. Angus sees her, stumbling from behind a big tree, forty, maybe thirty meters away from him. She's the closest to him, and Angus is impressed. "Look at that, you almost got to me."

Tanya seems furious. "I lost my footing there on that root. I could see you, though. Your shoulder, or your back, I guess, was moving."

Angus smiles, "So you could have taken a shot at me. Good job, Tanya. Maybe you have the making of a ghost."

Tanya smiles and throws a snowball at him, catching Angus on the shoulder. "Maybe that should be the name of our unit, The Ghosts."

Angus smiles and starts to make a snowball. "When this becomes a unit, it's a good idea. But there's a big road ahead of us until then."

Tanya replies, "I need to get back, I left my backpack some 200 meters that way."

Angus asks, "Who told you to do that?"

Tanya shrugs, "I had to get myself smaller. That thing on my back doubles my silhouette."

Angus looks at her half in awe, half in disbelief. "That's very smart, get your backpack and let's get ready."

As she turns around, Angus throws the snowball at her and hits her in the back. Tanya screams and starts to run towards her gear. Mischa throws a snowball at Angus, and for a few minutes, a whole snowball battle ensues, with no victims, no wounded, just a lot of laughter and giggles echoing through the forest.

After a few minutes, Angus yells. "Cease fire, cease fire!

It's getting late. Let's go back to that big clearing and let me show you how to catch a ride home in a helicopter. I've walked enough with you lot." Angus then makes a sign with their hands for them to keep quiet, looks around, almost sniffes the air, and smiles. Then the rest of the group hears the distant chop-chop sound of a Huey.

20

Chapter 20: The hunter and the hunted

Camp London, Krasnodar Krai,
February 6th, 1979

Richard checks left and right to ensure the pad is clear and he can take off safely. Then, he pulls on the collective, lifting the Huey into the air and gaining speed and altitude after a quick controls check. Accelerating, facing the wind, going through the transition speed, that crucial moment when a loaded Huey starts to generate lift with its rotor, looking after the lead Huey, turning towards him, and beginning to join up.

The flight lead comes on the radio. "Pontiac 1, on route!"

Richard replies, "Two is forming up with you. Took me a while to get going."

The other pilot grumbles on the radio. "Like a bunch of FNGs, you couldn't find the manual or what?"

Richard shakes his head, not dignifying that line with a response. James settles into a loose formation, trimming the Huey so he can fly it with his fingertips. He shifts slightly in his seat, enjoying yet another transport flight. He looks back at the flight crew, cramped in the middle of the helicopter with all the boxes. It will be hard for them if they have to open fire.

A few minutes into the flight, the lead comes on the radio. "Azovskaya!"

Richard replies. "Rogo. I'm with you! Do you know what's happening there at the drop point?"

The other pilot replies, "Negative. Just another camping trip in the snow."

Richard responds, "Just our guys?"

Lead replies, "Some of ours, and some of those young kids that are in the camp, you know the sort that enjoys this kind of thing."

Richard yawns and nods to Daniel to take the controls. "My bird, Rich."

Richard nods, "Your bird."

Richard turns to the crew chief, "Chief, you okay back there?"

Mark, the crew chief nods, "Yeah, just a bit cramped here. Looking at trees and more trees. You can hide a whole country here, and you wouldn't be able to find it."

Richard smiles, "You've seen that before, haven't you?"

Mark nods, "Yes, I did, not as thick as the jungle though, no triple canopy and all that crap."

Richard nods in approval, "If we go down in this place, you reckon we can make it?"

Marks looks out through the big side window of the Huey, "Neah, if you are not next to a village, you will either freeze or the wolves will get you. The snow must be six feet deep in here."

Richard shakes his head, "It will cushion the fall, though."

The minutes are flying by, miles and miles over the deep forests of the Caucasus Mountains, both helicopters travel at 80 miles an hour, 4,000 feet up in the air, in a blazing sun on a cold winter morning, with the peak of Mount Elbrus visible in the distance.

Daniel sees where Richard is looking, "Checking to see if Prometheus is there?"

Richard smiles, "Or looking to see if there's an eagle."

Daniel smiles, "Liver, so yummy."

Richard laughs, "Oh come on man, I mean it's Prometheus, stole the fire for us, you gotta respect that."

Daniel replies, "Actually, the better lesson here is that no good deeds will be left unpunished."

Richard smiles, "I hate it when you are right."

The lead comes on the radio. "We're getting close, LZ past the next village. The guys will pop smoke in a few."

Richard stretches his arms, rolls his head from side to side to relieve some of the tension in his neck. He places his hands on the collective and cyclic, his feet on the pedals. "My bird, Danny!"

Daniel replies. "Your bird!"

Both pilots now look ahead, seeing the small tents of the FARP, a standard setup for a Forward Arming and Refueling Point. A small area where troops and helicopters can operate and prepare for a quick turnaround. Two M113s are there, and a few M151 jeeps. Suddenly, white smoke appears on the corner of the FARP, and Richard sees four pads marked in the snow, with a windsock on the side. That's the place where they will land.

A voice comes on the radio. "Pontiac, Hawk 1, is your manifest accurate?"

The lead pilot responds, "That's affirm, Hawk 1, as far as I know it is."

Hawk 1, Major Henry Anderson, a Green Beret, continues on the radio, "Good, Pontiac 2, can you go to the clearing two and a half miles west of here and land there? We have some guys that need your stuff."

Richard responds, "Sure can do! Heading?"

Hawk 1 gives him the directions. "2 3 0. Thanks a bunch, it's hard to carry the stuff over there."

Richard replies, "No sweat, the guys there know I'm coming?"

Hawk 1 replies. "That's affirm. They will pop smoke when you get close. The LZ is cold."

Richard turns towards 230 heading, as he looks for the clearing. The clearing is past a ridge. Richard gains a bit of altitude and finally sees the clearing, oval-shaped with a few trees in the middle, smiling at Daniel, "Hey, a big clearing with a tight LZ, what do you know, eh?"

Daniel smiles, "It's not that tight, we'll be fine."

As soon as the Huey passes the ridge, a familiar voice comes on the radio, one with a distinct Scottish accent. "Smoke on!"

From the side of the clearing, blue smoke starts to billow. Richard confirms, "Pontiac 2 has blue smoke!"

Angus responds, "That's us. Come on down!"

Richard sweeps around, points the nose of the helicopter upwind, slows down, and comes in for landing 20 yards from the smoke, slightly to the side, ensuring the smoke does not obstruct his vision. Settling slowly in the snow, not knowing how deep his skids will sink, the Huey settles down an inch or so into the crunching snow. Richard grimaces. *I have to be careful taking off from this.*

Richard twists the throttle to a minimum, letting the rotor slow down, but keeping the turbine going. The warning sound of the "Low RPM" alarm starts to beep in the helicopter. Richard silences it and then turns around towards the Crew Chief, "Let's go, open doors and help them out with the unload, Chief."

Angus comes towards them, and Richard opens the door on his side. Angus shakes his hand quickly and pops his head inside so they can talk easily through the noise. "Hey guys, you found the place alright?"

Richard smiles, "Hey, Angus, nice to see you around. Quite a day for a stroll in the park, isn't it? And yeah, it was easy, you know, just point the nose where you want to go."

Angus grins, "You joker!"

His face becomes serious. "Hey, either go low and fast when you go back, or go high, there's something in this forest around here."

Richard nods, realizing that this may not be a milk run. "Low and fast, it is, pal. We'll be on the other side. One more bird with us. Call us if you need a getaway car!"

Angus slaps his shoulder. "Off you go! We're done. Thanks for the help, Chief."

Angus helps him close the door. Richard checks left and right, turning his head back to check behind him. Then, he increases the throttle, and the rotor picks up speed. He pulls the helicopter out of the snow quickly and takes off, gaining speed as he zooms over the trees and accelerates rapidly.

A mile or so from the base, jumping over the ridge on his way back, the forest opens up a bit, and Richard starts to see, on the tree line, multiple muzzle flashes and streams of tracers converging on his Huey. Richard flicks the helicopter on the side, gaining some distance, while keeping it moving. "Enfield 2, we're taking fire, taking fire! One mile from the base!"

Hawk 1 responds first. "Hawk 1 confirms. I see the tracers. Come back. We'll deal with it."

Richard yells on the intercom. "Chief! Open the damn doors and fire back."

The Crew Chief slams the door open, picks up his M60 machine gun, and starts to spray bullets into the tree line. "I'm on it! Can't see shit through those trees."

Angus gets on the radio, "Bastards! Couldn't keep it quiet. All right, lads, get back. We'll deal with it! "

Richard replies, "Roger!"

All quiet now, it all ended as quickly as it started. Richard lands on the pad, where a soldier on the ground signals him to put the helicopter down, and he goes through the shutdown motions. "Like a walk in the park. Chief, the LZ here should have some miniguns. Can you install them? We may need them later. The whole crew can help.

Mark, the Crew Chief, smiles. "Sir, I can do it by myself with the gunner, but I wouldn't say no to something warm to drink, though."

Richard nods. "I got you, buddy. I'll see what these guys have here."

An hour and a half later, the hill behind the LZ explodes in a cacophony of shots fired, grenades exploding. The radio in the tent crackles with short commands and calls. Richard and his crew are running out towards their helicopter, with the miniguns already installed. Dashing in, Daniel straps quickly and yells at him, "Get the radios up as soon as possible!"

Richard nods, "Let's crank it, things are crazy on the other side of the hill! Chief! Doors and guns!"

Getting the Huey started as soon as possible, the turbine comes to life in less than a minute, and the rotor blades begin to turn slowly.

Angus comes on the radio. "Pontiac flight, you up on this frequency?"

Richard responds, "Affirm, go ahead!" Angus continues, "We're pinned down in the clearing where you dropped your supplies earlier. Requesting MEDEVAC. The LZ is hot!"

Richard is relaying the information to the controller at the London Camp. "London, Pontiac 2. I have a MEDEVAC request. Troops in contact, they have casualties. The LZ is hot!"

On the other side, the implacable voice of the controller. "Stand by Pontiac."

Another voice on the radio. "Pontiac 1 here, my bird is down! Can't start it! I'll need a whole crew of mechanics to get this crap in the air."

Richard groans and acknowledges. "Charlie Foxtrot! Two Roger! Screw it! I'll go alone!"

Richard looks at the rest of the crew, all of whom nod, understanding what they will do. "London, Pontiac 2. We are going for MEDEVAC. Pontiac 1 bird is NO GO with mechanical problems."

London responds, "Roger, be advised. No other units in the area!"

Richard checks the cockpit one more time and starts taking off. "How about getting some of them Cobras here, London?"

London camp replies. "Negative, that's not my call to make."

Richard turns the Huey around, accelerating at low level, heading towards the battle. "Chief! You shoot at anything that's not wearing our colors or shoots back!"

Mark grins at him. "Will do! I'll show them scumbags!"

Richard concentrates on flying, not having the rockets, while Daniel is already on the flex miniguns. "Here we go, boys! Keep your eyes peeled!"

Three minutes later, Richard sees the battle unfolding beneath him, Angus and his group taking cover behind the trees in the middle of the forest. At the same time, the Soviet forces attempt to flank them, still positioned in the trees around the clearing. "Goat 1, Pontiac! Pop smoke!"

Blue smoke billows in the clearing, but not from the position Richard identified.

Angus talks on the radio. "Smoke on!"

Richard responds, "I have blue smoke!"

Angus responds, "That's not us! How about now? I took my time with it!"

Richard scans the clearing. The gunner is already firing in the forest, and some tracers are flying by. "Orange smoke, Southwest of the LZ."

Angus confirms, "That's us. Put it down there when you can. The LZ is bloody hot."

The last word from Angus sounded like a grunt, and another voice came on the radio. A feminine voice with a Russian accent. "Goat 1 is hit! Goat 1 is hit!"

Richard clenches his teeth and yells on the intercom! "Damnit! Come on, guys! Shoot the damn bastards!"

Pointing the helicopter for a few seconds, facing the Soviet troops so Daniel can work them with the flex guns, then swooping down to land, half covered by the trees, but still allowing the door gunner to have a line of fire and give them some protection. Landing quickly in the snow, happy that he found a patch of hardened snow, not sinking the Huey skids into it, making it easier to take off that way. "Cover them! Chief, help them in"

The Crew chief jumps out and helps the soldiers climb in, some of them hurt pretty badly, limping, one of them jumping on one foot to make it to the Huey, pushing them and shoving them in. Blood is already covering the floor of the helicopter, making it all slippery. Blood mixed with brass and spent cartridges from the M60 machine guns, thirteen soldiers, ten US Army troops, and three Russians dressed in some British camo. The Crew chief jumps in and mans his M60, "The Scottish guy was not with them! Go! Go! Go! Land at the FARP, I have a lot of hurt guys around here!"

Richard pulls on the collective, the turbine whining as it reaches maximum power, nearly redlining. The low RPM light flickers a bit as the overloaded Huey gets light on the skids and lifts off a few inches from the ground in ground effect. Snow lifting, surrounding the Huey, while tracers are zooming by, Richard hears the ting-ting sound of some of them finding their target. Richard glances at Daniel. They both know that they are grossly overloaded, and the Huey, in a hover, wouldn't go up more.

Daniel says, "She doesn't like this weight."

Richard's face is set. "She's gonna like it. I have enough room to get some speed, get on the flex guns."

The Soviet troops are now dashing through the open snow in the clearing, trying to bring down the Huey. The door gunner changes another ammo belt in his M60. Richard puts the nose down, accelerating the Huey like this, turning round the trees in the middle of the clearing, the nose of the helicopter facing the Soviet troops, Daniel is firing his flex miniguns, while Richard keeps accelerating like this, going round the trees, the Crew Chief joins with his M60, finally the Huey goes past 40 miles an hour, no longer in transition flight, able to climb. Richard jumps over the treeline and dashes in the opposite direction for a few seconds, then turns around towards their safe LZ. Richard keeps looking around, hoping to spot Angus through the trees, but nothing can be seen. The Crew Chief safes his weapon and starts to help the wounded men. Groans and moans are being heard as the Chief tries his best to cover some wounds and help the soldiers. As they fly towards the LZ, one of the radios, the FM direction finder, is usually tuned to the emergency frequency, and Richard and Daniel hear the familiar two-tone beep of an emergency beacon in their headsets. For just a second, the direction finder needle turns, then, as the transmission stops, it returns to its neutral position.

Daniel looks at the radio, "That sounded like a Prick Ninety beeper."

Richard nods. Prick Ninety is the radio that pilots and operators in the area are using. The official name is PRC-90, but it is commonly referred to as a Prick radio. "Let's land and take care of these guys. We load ammo and get back up."

The Crew Chief chimes in. "We have five new holes. They will leak. I hope it won't rain soon.

An hour later, they get back into the battered Huey, conducting a quick check to ensure that nothing vital has been hit. The Crew Chief shrugs, looking at the bloodied floor, "There's no running water, sorry, Rich."

Richard nods, "No worries, Chief, we'll clean 'er up when we get back home."

They take off and turn towards their previous battle, the

LZ now with fewer troops, the M113 gone, and the jeeps. The US forces chase the Soviet forces that remain on the ground, trying to make contact with them. Just a few orderlies are left, waiting with the wounded to be evacuated.

Daniel checks the radio. "We're on the SAR frequency. I'll listen up, get up, and go slow. We need to see better."

Richard nods and climbs to 2000 feet, keeping the Huey at 50 miles per hour, while the rest of the crew scans the forest. Suddenly, the two-tone beeping sound is heard again, and the needle jumps, pointing 40 degrees away from their direction. Richard turns the helicopter to match the needle heading, speeding up a bit. "He must be in a clearing somewhere. So, we can pick him up."

Daniel nods, "Either this, or we're just about to spring a trap."

The sound stops after a few seconds. Daniel gets his map, finds their position, and draws a line on the heading of the beeper, trying to work out a triangulation. Richard changes his heading, 20 degrees to the right, waiting for another signal. "He's keeping them short, to make it hard to triangulate."

Two minutes have passed, and the signal comes to life again. Richard turns towards it, and Daniel draws another line, looking where his lines intersect.

Shaking his head, "I don't know, not exactly accurate."

The radio signal stops again, and Richard swears under his breath, looking around. With the corner of his eye, he spots two shadows skimming over the trees. "Helicopters! Hips! What the hell are they doing here?"

Daniel replies. "Up! Up! Get up on top of them so they don't see us. They must be looking for the same radio bursts."

Richard responds. "Damnit! Chief! Doors! Get the guns

ready!"

Daniel is asking, "What's our ROE?"

Richard shrugs, not giving a damn about the Rules of Engagement at this moment. He speaks again, talking with the London controller, "London, Pontiac 2! I have two Russian Mi-8 looking for the same radio signal. I believe they want to snatch our guy before us. Declare!"

London replies, the poor guy on the other side, probably trying to rustle up some officer. "Pontiac, stand by!"

Richard replies, "Negative stand by! Declare!? They have door gunners and pods with rockets hanging. They are armed!"

Another voice comes on the radio. "This is Hawk 1! Pontiac, I have authority over this area. Declared hostile!"

Richard half grins, "Roger, hostile! This is a first! Tally-ho!"

Using the term fighter pilots used when identifying an enemy and going offensive. Richard drops down, working to get behind the two unsuspecting Mi-8 helicopters, unaware of how much the door gunners can see, not knowing that the Mi-8 carries a gunner in the back. Suddenly, the two Mi-8 helicopters are turning. They have been spotted. Richard is coaxing the Huey at its maximum speed, knowing that in any aerial battle, speed and height are the main advantages.

He tells Daniel, "Take the right one! Chief, when your gun can bear, take the left one."

Daniel aims through his flex gunsight and opens fire. The guns, with their familiar sound of a zipper ripping through the sky, fire two streams of tracers chasing the Mi-8, falling short, then catching up to it. Bullets ricochet from the Mi-8, and Daniel talks through his clenched teeth, "That bastard is armored like a tank!"

Richard replies. "Keep shooting! Some are getting through."

They could see the Mi-8 shuddering, a sign that some controls and parts of the helicopter had been hit. Richard gasps as he sees red tracers coming towards him, big ones. He turns the helicopter to avoid them, but Daniel's aim goes awry. Still, he is able to adjust quickly, pouring another stream of bullets into the battered Mi-8. Richard zooms between the two helicopters, both door gunners firing now. Pitching the Huey up, almost going vertical, losing speed and gaining altitude, he stands the helicopter on its tail, then pedal turns the other way with a quick 180-degree vertical turn. Facing the other helicopter now and diving at it.

"Get it! Get it!"

Daniel starts firing, his rounds hitting the rotor and the turbines, while the Mi-8 belches smoke and flames. He turns away, trying to make it back, losing altitude, shuddering, and trying to stay in the air. Richard passes by the other Mi-8, and the Crew Chief fires his M60 at it, hitting the tail boom with a few lucky rounds. The tail boom separates, and the tail rotor flies away. The helicopter is now doomed. No tail rotor, no controls, spiraling down towards the forest.

Richard goes on the radio. "Splash one! Splash one!"

He circles around and sees the other helicopter in flames, low over the trees, catching the treetops and exploding. Fuel spreads all over the forest, and the trees engulf the remains in a big fireball.

"Splash two! Splash two!"

Richard turns the Huey in a big circle, looking around, spotting a small clearing on top of a hill. Daniel looks at his map and then points at the same clearing. The FM radio comes alive with a faint voice in a Scottish accent. "Quit playing around and come get me! You have my spot?"

Richard replies quickly, "Roger, don't pop smoke. You have something smaller? A flare?"

Angus responds, "That's affirmative, I'll put one out when I hear you close."

They lose altitude, scan the small clearing, check the wind direction, and prepare for landing. A red flare pops out into the air, and both pilots see Angus and another smaller person next to him, without a helmet, with unruly curly blond hair. Daniel speaks in the intercom, "Got him, land there next to the trees."

Richard nods, "Yeap. Will do! Any movement in the trees?"

The Crew chief responds, "Nothing so far. We'll see when the skids touch the snow."

Mark knew that the moment they are most vulnerable is right when they land, a lesson learned the hard way during his tour in Vietnam. Richard puts the helicopter down next to them, and Angus starts to walk, helped by Tanya, more than helped, leaning hard on Tanya.

"Chief, go and help them." Yells Richard.

The Crew Chief helps them in, "Go! Go! Go! He's hurt quite badly! He lost a lot of blood."

The Crew Chief helps him out and talks to Tanya, "Keep the pressure on! Keep pressure there!"

Getting out his med kit and putting a hemostatic gauze on Angus's wound, then getting out a chest seal.

Richard gets on the radio. "London, Pontiac! We got him! We'll come directly to London. Have the medics ready!"

London replies quickly. "Roger Pontiac, the medical team is

ready for you!"

Richard and Daniel are heading towards Camp London, starting to climb gently as they maintain the Huey's speed.

Angus, with a headset on his ears, said, "Thanks, lads. I got one in the leg and something in the chest. Broke some ribs and what feels like a collapsed lung. Don't go too high."

The Crew Chief is attending to Tanya. She's not hurt, but she's obviously in shock. Sitting with her feet up, curled in a ball, gripping at her sleeve where there is a patch of dried blood. The Crew Chief talks to her, gripping her shoulder tightly, and then gives her some smelling salts from his med kit. Tanya sniffs them and shakes her head, sneezing loudly, her breathing starting to calm down after that.

Richard keeps flying low at treetop level, and he goes on the intercom again, "Hang in there, Angus, we'll be home before you know it! Why the hell did you run away?"

Angus groans and responds, "Who the ruddy hell draws their fire away from you, eh? I told the guys to evac and ran away over that patch of forest and flanked them. I put some grenades up their arses and made a nuisance, so you have time to land and get the other guys out. Tanya here, despite my orders, stuck around with me and helped."

Angus takes a pause, breathing, coughing a bit, then continues. Richard replies, "Damn, I didn't see you going across and flanking them."

Angus smiles, "It's my job not to be seen. They sprayed the forest with bullets, and it looks like some got lucky."

Richard continues, "Damn man, you should be put up for a medal or something."

Angus shakes his head, "Neah, just another trinket. I'm just glad that everyone made it out."

Richard shakes his head, "Just relax now, we'll get there soon."

Angus keeps talking. "You guys see where those choppers came from?"

Richard says, "No, I just saw them approaching, and by the way, I believe it's the first time a Huey gets two kills in one battle. We must paint the kills on our battered bird."

Angus smiles, "They must have some base nearby, they were on top of us in about 10 minutes after my first radio burst. We had to move around. Poor Tanya had to deal with the old, fat me."

Daniel smiles and turns around and looks at Tanya, "Miss, we have to stop meeting like this. One day, I promise you, we will have a helicopter that's clean and presentable, not like this, covered in grime and other things."

Tanya looks at Daniel, realizes she is safe now, and starts to laugh. Laughing uncontrollably, all the shock and the nerves and the tension of that close battle piled up in her, and now getting out all of a sudden. Everyone in the helicopter has a smug grin, another close shave, but they made it out alright, and everyone is more or less intact, except Angus, but Angus will be back on his feet before you know it.

21

Chapter 21 SAM Country

Over Veselovka, Krasnodar Krai,
February 6th, 1979

Twenty-seven thousand feet in the air, James is shifting in the seat of his F-5, flying in a formation of four airplanes, on their final leg before arriving at their destination, Krimsk Airport in the Republic of Krasnodar Krai. His F-5 was sluggish with the three additional fuel tanks, the three bags, as the pilots call them, but much needed now on this final step of their journey. Taking off from Timisoara, in Romania, the formation flies over the Carpathian Mountains, then over the Black Sea, skirting Ukraine, which has emergency airports, but avoids crossing into Ukrainian airspace so that the Russians wouldn't see this as a blatant act of aid from the Ukrainian side. Even in transit, politics, policies, and treaties make their way into the life of a fighter pilot.

Looking ahead, James sees the contrails of the three C-130 Hercules as they take off, bound for Krimsk, with MiG-21s nearby. The final stage of their flight is an escort flight, where they have to babysit the slow Hercules. James, at 400 knots, is getting closer to them, adjusting his heading so he comes on a parallel course, looking left and right at his formation, flying in a loose fingertips formation, he makes a hand sign changing the formation to echelon right, so they don't interfere with the Hercules as they get closer. Slowing down to match the Hercules' speed, getting closer to the plane on the right of the formation, 300 knots, the F-5 at that altitude, not liking this speed, close to its maximum angle of attack, flying with its nose up, James groans in his mask, *Oh man, trudging like this, we'll burn more fuel.* James checks his fuel, looks down at his kneeboard, and makes some mental calculations. *There's plenty to go around, even if we have to dash about a bit. We have enough.*

The Hercules copilot in the right seat sees them and nods. Putting his hand forward, making a fist and pushing, showing that they are going as fast as they can, then putting his hands up in an excuse gesture. James nods back and settles into this formation with the Hercules, half an hour away from Krimsk, plus however long it will take for them to land all seven planes. A few minutes after joining up with the Hercs, the copilot makes the sign to change the frequencies. James checks his kneeboard, looking for the right channel. Overlord, the E-2C Hawkeye, also known as "The Hummer," is on loan from the Navy, acting as the controller for all airspace and military operations. Three Hawkeyes should operate around the clock over the airspace of Krasnodar.

James hears a voice coming on the radio. "Albert, Overlord, Check!"

Overlord, a feminine voice with quite a high pitch, giggles

as James realizes that the callsign does not match the voice in any way.

Albert, the Herc formation responds, "Overlord, Albert with you, 25 miles northwest of Anapa."

Overlord responds, "Radar identified Albert. Continue."

Overlord continues the roll call. "Enfield, Overlord! Check!"

James replies, "Overlord, Enfield with you, flight of four, in formation with Albert."

Overlord replies, "Identified Enfield! Fuel state?"

James checks his fuel. His external tanks are empty now. "Enfield fuel state 1.6!"

Overlord continues. "Roger, 1.6, continue as fragged. Picture clear."

James nods, picture clear means that Overlord, with its powerful radar that can look over two hundred miles, does not see anything concerning.

Two minutes after this, Overlord speaks again. "Welcome to Krasnodar, boys! I'll guide you with your approach. Follow the coast until you reach Glebovoskoe and then turn left for the Krimsk approach."

Overlord makes a short pause, and then she continues. "As you can see, the snow is melted here, but the weather still turns nasty here at this time of the year. Novorossiysk and Gelendzhik airports can be used as Emergency Landing Strips, but do not count on any support there. The only manned airport in this area is Krimsk. As you turn towards Krimsk, you will see three lakes, one of them, the round one, is the Krasnodar reservoir. West to East, use them as visual landmarks. South of the lakes, you are in SAM country."

The last line drops on James, and he checks his RWR one more time, turns up the volume, and then performs a quick test to ensure it is functional.

A few more minutes into the flight, James sees the Alberts, turning gently left and starting to descend slowly, with Krimsk Airport some 25 miles away. The radio comes alive.

"Enfield, Overlord! Break formation and VIS ID target on bearing 1 2 0, altitude 18,000! Maintain ROE! Do not fire unless instructed to do so! I repeat! Do not engage! Maintain contact and escort the target outside Krimsk airspace! You will be under SAM range, monitor your RWR!"

James confirms, "Enfield! Roger! 1 2 0, 18,000! Enfield flight! Drop tanks! Spread formation!"

James turns the F-5 towards 120 heading, checks left and right, and sees the rest of his flight spreading the formation. They have a better chance of spotting an airplane this way. He is making sure that nothing is underneath him and jettisoning his external fuel tanks. The tanks go off with a thud, and James sees them tumbling through the air. The F-5, clean, nimble, without all the drag from the massive tanks, is accelerating already as James dives towards 18,000 feet. A touch of afterburner to accelerate a bit faster, settling his speed just under the speed of sound. James turns his radar on, grunting in his mask. *The sun is in my eyes. cloud coverage is at 10,000, so I won't see a lot.*

Overlord comes with more instructions, "Enfield! Target BRAA 1 5 5. 35, 18,000, flanking!"

James replies, "Roger! Enfield is intercepting!"

BRAA is the term used to give the correct and consistent information about the position of an enemy airplane, referencing the Enfield flight position, Bearing, Range, Altitude, and Aspect. James works out the geometry of the intercept in his head, using his radar, which is not as performant as the radar in the F-4. With this intercept angle, nearly 90 degrees from the target, his radar will not pick up the contact. James tries to sweeten the intercept solution by turning left a few degrees. Pushing the throttles into the afterburner, the F-5 accelerates past the speed of sound. James quickly checks to his right, his flight spread out over 2 miles. Suddenly, his RWR comes to life, symbols appear on his circular screen, and chirps of radar sweeps are beeping in his headset.

Overlord talks to him in the same instant. "Enfield, Overlord! Be advised! I see SAM radars coming up! Keep your eyes open!"

James responds, "That's affirm, Overlord. I have SA-6 and SA-3! spikes" The RWR in the F-5 indicates that the radars are not a threat yet but are merely searching for his flight.

A few seconds later, James sees a blip on his radar screen, a few degrees to his right, twelve to thirteen miles in front, turning the plane onto an intercept course, now traveling at maximum speed with full afterburner. Scanning in front, trying to see what target he is intercepting, finally catching a glint of light from a wing or the cabin, his eyes are focused on a single dot in the sky, closing on it, gaining on it second by second, until James manages to distinguish the slick silhouette of a Su-24. Closing on it more, not locking the SU-24 on its radar, James sees that the plane is not carrying any ordinance, just a recon pod underneath, probably on a mission to photograph the port and the UN lines.

James goes on the radio, "Overlord, I have the Su-24 in sight, recce flight, no weapons!"

Overlord replies, "Roger Enfield 1. Maintain contact and push him out of the airspace."

Suddenly, his RWR starts to beep, the radars now in the danger threat circle, guidance radars illuminating him. Enfield

2, his wingman, comes on the radio. "SA-6, launch! Take it down! Take it down!"

James looks to the right, hearing the call he heard so many times in his F-105 over Hanoi, or crossing the Thud Ridge in Vietnam when SA-2 missiles were launched against them. Scanning the sky in the direction of the radar, with the cloud coverage preventing them from seeing the launch. Pressing the "chaff" button two times on his stick, releasing some countermeasures, the radar still locked on him. The SA-6 symbol was flashing on his RWR. SA-6 medium-range missile, Mach 3, manoeuvrable, and way deadlier than the SA-2s he had to dodge in Vietnam. James spots the missiles, tracking away from him, and they are locked on one of his wingmen. James sticks with the Su-24. *Go home, you idiot! Go home! I can't shoot you down, but do you trust the radar guys down there on the ground? Do you trust that they will get me and miss you?* His RWR beeps again, the SA-6 symbol flashing again. James sees two more missiles popping from the clouds, their engines still burning, and their aspect is not changing. *Oh crap, these have my name on them!*

"Enfield 1! Engaged! Defensive!" James flips the F-5 upside down, diving down, turning his head around, and seeing the missiles, one going stupid, and continuing to go up in the sky, the other following him down, adjusting his course a bit, pulling away from the missile, but not wanting to lose the Su-24, pushing through the clouds in a steep dive, seeing the earth rushing towards him, easing up the dive, going close to the ground, at the max speed his F-5 could go at this low altitude, the missile popping from the clouds, still tracking him, but low on speed and energy. Frantic calls on the radio, everyone in his flight is taking it down, dodging them. The missiles get closer, and James squeezes his muscles in his belly and feet to keep the blood in his head. Hocking as he pulls on the stick, arching the plane up on a steep climb, flicking the stick and turning into the missile, knowing that the missile doesn't have energy to follow him up, the proximity sensor on the missile finally gives up, and James sees the explosion of the missile some 500 yards behind him, way outside of its lethal range. James keeps going up, now himself like a rocket with wings, pushing out of the clouds and re-acquiring the Su-24. *Go home, damn you! Go home before I make you!* Getting closer to the Su-24 again, locking him now on his radar, to show him that there's someone there on his tail. The Su-24 banks from side to side, the pilots looking back, when James's RWR beeps again, the SA-3 symbol now flashing.

"Enfield 1! SA-3! Defensive!"

Through a gap in the clouds, James spots the launch, the missiles launching from the ground in quick succession, bellowing white smoke as the rocket engines propel the missiles towards him. Both tracking him, James pulls closer to the Su-24. Laughing when the Su-24 pilot pops chaff. *Not so brave now, isn't it?* Flicking the plane on its back and pulling towards the ground, SA-3s are supposed to be easier to deal with at low altitude. As they dive down closer to the ground, the missiles on their intercept course track where he is going to be. James dives down into a valley and sees both missiles exploding in the forest. Pulling the plane up again, checking his fuel, *I got two or three minutes left of this fun.* Pushing through the clouds again, trying to spot the damn Su-24.

Maykop, Krasnodar Krai,
February 6th, 1979

Vanea and Piotr, the two alert pilots on duty today, are glued to the radios in the readiness building. They are equipped and ready to be launched within five minutes of receiving the takeoff order. The two pilots already know from the controllers working the radars that there are at least eight American planes in the air: three or four transports and four fighters, probably F-4s, Vanea thinks. *How I want to tango with an F-4, all those guys that went to Vietnam and instructed the pilots there, and flew those clandestine missions, they all speak so mighty of the F-4, how I want to face one.*

Vanea looks at Piotr, "If the guys in the tower don't send us out quickly, that Su-24 is going to be shot down."

Piotr shrugs, "I don't know, probably not, they would have shot him down by now, after eight missiles. I know for sure that in their place, my finger would've probably slipped."

Vanea grins, "I know, I would've done the same, but Americans, they are cowards, all they do is just follow orders."

Thc phone rings, and Vanea picks up, nodding a few times. "Understood! Flight 116 is taking off!"

Vanea puts the phone down and grabs his helmet bag. Piotr is already starting to run. They run together towards their planes, the mechanics hearing the phone and already getting everything ready.

Vanea yells at Piotr, "6000 meters, 240, stick with me! Channel 10 for the controller!

Vanea climbs into his Mig, starts it up quickly with well-rehearsed choreography, and checks left and right, signaling the crew chief to pull the chocks out. He looks at Piotr and sees his nod, indicating that he is ready. Pushing the throttle forward and taxying the plane, one hundred meters from where they are parked to the runway, getting there in a few seconds, and lining up on the left side of the runway, making room for Piotr on the right. Checking on his right, to see Piotr lining up with him, Vanea makes a forward motion with his hand, then pushes the throttle to full military power, letting the engine spool up. He holds it on the brakes, then pushing the throttle in the afterburner. The Mig accelerates on the runway. They take off together. Vanea cleans the plane, gear up, flaps up, and accelerates to 900 kilometers per hour, then climbs to 6000 meters.

Turning the channel selector to channel 10, Vanea goes on the radio. "116 flight check!"

Piotr responds, "117 five by five."

Vanea contacts the controller. "Maykop control, 116 flight with you, climbing to 6000, heading 2 4 0."

The controller replies. "116 received, continue on this heading at maximum speed, four targets, at 100 kilometers from you, closing in on a Su-24. Escort the Su-24 to base, weapons free! I will guide you when you get close."

Vanea grins on his mask, "116 received! Weapons free!"

Looking at his speed now, well over Mach 1, he pulls the throttle back from afterburner, the MiG slowing down a bit, right under Mach 1. At this speed, 100 kilometers is about 5 minutes. But five minutes in an aerial battle is an eternity. Vanea energizes his radar, his RWR, already chirping and bleeping from all the radars on the ground and in the air. His RWR, not as refined as the American ones, but provides him with enough information for what he needs to know. Vanea sets up his missiles. Four real ones on his plane, two radar-guided ones, R-3R, and two infrared, R-60, small missiles, but deadly, far more maneuverable than the AIM-9 Sidewinder the Americans use. Vanea keeps pushing towards the American formation, turning on his radar, and looking at it. His radar will not pick up anything this small at a distance of over 25 kilometers. Placing the radar back on standby so it doesn't overheat, he prays in his mind that the mechanics didn't siphon the alcohol used to cool his radar, pure ethyl alcohol diluted with a bit of tea, which makes excellent vodka.

Over Veselovka, Krasnodar Krai,
February 6th, 1979

James finally spots the Su-24, his head moving around, one glance up at the plane, one at the RWR, one back trying to count the planes behind him, one around over the horizon to spot another threat. The Su-24 turns right, finally going home, and James increases the distance between them, turning to the left a bit when Overlord comes on the radio.

"Enfield, Overlord, break! Break! MiG-21s from Maykop, 40 miles. RTB Krimsk. 280 for 35 miles."

James turns the plane towards Krimsk, "Roger Overlord, Enfield is RTB."

James looks back and counts his planes, all 3 of them starting to form up. "Enfield check!"

He hears the voices in order "2", "3", "4".

He replies to all of them. "You heard the Overlord, let's go home."

Vanea keeps getting closer, and he finally spots the Su-24 on an opposing course, going fast towards the base. Vanea keeps pushing, knowing that the chances of catching the Americans are getting slim.

All of a sudden, his RWR lights up, with all four lights blinking, and he is being locked. "Maykop control, 116 is being locked by radar."

Maykop responds, "Maykop received, that is the Hawk battery, 116 return to base."

Vanea replies with disgust in his voice, "116 returning to base."

Turning the Mig around, following the Su-24 back home, Vanea keeps brushing his finger over the radio transmit button, when finally, not able to hold it in, he transmits, "Maykop control, 116, may I suggest being launched earlier next time? We had a good chance to catch them if we had had a few more minutes."

The voice of the Colonel comes on the radio. "Comrade Gureevich, when you are in a position to suggest tactics, we will listen to your valuable suggestions. Until then, Comrade pilot, maintain radio silence."

Vanea mutters a swear word. Being called by name on air is a significant breach of radio procedure. Now, the Americans will know who 116 was. It could be used against him if he were shut down and taken prisoner. Vanea makes sure that his finger is nowhere near the radio button and mutters, *"I will suggest where and what to shove and how many times, Comrade Colonel, you fat bastard, I'm here risking my life, and you bark at me. Checkist bastard!"*

James looks at the Krimsk airport from the air, seeing it for the first time, getting clearance from the tower to go on the pattern, with an overhead break, seeing the last of the Hercs landing. *What the hell, we fought a whole battle, and these just made it home. Time must pass differently for the transport guys.*

If that's how it is in the airlines, I'll stay in the Air Force for good. Diane sure will kill me, but look how slow they are. James wags his wings, pushing the guys to keep their formation tighter. These are the first fighter planes arriving at Krimsk. They must look sharp. Coming fast, 400 knots for the overhead break, over the airport, at the middle of the runway, he banks the plane left, pulling on a 5 G turn, looking down, astonished for a moment when he sees the Hawk battery there close to the airport, the missile launchers tracking something over the horizon, shaking his head and getting back into flying, continuing his turn, dropping flaps and gear down, lining up the F-5 on the final approach, coming down to land, a perfect, smooth landing, keeping the nose of the plane up, aerobraking, not using his brake chute, not knowing if they have spares or not. Letting the plane roll to the end of the runway, where a Jeep is waiting to guide him through the unfamiliar airport. James opens his canopy and gulps fresh air, inhaling for the first time the air in Russia, grinning as he thinks to himself that that's another first for him. Looking back and seeing the rest of his flight lining up behind him, he watched as the Jeep started to move and guided them to their parking spaces. After the plane is shut down and chocks are placed, James climbs down from the cockpit and hands the maintenance logbook to the Crew Chief.

"It's Code One, Chief, but I pulled a bit on it, not over G, but make sure that everything is okay."

The Chief salutes, and James walks towards Ronald and shakes his hand. Shaking hands with the other two pilots. Their flight suits were all wet from perspiration during their dance with the SAMs.

Ronald grins and tells them, "Man, this is like that night

when I came home after too many wobbly pops. And Jayne got mad at me from the moment I put the key in the door, and she started to give me a hard time. I told her. Darling, let me get my foot in the door, and then you can start to yell at me. The same thing with the Russians, didn't even make it here, and they started shooting at me. Come on. That's not classy at all."

Krimsk, Krasnodar Krai,
February 6th, 1979

A few hours later, James and Ronald make their way to the O Club. For now, it's just a room with a few tables and a makeshift bar. Not much has been done here to make it feel like an Officers' club. The austerity of the Soviet Union's base is still evident throughout the entire building. They order a beer and make their way to a table. They are the only customers so far, as just eight F-5 pilots have arrived today, with the rest of the squadron scheduled to arrive tomorrow.

James clinks his beer bottle onto Ronald's, "Cheers, man, look at us, going halfway around the world again."

Ronald nods, "Yeah, the US Air Force traveling circus."

James takes a sip from his beer, thinking of their arrival in this area and of the dance they had to do with the missiles. "I'm telling you, though, that Su-24, that Fencer, was quick."

Ronald nods, "And with the angle we intercept it, and our radars, I did not have it until I was maybe 12 miles from it, right there at the visual range, and with the sun in my eyes, it made it worse."

Ronald ponders for a few seconds, then continues, "And you think we'd be used to SAMs, but I'm telling you, when the first ones came, my voice went up a few octaves, and my ass was chewing on the seat cover. I froze for a fraction of a second."

James laughs, "I know, I felt exactly the same way. I saw the first two and realized they are not coming for me, but with the second salvo, when they start to track me, man, oh man. It got intense quick, and that Fencer, he was cruising like it's nothing. Just when they launched the SA-3s, he popped chaff."

Ronald smiles, "Really? I'm sure they have IFF, but he didn't trust his mates on the ground?"

James shakes his head. "It looks like he didn't."

At that moment, another crew is coming into the Club. Four people in Navy flight suits, three men and one woman.

The woman looks around, sees them, and then tells the rest of her crew. "Hey guys, these must be the new folks, the Enfield flight we had to guide in today."

The woman turns towards them, and the rest of the crew follows, as James and Ronald get up. She gives a quick salute, and James and Ronald return the salute. "Lieutenant Katherine 'Cali' Mueller, nice to meet you."

Everyone is shaking hands and getting acquainted. This is the crew of the E-2 Hawkeye that guided them earlier. "Y'all can call me Kate, or Cali, or Overlord."

Kate smiles. She's pretty short, at 5'1", but willowy and very attractive, with a tanned complexion and a big smile on her face, the typical California surfer girl with a big and radiant smile on her face.

She turns to the rest of the crew, "I'll go get beers, we'll park here, if that's okay with you guys."

James and Ronald bring more chairs to their table. Ronald glances at Kate, "She's quite a pistol, isn't she?"

One of the Hawkeye pilots smiles. "She graduated from MIT,

and she's smart as a whip. She wanted to be a pilot, but that's not a typical career path for women in the Navy. However, she excels as a CICO, and you'll be lucky to have her as your eyes there."

James nods in approval, "That's not bad at all."

Kate comes back with eight beers, knowing that her crew won't stick with just one. "Now, you fellows talked about me while I was there at the bar, yeah, I am Overlord. I like it and it suits me. Not too many jobs in the world where I get to order a Colonel and his squadron to fly how I want to and to make him do what I want him to do."

Kate flashes a big smile at James and Ronald. Ronald laughs, "Ma'am, we're just Majors, we follow orders even better than a Colonel, we're used to it."

Kate laughs, "Ma'am is my grandma, but I do like your attitude."

The conversation continues, with James and Ronald asking the Hawkeye crew what they know so far and how their three days have been since they arrived at Krimsk. They are already trying to familiarize themselves with the airspace, threats, weather, and the locals. Three days in the country is not much, but it's a start.

James looks around the O' Club, "Guys, we're missing something here."

Everyone looks around, and Kate responds, "We're missing a lot of things. This room has nothing in it."

James shakes his head, "Nope, we need the missing man table."

The table falls quiet for a few seconds, as everyone realizes that despite the banter, laughter, and technical discussions, this is real. There will be fallen pilots, missing pilots, and friends who will strap into a plane and never come back.

Kate bangs her beer bottle on the table. "Tomorrow morning, we suit up, I have my whites, and we set it up."

22

Chapter 22: The Fire Begins

Kremlin, Moscow, USSR
February 7th, 1979

Secretary General Ustinov is with the General Staff. These meetings now occur daily, compared to the weekly meetings of the Politburo. The Secretary General is now relying on the advice of his armed forces and the members of the General Staff. Ustinov is enraged. "Comrades, now there are fighters, American fighters stationed at Krimsk! Not helicopters used for humanitarian purposes, not for keeping peace, but these are American fighters on the territory of the Soviet Union. Our forefathers are turning in their graves, where heroes gave their lives in the Great Patriotic War, there are American fighters, where people died, there are German tanks again, where I have fought! At Anapa, at Pshada! There are German tanks! This has gone on for too long, Comrades."

Ustinov looks around the room, and not a single sound is heard, nobody dares to breathe. Ustinov sits down in his chair, still looking from one member to another of the General

Staff. "Today, in two hours, a declaration will be made by the Minister of External Affairs that any foreign troops in the territory of the Soviet Union are considered hostile, despite any UN resolution, and any hostile troops will be dealt with according to our rights to defend our country."

Ustinov makes a quick pause, looking for any reaction. "Also, the Minister of Internal Affairs will put a notice that any citizen of the Soviet Union who's caught helping, fraternizing, or maintaining any relations with separatist movements, separatist propaganda, will be tried on the spot under martial law and shot. All propaganda will drill on that. People will learn that going against the will of the Party is a mistake."

Another pause from Ustinov, "Now, Comrades, let us see how we throw these Americans and Germans into the Black Sea, and once we deal with that, we can focus on bringing the other nations into the big brotherhood of the Soviet Union. But first, we must stop this! Root and stem! Therefore, no other UN or NATO intervention will even be considered. I believe that after this, the Soviet Union will emerge stronger than ever!"

Everyone started to applaud in the room. The thought that they might still be able to salvage this was a possibility in the minds of the Generals and Admirals in the room.

Marshall Ogarkov clears his voice and starts, "Comrade Secretary General. Our forces came out prepared for an offensive after the winter. The weather is not ideal, but we can commence the offensive in the following days. We have forces amassed on each side of the Caucasus Mountains, and they will be able to offer mutual support. The shortest road for us would be through Pshada. By achieving a breakthrough there, we can quickly take their main supply route, the Novorossiysk port. Stopping that supply route would mean the end of the

UN forces. The other groups will push on the eastern side of the Caucasus Mountains, towards Krasnodar. Although the terrain will be less complicated, the distances are greater, and our supply routes will be more exposed. However, where we will achieve a breakthrough, the rest of our forces will take advantage of that and continue to move forward. Of course, in all this, we need the support of our air forces. We have good Anti-Air coverage, but in all conflicts, Anti-Air is never enough. Our forces in the air will have to achieve superiority, and with Frontal aviation, we will help the soldiers on the ground."

Marshal of Aviation Batitsky is the next to talk, "Comrades, our pilots are ready, and our equipment is ready, we will not only achieve air superiority and protect the forces on the ground, but our bombers will start to cut their supply routes, a large maritime convoy is transiting through the Dardanelles strait as we speak, it will be tomorrow through Bosphorus into the Black Sea, our bombers will attack the convoy and it will never make it on land, my commanders are organizing the attack as we speak, our initial plan is to attack it far into the sea, but one of my commanders pointed out that the UN cowards will complain that we sank food and aid, but, if we attack it closer to the coast, we may be able to tackle that fighter group that was sent out yesterday, this way, we may be able to contain both threats, also, only a convoy of military importance will have air coverage. As soon as the ships are in range, our bombers will attack in droves. Su-24s and Su-17s are capable of taking on this threat, with MiG-21 and MiG-23 fighter escorts."

Ustinov looks around the room, and the mood has improved since the meeting began. He gets up and prepares to leave. "Glory to our soldiers! Glory to the Soviet Union!"

White House, Washington, USA
February 7th, 1979

In the Oval Office, Secretary of State Cyrus Vance starts to talk, "Mr. President, this is it, we're at war with the Soviet Union, actually, not all of us, but the forces in Krasnodar Kray. The declaration was carefully crafted to impact only the forces in Krasnodar. I'd say it's a good thing. Otherwise, we would have this conversation in a bunker fearing a nuclear attack, but this way, at least for now, it will not escalate."

President Carter runs his hands over his face in the familiar gesture he makes when he is stressed. "We're in contact with them. And all the moves we make in accordance with the UN resolution are publicly available, is that right?"

Vance nods, "We're telegraphing them every move we make, and we keep it public. It's good for public opinion, but I know that General Emerson hates it."

The General is participating in a teleconference during this meeting. There is a second delay in the conversation due to the lag in the satellite link. The General speaks, "Mr. President, I truly hate this, I understand the reasons, and they are sound, nonetheless, I hate it, that we don't have the element of surprise, and in all honesty, when we are in country we can operate however we want, just getting there, they know every soldier, tank, airplane and piece of equipment is on that ship or airplane. They probably have the manifest before I do."

President Carter nods, "General Emerson, I understand the position you are in, but because of that, we're not in total war with them. I believe this is an acceptable trade-off, one that does not overwhelm them. And I know, once again, you have to fight with a hand tied behind your back. My question is, can you do it?"

General Emerson responds after a second, "Mr. President, we can. Our aviation is getting in there, and we will have all four squadrons available. The maritime convoy, which is expected to arrive in two days' time, will enable me to consolidate the Eastern flank. In the West, we have the crossing at Pshada well locked. If they attempt to cross that river, we will chew them well. In the East, we make a lot of noise with special forces, but we're thin, for now, but in five days' time, we should be in a better spot. Now, keep in mind that all the plans in war last about 5 minutes after the battle starts. Five days from now, if you hear a different story from me, be sure that I have not lost my mind, yet."

At this last phrase, President Carter bursts into laughter. The General did not lose his sense of humor. That's one of the most reassuring gestures that someone can show, still maintaining your sense of humor on the verge of the battle, which shows nerves of steel.

Krimsk, Krasnodar Kray
February 8th, 1979

The first briefing at Krimsk, in an austere briefing room that the Russians used at the Krimsk airport, everyone is gathered in, the twelve F-5E pilots from the 426th Tactical Fighter Squadron, the helicopter crews from the UH-1, and AH-1 squadrons, the crews for the E-2 Hawkeye, the meteorological officers, Ops and all the people that will be involved in the operation Black Sea Resolve, the name came from the UN a few days prior. The room, just like any other briefing, has three maps. The operation areas, the meteorological map, and a detailed map of their sector around Krimsk and Krasnodar. Blue and red dots and markers have already been placed on the map to indicate the locations of the troops.

General Henry "Hank" Emerson steps into the room, "Good morning, folks. I'll keep my speech brief. The rest of the folks have more interesting things to say. As you well know, as of yesterday, the Soviet Union forces declared that all forces in the former territory of the Soviet Union are hostile."

The General emphasizes the word former. "That means that from now on, we must expect a strong offensive from the Soviets. Nonetheless, this was to be expected. My expectations are simple in this matter. We must do everything in our power to protect these folks in Krasnodar Kray and to come to a quick resolve of this conflict. I have met with the local leaders here, and they are all behind us and believe in what we are doing. A few things I can promise you. We will fight! And we will fight hard, and we will fight an enemy that's determined, trained, and willing. I will do my best to keep the pressure on Washington and ensure that we have all the necessary tools to fight effectively. With some constraints, I believe we are well-positioned to succeed. I'm working to break those constraints. We will ensure that no one is left behind. For the flyboys, we will have rescue ops over the sea and SAR over the ground. No matter what, if you eject over areas that the Soviets control, we will do our darnedest to bring you back. Evade and escape, and work your way towards us. You will be able to get support on the ground from the folks in the villages and cities, but be advised that the folks helping you will be punished by death by the Soviets if they ever get the word. My personal recommendation would be to work on your own. Preserving the local infrastructure and preserving life are paramount. No ordinance should be dropped if there is any doubt that civilians may be affected. Remember, despite all the fighting that will happen, at the end of our mission, these folks should still have a country and not a heap of rubble. I will not wish you luck. I am confident that you can do this right!"

The General nods and turns around, walking out.

The meteorological officer comes to the podium. "Good morning, first of all, remember, we present the weather, we predict it, with some degree of success, but despite everything that's being said, we can't change it."

The officer smiles, the curse of every meteorologist, being blamed for bad weather and not receiving any recognition for the clear skies. "Yesterday we had all four seasons in one day, we started with winter, then it turned to spring, with a brief hour of summer time, then it all turn to fall, however, this is the weather in February, expect the temperatures to rise, but be aware of icing conditions, fog will form in the valley, especially in the mornings. Low cloud coverage is expected for the next five to seven days, after which the weather is expected to improve, and temperatures will start to rise as we approach March. Historical data shows a clear pattern. Weather updates will be provided every eight hours for briefing and mission planning purposes. If there are any immediate changes, METARs will be updated accordingly."

The weather officer walks out, and Kate "Cali" Muller takes his place.

"Good morning, everyone, I'm Lieutenant Kate Mueller, callsign Cali, and you will hear me on the radio as Overlord."

Kate pauses for a second. "I am the Combat Information Center Officer in the E-2C Hawkeye, and chances are, I will guide you through this as well. My job is to make you smarter with all the intel we gather from the air. During our brief stay, we observed the following threats in the air. MiG-21s, which operate from Maykop and Sochi. The squadron at Maykop is quick, and they can be here in a few minutes if needed. They operate in a Soviet fashion, with two radar controllers overseeing this area. There is one at Maykop and one at Sochi. From what we got on the radio, they are good, and they guide their airplanes well. The second threat is the MiG-23s stationed at Sochi. The Floggers have longer legs and long-range missiles, including the semi-active AA-7 Apex, which is comparable to our Sparrows. However, our reports indicate that the Flogger is not as maneuverable as the Fishbed. Su-17s and Su-24s are the main frontal bombers. Both are high-speed airplanes. Mach 1.7 capable and quick on the deck, with a swing wing, they are able to accelerate quickly. However, just like the Flogger, they are easily outmaneuvered by the F-5. Keep in mind that both bombers carry the short-range AA-8 missile. This is rumored to be more maneuverable than the AIM-9, but with a shorter range and with no front aspect capabilities."

Cali takes a pause, "Any questions so far?"

She surveys the room, and all the pilots are writing down notes that will be used in the briefings later. "Alright, in the air, there are rumors that a new plane is being introduced, as an air-to-ground, close air support platform. The Su-25 is a subsonic aircraft, highly armored, built to survive ground fire, so if you face it, it will take more than one shot to bring it down. There are also plenty of Mi-8 helicopters, and the Soviets employ them in various roles, including transport, gunship, and rescue operations. Here, you will operate under our direct control. We will be your eyes and ears in the air and on the ground. We will coordinate with ground forces if you are transferred to a Forward Air Controller on the ground. Please ensure that you use your authentication cards to identify the FAC correctly. Make sure that you properly identify the marker on the ground, smoke, flare, or any means of identification, and if you don't have a positive visual on a target, DO NOT DROP! Remember our mandate. We must avoid blue-on-blue casualties and civilian casualties. Gentleman, I'll see you in the air! Remember, if I sound strict on the radio, it's because I want you all to come home!" Kate nods and walks out of the room.

23

Chapter 23: Black Sea Intercept

Sochi, Krasnodar Kray
February 10th, 1979

Vanea is sitting in the cockpit of his MiG-21 in Sochi. His squadron returned yesterday, while the other squadron of MiG-21 rotated to Maykop. The Generals in command decided that it was best for both squadrons to know the Maykop Area of Operation. Vanea holds his hands outside the cockpit, tapping nervously on the side of the airplane, 15 minutes before the takeoff time. He glances at the big Tu-95 starting its takeoff roll, the big counterrotating propellers biting into the air, as they begin to move the big lumbering beast. The Tu-95 Bear will provide naval radar for the strike airplanes. Four Su-24s lined up as soon as the Bear started its takeoff run. The Bear accelerates slowly, gains speed, and uses almost the entire runway at Sochi before finally lifting off into the sky. Vanea shakes his head. *This is not flying, it's more like clinging to the sky. If I ever get moved to bombers or naval aviation, I'll quit.*

Anything would be better than this, even agricultural spraying. I would rather breathe fertilizer than fly with that lumbering beast. Vanea chuckles. *I bet they have a tea kettle in there, and probably they could fit a whole samovar.*

Vanea looks at the four Su-24s taking off in pairs, grinning as the afterburners kick in, leaving a cone of flames behind them. They accelerate quickly, with four Kh-29 missiles slung on the pylons and two R-60s for self-defence, totaling 16 missiles for a convoy of 25 ships. The Su-24s take off, turn to the left, and start to form up and curve away. Vanea sets the stopwatch in the cockpit, checks the time, and waits for five minutes until his start time. As time passes, five minutes gone, Vanea glances at the other three Migs lined up beside him, seeing the nods of the helmets and the thumbs up. Vanea puts his arm up and rotates his hand to signal the start of the engines. He's glancing down in the cockpit, going through the startup procedure of his MiG-21.

"110 flight radio check!"

"111 reads you loud and clear!"

"112 five by five"

"113 loud and clear!" Vanea talks with the tower. "Tower, 110 flight of four, ready to taxi!"

The tower replies, "110 taxi to runway 06, left from the apron, hold short at runway 06."

Vanea confirms, "Received, runway 06, holding short."

Lining up his flight short of the runway.

Vanea hears on his helmet. "110, line up, runway 06, clear for take off. Wind 060 for 10."

Vanea replies. "Clear for lineup and takeoff 110 flight."

Vanea enters the runway and lines up on the left side, making room for the rest of his flight. Checking behind to see the rest of his formation on the runway, Doing one final check on the cockpit, engine parameters, flaps, gear, controls, Vanea pushes the throttle forward, all the way into military power, watching the engine spool up, holding the Mig on the brakes, glancing right to check the rest of the flight, releasing the brakes and letting the Mig accelerate, not using afterburner on this takeoff, trying to save fuel for the long escort flight ahead of him, checking the speed, the Mig accelerating, finally making it to 300 kmh, Vanea pulls the nose up slowly, holding the plane in the takeoff position, feeling the Mig bouncing on its stubby wheels as it gets light, the delta wings finally giving him lift, getting the Mig in the air. Vanea holds the Mig steady, as the plane climbs over 100 meters, accelerating more, bunting the nose down a bit to increase speed, flicking the gear up, waiting for the familiar thud of the wheels being locked inside, pressing the flaps up button, reducing the power, and allowing the airplanes on his flight to join back in formation. Wagging his wings as the formations tighten up in an echelon right formation, spaced about one hundred meters apart between the planes, Vanea continues to climb, curving over the sea, already climbing at 550 km/h, up towards 8,000 meters, the altitude for their escort flight.

As they reach 8000 meters and their first waypoint, Vanea begins a series of wide turns, locating the contrails of the four Su-24, assessing their position Vanea starts to close on them, sliding on the right of the bomber formation a few hundred meters higher than them, happy that the SU-24s are keeping their speed, not having to rush in afterburner to get them it's a good thing.

"Sochi Control, 110 in position with the 204 flight."

Sochi control responds, "Received 110, no threats on my

scope, just the radar plane, 150 miles north of you."

Vanea lifts his shoulders. *Nothing to do about that one.* Checking on his engine, his fuel, glancing in the cockpit, and keeping his head moving all the time.

Vanea hears the Bear pilot coming on the frequency. "204, 313. I have radar contacts on your target, position sent!"

The Su-24 flight lead replies. "204 acknowledged, plots marked."

The Bear's powerful search radar has detected the ships and transmitted their positions to the Su-24s via a data link between the airplanes. This way, no communication is sent in the air.

As the flight continues, Vanea transmits on the radio. "110, 204, will proceed with the escort."

The Su-24 flight lead responds. "204, received!"

The Su-24s slow down a bit, allowing the MiGs to overtake them, creating enough forward separation for Vanea's flight to clear the skies ahead of them.

KRIMSK, Krasnodar Krai

February 10th ,1979

James sits in the cockpit of his F-5, his first operational alert since arriving in Krasnodar. Since there is no hut or building nearby, all the alert five flights will have the pilots in the cockpits and the crew chiefs around the airplanes. Shifting from side to side, *Damn, my ass is going to go numb like this.* James looks to his right, and Ron is sitting there on his plane, grinning at him. A few moments pass when an alarm is heard, an old-style alarm being cranked by hand by someone in the control tower. The loud, wailing sound grows higher and higher. *Damn thing is effective. It makes your heart go.* Thinks James as he starts to work through the startup procedure of his F-5, the crew chief already under the plane hooking up the compressed air hose on the left engine, James energizes the plane, looking at the crew chief then glancing down in the cockpit to see the engine being spooled by the compressed air, mashing the start button and watching the engine coming to life, hearing the whine of the jet engine as it spools and starts, watching the engine indicators, flicking on the hydraulic pump on the left engine, signaling the crew chief to switch the compressed air hose to the right engine, checking the fuel settings for this flight with two bags, James sees the crew chief signaling that the air is connected on the right, mashing the start button and repeating the same process for the right engine. Checking on the cockpit again as the engine comes to life, doing the final checks. The crew chief went through the motions of checking the flight controls, ailerons, elevators, flaps, and brakes, pulling up, dropping down, and pulling up again. One final nod from the crew chief as he holds up all the lanyards and pins. James nods, lowers his canopy, checks it, and pressurizes it.

"Krimsk Tower, Enfield flight!"

The tower responds, "Enfield flight, taxi to runway 090, clear for takeoff, 090, wind 060 for 5!"

James replies, "Taxi, lineup, and takeoff, Enfield flight!"

James then checks with the rest of his flight. "Enfield check!" they all reply in quick succession. "Two!", "Three!", "Four".

The planes are parked a few yards from the runway, with the throttles pushed forward. James taxis from the apron to the taxiway, holding short of the runway for a fraction of a second, then lines up for takeoff, aligning on the left side of the runway to make room for the rest of his flight. He turned back and looked at the rest of his flight, making sure they were lined up. Holding the F-5 on the brakes, pushing the throttles on, feeling the engine spool, then pushing the throttles into the afterburners, the F-5 starts to accelerate, speeding on the runway, nose getting light, the plane bouncing on the not-so-even runway of the Krimsk airport. James holds the nose up as the F-5 takes off, climbing slowly, gaining speed. James brings the gear up. The flaps are in their automatic position, lifting up as the plane accelerates through 300 kts. James looks back and sees the rest of his flight behind him, reducing his speed to let the rest of his flight join in.

"Enfield flight, Krimsk tower, switch to Overlord!"

James responds, "Roger, Enfield flight switching to Overlord. Enfield! Push channel 10!"

Instructing his flight to change the frequency. A few seconds after this, James talks on the radio." Enfield check!"

The flight replies in quick succession, all checking in on the right frequency. "Overlord, Enfield with you!"

Kate, using the Overlord callsign, replies. "Enfield! Identified! Climb to angles 26000, heading 260! Expedite! I'll give you a picture in two minutes."

James replies! "Roger, 26000, 260! Pushing the throttles into the afterburners, zooming up, expediting the climb, and accelerating close to Mach 0.95.

The Enfield flight is reaching an altitude of 26,000 feet, with a solid layer of clouds extending down to 18,000 feet. This makes it easy for an airplane to escape the cloud coverage but difficult for a pilot to see an incoming missile.

James talks on the radio. "Overlord, Enfield, picture!"

Overlord responds, "Enfield, two groups, eight plus, bandits, BRAA 210, for 130 miles, 26,000, hot! Maintain this heading and altitude. I'll put you over the ships and then vector you to intercept."

James responds, "Roger Overlord, can we get a radio bearing from the ships? Visibility is stinko."

Overlord responds, "Negative, Enfield, the bad guys would read that too."

James checks his fuel. There's still plenty left in the tanks, holding the plane in military power, not touching the afterburners, cruising under Mach 1. Turning his head left and right, he checked on his flight. All three pilots nod their heads when they make eye contact. James checks his RWR, rechecks the fuel and fuel flow, and verifies his armament switches. He scans the distance towards his 10 o'clock position, but the bandits are over 100 miles away, making it impossible to spot them.

Minutes into the flight, Overlord comes on the radio. "Enfield, Overlord, bandits, two groups, one group Fencers, one group Fishbeds, BRAA 190, for 90 miles, 26,000, hot!"

James clicks his microphone button twice as an acknowledgment, signaling his flight to go on spread formation, four planes now covering over a mile of sky.

Over Black Sea, Krasnodar Kray
February 10th, 1979

Vanea comes on the radio, "Sochi control, 110, any work for us?"

Sochi control responds, "110, I have four contacts, 330, 150 kilometers, flanking aspect."

Vanea replies, "110 received."

Vanea pushes the throttle into afterburner for a few minutes, the MiG-21 accelerating over Mach 1, overtaking the Su-24s.

Vanea is trying to sanitize the air in front of them.

Vanea looks left, and he notices that the Fencers are keeping up with him. "204, 110 maintain your briefed speed! Maintain your briefed speed."

The Fencers respond, "204 received." Vanea remains with the afterburner plugged in, burning fuel, as the Su-24s slow down and stay in the rear.

"Enfield, Overlord, picture! 1st group, BRAA 180 for 60 26,000 hot! 2nd group! BRAA 185 for 65, 26,000 hot! Fishbeds are the first group."

James replies, "Roger Overlord, call our turn!"

Five minutes later, Overlord comes on the radio again. "Enfield! Turn left 180, weapons hot. Priority for bombers! You are over the ships! Priority for bombers! Be advised, the Fencers are getting tracks from a Bear 200 miles south! Most likely they carry guided munitions!"

James flicks the plane to the left, turning towards a 180-degree heading, pushing the throttles all the way forward, and pressing hard on the afterburner. His flight follows into the turn, realizing they will fall behind. Still, he kept pressing on, turning his radar on, and scanning the sky ahead for the telltale of the contrails.

"Overlord, Enfield! Picture!"

Overlord responds. "Enfield 2 groups. 1st group BRAA 175, 30 miles, 26,000! Second group, 185, 35 miles, 25,000."

James responds, "Enfield 1, Roger!"

James comes on the radio, "Enfield 3 and 4! Sort right! Enfield 2. With me, sort left!"

James splits his flight, taking the Migs with his wingman and instructing Ronald to go for the bombers. The flight shifts slightly, but they are still maintaining their formation, going as fast as the F-5 could go at this altitude with two fuel tanks, reaching Mach 1.3

Vanea hears on the radio, "204, 313, ship position updated! Clear to attack!"

The Fencers respond, "204 received, attacking!"

Vanea swears as he sees the Fencers with their afterburners on and wings pulled back, accelerating and gaining on him. The bombers become more vulnerable as they close the distance. Instinctively, Vanea plugs in his afterburner and punches the now-empty belly tank. He still has over 2000 liters of fuel, but at this rate, it will be empty soon. Cursing again, realizing that he can barely keep up with the Fencers, looking forward to spotting the contrails.

James looks at his radar, eight dots being painted on his radar, four on the left and four on the right of his nose, slewing the radar cursor on the closest left contact and locking it, to get a better distance reading, "Enfield! Drop tanks!"

Mashing the jettison button, dropping his tanks, checking the fuel level, arming his wingtip missiles, turning the weapon selector for guns and missiles, hearing the growl of the Sidewinders. This will be a surprise for the Migs, as the AIM-9 P5 missile can track a hot target coming towards them. The forward aspect missile should negate the advantage of the R3R radar-guided missiles the Russians are using. James spots the eight contrails, closing on him, the MiGs in a finger four formation, while the bombers are strung in trail formation.

"Enfield1 Tally ho! Three get the bogies on the right! Two cover me! Weapons hot!"

Ronald responds, "Three Roger!"

James's wingman replies also. "Two Roger! Weapons hot! Give 'em hell!"

Vanea spots the four contrails. Looking at them, the F-4 should have smoky engines, but these don't, and they are smaller.

"110 I have spotted contacts in front! 110 flight attack! 111 cover me!"

Vanea locks the first contact on the radar and keeps it in the center, watching the distance decrease and waiting for the range to be within the launch parameters. Seeing two planes turning right, towards the bombers, facing the decision now, to defend the fighters coming for him or to engage the fighters going for the bombers he was supposed to escort. Finally, he discerned the shape of the planes in front of him.

"Sochi control,110, we are facing F-5 airplanes! F-5!"

Sochi responds quickly, "Sochi control received!"

Vanea is watching the radar indication for his locked target as it gets inside the launch parameters, with the nose of the F-5 pointed straight at him. Waiting for two more seconds to sweeten the solution, then mashing the button on the stick, the R3R missile launches with a whooshing sound of a bottle rocket, hanging in the air for a second, then accelerating towards the F-5 in front.

James has his eyes locked on the first Mig, watching the distance drop. His Sidewinder growling in a high pitched sound, the seeker locked, but knowing that the missile won't make it at this distance, 3 miles now to the first Mig, James sees a plum of smoke from the Mig wing and a missile curving towards him, another missile from the third Mig doing the same, but not tracking him, James pushes the nose down, dropping chaff and flare, going under the nose of the Mig-21 in front of him, watching the missile coming towards him. The aspect changes, the missile falters for a second and trails upwards, loosing lock, James pulls back on the stick, grunting under the G load, not able to catch the first Mig, but hearing the growl of the Sidewinder, locked on the second Mig, James uncages the missile and pulls the nose up more, leading the Mig, and mashes the trigger on his stick.

"Enfield 1 Fox2! Fox2!"

James eases up on the stick, turning towards the other Migs, watching his missile curving towards its target, following it, tracking it, closer and closer, seeing the Mig popping flares, but with no result, the missile is locked on its target, the Mig wings streaming vapors as the pilot pulls to save his plane, and the proximity fuse of the Sidewinder makes the missile explode, 70 kilograms of explosive and shrapnel on the right side of the Mig, between the wing and the stabilizer. The Mig belches smoke, black and white, and makes a quick roll, pulling down and curving towards the clouds.

"Enfield 1! Splash 1! Splash1!"

Vanes curses as his missile loses lock and goes stupid, trying to follow the F-5 on its dive, but unable to. His Mig will lose the engine at this speed under negative G, and at this speed, he can't follow the F-5 down. Glancing behind him, he saw his wingman pulling the Mig around, then being hit by a missile.

"111 Eject! Eject! Eject! 110 flight. Forward aspect missiles! Protect the bombers! Protect the bombers!"

Vanea turns left, locking on the other F-5s looking at the two airplanes positioned behind the first two Su-24s. At unison the Fencers are dropping towards the cloud bank below, Vanea locks onto one of the F-5s and looks at his radar, not quite there yet, pushing the throttle forward into the afterburner, trying to catch them up. Watching as two Sidewinders are converging towards the first Su-24, one being spoofed by the flares. Still, the second one finds its target, hitting the right engine. The Fencer tumbles through the air, tearing itself apart, tail breaking, wings separating. Vanea watches one pilot ejecting, clenching his jaw, realizing that only one pilot made it out of this wreck.

James turns around, watching the fight below him. Fencers trailed by F-5s trailed by Fencers and trailed by Migs, and behind all this, James and his wingmen, diving towards the cloud bank, trying to go down quicker than the others and finding them down. *Damn, the clouds will hide them and us and missiles, not to mention that we will probably run into each other.* James keeps pushing down towards the clouds, looking at his radar, which is a mess with all the contacts and clutter from the clouds.

Vanea gains on the last F-5, holding the contact there in the middle of his radar screen, seeing a missile passing him, glancing back at the Mig that launched too early, the missile losing speed, then diving, exploding harmlessly some 400 meters behind the F-5. Gaining more speed, as the procession of planes dives towards the clouds, finally in range,

Vanea shoots another R3R missile. "110 locked! Launching!"

Watching it accelerate, track, and get closer and closer to the F-5. In the final moment, the F-5 turns upside down, expelling flares and chaff, and the missile detonates. Vanea sees the plane dive towards the clouds, and one of the engines starts to smoke, and red hydraulic fluid spills from the damaged F-5.

"110 Hit! I got one!"

James pops out from under the clouds, seeing the sea below him, 6,000 feet below, as he tries to get his bearings. From the clouds, an F-5 belching smoke comes down straight towards him, the plane rolling left and right as the pilot struggles with the controls. *Holy crap!* James thinks, avoiding the stricken F-5.

"Enfield 4! Bail out"

Enfield 4 replies, mustering all the coolness needed in this situation, but his voice is three octaves higher. "Negative, I got it! I lost my bearings in this soup. Enfield 4 is RTB."

James replies, "Roger that! Bail out if you need to, make it close to shore!"

James hears Overlord's calm voice: "Enfield four, heading 075 direct to Krimsk, heading 060 direct to Gelendzhik if needed!"

"Roger, and thanks, Overlord. I think I can make it to Krimsk."

James sees the procession of planes popping from under the clouds one by one, Fencer, F-5, Fencer, Mig, locking into a Mig and pointing the nose at it, hearing the growl of the Sidewinder and launching it, the missile shoots and goes completely stupid, pulling away on its right, not guiding at all. James curses in his oxygen mask, getting closer to the last Mig. In that moment, the Fencers are launching their rockets. At the exact moment, Ronald, trailing the first Fencer in formation, launches his AIM-9. The missile goes straight and accurately, and hits another Fencer.

"Enfield 3! Splash! Splash! Sierra Hotel!"

The two Fencers left are lighting their burners and pulling up and away from the ships, their missiles sailing towards the ships, five missiles that will most likely find their targets. James groans and keeps pulling after the Mig, spotting 110 on its nose, getting closer and closer, then pressing the trigger to shoot a stream of 20 mm rounds.

Vanea hears on the radio, "110 break! Break!"

Glancing back and seeing an F-5 with smoke from the guns on its nose, Vanea pulls on the stick and pulls the throttle down, slowing down his Mig, letting the F-5 to overshoot him feeling the Mig shuddering the warning lights of high angle of attack blinking at him and rolling the Mig on its back and pushing forward on the throttle, unloading towards the sea to gain back the lost speed, finding his attacker and pulling towards him.

James gasps as he is realizing that he was too fast, not able to follow the Mig, as the Mig jinxes into him, making him overshoot, looking back seeing the Mig doing a quick roll to his tail, James extends, using his speed, not letting the Mig gain that turn, then realizing that his is going to give the Mig a missile shot, James pulls on the stick, turning towards the Mig, popping flares, as he sees a missile zooming past him, right where he was a fraction of a second ago. *Damnit! This is becoming dangerous fast. And this guy is good. I overshoot him like a novice!* James pulls on the stick, using both hands, tightening the muscles in his feet and gut, fighting the G-forces, as he pulls the F-5 across the horizon in a tight turn. Seven and a half G's. Grunting with the G strain, his head turned back, locked on the Mig chasing him.

"Enfield 1! I have cornered a Mig on my six!"

Pulling harder, bleeding speed and energy, turning into the Migs turn. James hears on the radio the voice of his wingman, "1 turn right at my mark!"

James looks behind the Mig, seeing an F-5 turning into the Mig's tail. "Break right, Enfield 1 Break right!"

James unloads for a fraction of a second, pointing the nose down as he rolls the F-5 on the right, letting the speed build up a bit, then pulling again on a right turn, swearing loudly as he sees big balls of fire flying over his canopy. The Mig is using his guns. Not very effective, more of an instinctive shot.

Vanea is chasing the leading F-5, gaining on him slowly, focused now after he wasted another R3R missile on the moving F-5. Trying to match the turn rate of the F-5, straining with the G forces, pulling the Mig at the limit, feeling the wings shuddering, almost losing lift and stalling, keeping the airplane there at the limit of its flying envelope, pushing the throttle forward again, lighting the afterburner the Mig turning tighter now, pushed more by the added propulsion in the back, Vanea sees the F-5 bunting the nose down then rolling the other way, glancing in his mirror and seeing a shadow, turning his head back, freezing for a fraction of a second, an F-5 waiting there for him to follow him. Vanea continues his roll on the left, diving down towards the sea and disengaging for now from this fight. *Live to fight another day, Vanea. These guys are good, and you lost your flight integrity in all this.* Vanea hears on the radio.

"113 I'm blind."

Vanea replies. "110 received. 113, return to base, the bombers launched."

James continues his turn, trying to locate the Mig behind him, cranking his head backward more.

"Enfield 1, you are clear! I scared him off."

James replies, "Thanks, Enfield 2! Stick with me!"

Easing off on the stick, checking the sky around him, checking his fuel, maybe seven minutes before bingo, James spots a Mig three miles in front of him, doing a lazy turn on the right, going south, " *You are mine now!* He pushes the throttles forward all the way, the afterburners accelerating his plane, diving down a bit, keeping the F-5 hidden in the Mig blind spot, making sure that the pilot cannot see him from his own wing, James accelerates, selecting his dogfight mode on his radar, getting closer and closer and on the final moment locking on the Mig, lining up the pipper on the belly of the Mig and pressing the guns button, a long ripple of 20 mm bullets are flying from the two cannon on his nose, ripping into the belly of the Mig, the Mig jerking up, almost hung upside down in the sky, the engine tearing itself apart. James yanks the stick left to avoid the flying debris.

"Enfield 1! Splash one! Splash one!"

Hearing Ronald's voice on the radio, "Sierra hotel! Sierra hotel! Confirm splash one!"

James breathes deeply a few times, his mask all sweaty, his flight suit all wet.

Looking at the watch in the cockpit, all of this had taken exactly three and a half minutes. It all felt like a small eternity.

"Overlord, Enfield 1, picture?"

Overlord responds, "Enfield flight, contacts are cold. I have reports from two ships hit by missiles. RTB."

James clenches his teeth, "Enfield 1! Roger! We got tangled with the Migs. Couldn't clean the bombers. We could have done better."

Overlord replies. "Chin up, Enfield, 18 ships are untouched thanks to you."

James takes his flight back to Krimsk, keeping them under the cloud layer, as they transit from the sea towards Krimsk, James's RWR gets lit with radar warnings from the SAMs. James swears, *Come on, you bastards, I'm not in the mood for this. You don't have the range for this."* Just to be safe, James turns left a bit, extending the distance between him and the SA-3 and SA-6 guarding Pshada.

After landing, James walks past the Enfield 4 Tiger. Ken, the pilot, has made it to Krimsk, but the aircraft's vertical stabilizer looks like a sieve, hydraulic fluid drips from the belly, and there are scorch marks on the left engine. James nods to one of the fitters already working on the plane.

James asks, "How bad is it?" One of the fitters responds, "We don't know yet, but the left engine is done for, we'll have to do the hydraulics, and I've had a pasta strainer with fewer holes than this."

James chuckles, "I'm sure you guys have enough speed tape."

The fitter laughs, then continues working on the airplane, with the rig to replace the engine already in place. James gets in the dirty shirt room, takes off his anti-G suit and all the strapping, kneeboard, survival bag, and the rest of his equipment, wiping his face with a towel, slamming the door of the locker, he got two kills today, but somehow, the frustration of not able to protect all the ships gets to him, the fact that he overestimated the Migs and how quickly that Mig fell behind him adds to all the pressure after the flight. *Get it together,*

James, you bagged two, and you did the dance with a good Mig pilot. Get it together. James walks out of the dirty shirt room and steps into the debriefing area, where the rest of the flight is already present, and Ronald is preparing everything for the debrief.

Grinning from ear to ear, Ronald shakes his hand. "Good job, man, a few more like this and we get to be aces!"

James smiles. "Man, I got to tell you, when that Mig glued to my backside and I saw his missile and bullets zoom past, my voice went up a bit, I was squeezing the black out of the stick."

Ronald smiles, "That's nothing, man, we came on top. You bagged two, I bagged one, and Ken bagged another. Ken made it back. It's all good."

James turns towards Ken, "How did you get it back?"

Ken shrugs, sipping on a cup of coffee, looking a bit dazed. "I got hit, like an idiot, I lost hydraulics, and stalled, got in the cloud and I lost my bearings, I didn't realized I was spinning, The moment I saw the sea, everything clicked together, I still had controls, I had one engine, I nursed it back, lowered the gear with the emergency system, and lucky for me the chute worked, I had no flaps and no brakes."

Ken grins, "But at least I didn't lose the bird, and I scored a kill, I'll take it."

James shakes his hand. "Good job, we can do better, I'm pissed off I broke the flight integrity, but I don't know how I could have countered the Migs and Fencers."

At that moment, the Colonel steps into the room. "At ease! You guys did well! I know you are beating yourself up, but you will never be able to stop them all. We'll have a constant fighter sweep over the convoy now, but I will need you guys back out there in five hours!"

James looks at the Colonel, "We have one bird down, Sir. We could go with a pair, but we need to stay ahead of them to be able to tackle them. If we could have been ten miles closer to them, we could have worked better."

The Colonel nods. "We'll get the F-4s today, and we'll have a better chance to intercept them. I need a pair in the schedule when the Phantoms are scheduled to come in. You and Ronald will go out! Ronald, you gotta wipe that grin off your face, I swear, the oxygen mask won't fit your face."

Ronald tries to keep a straight face. "Yes, Sir, I'll work on that. Once we finish the debrief, I'll shower the smile off."

The Colonel's face twitches in what could be a smile, "What you do in the shower is not my concern. Do your debrief, guys, and get some food, and if you can, get some sleep. Good job today. But stay on your toes."

Vanea steps into the operation room, still waiting for news from his downed pilots. The Colonel was already there, chewing the Su-24 pilots.

Turning around, he sees Vanea and speaks with him. "Comrade Gureevich, how can you explain the loss of a Su-24, another one being damaged and probably a write off, and the loss of two of your MiGs?"

Vanea looks down, takes a deep breath, his jaw clenched, the pressure of losing two Migs and one bomber sits heavily on his shoulders. "Comrade Colonel, reporting with your permission. We couldn't support the Su-24. They pushed too soon, and we had no chance to sweep in front of them. If I had had a three or four-kilometer separation, I am confident that all the bombers would have gone through. I take responsibility for this."

The Colonel looks at him. "This is not your responsibility, Comrade Major. Your tactic was correct, but the execution was not. This was on the 203 flight, but we all make mistakes in times of war. I trust you all to do better. Now rest and get ready for the next one. Two of your pilots have been recovered, but we have also suffered a loss. One of the Su-24 pilots did not make it.

24

Chapter 24: Hell from Above

Defanovka, Krasnodar Kray
February 10th, 1979

Henry "Hawk" Anderson clasps Mischa's arm and holds him tight, pushing him down in the snow, not letting him move, seeing that Mischa pulled his knife from its sheath, "Don't make a move, Mischa, don't make a move, they won't see her. If you move now, we're all dead."

Mischa stops struggling and stays still in the snow, his eyes following the Russian soldier as he walks towards Tanya. Tanya is twenty-five meters away from them. A Russian soldier was walking through the snow, getting closer and closer to her. Tanya lies down, almost one with the snow, covering her face and mouth with her gloved hand, becoming one with the snow. The soldier stops behind a tree and starts to relieve himself. Tanya thinks, *I should blow your pecker off, you communist bastard, but you got lucky today.* The soldier turns away, and finally, Tanya makes it back to the others. The group pulls away from the Russian camp, and a few kilometers away, they put together the information they gathered.

Mischa starts first, "On the North side of the FARP, there are two ZSU enclosures, and I was able to see a few Strella launchers. I could see a total of six landing pads for helicopters, two Mi-8 on them, and two Mi-6."

Hank nods, "Those Mi-6 can carry a lot. I'm willing to bet that the Russians are planning more than just a FARP here; they could use this as a rally point and could launch a sustained offensive from this."

Tanya, what could you get?"

Tanya checks her notes, "Same six pads and with helicopters, there are also four more ZSU enclosures, here on the West side." Tanya points on the map, "Also, I could see Strella's, at least five soldiers with them, and four BTRs here on the East side of the FARP."

Hawk nods, "Well, this is already quite a well-equipped base. They are quite an independent base at this point."

Mischa asks, "How do we take it out?"

Hank responds, "We move back a few, back towards the Zulu FARP that we have in the mountains, and I'll get on the radio and organize a strike, a six to eight Cobras could really do a number on this place. Once we have an ETA for their strike, we go back and observe their strike."

Tanya nods, and Hank continues, "Gear up, let's go."

Two hours after this, Henry "Hawk" Anderson is in a UH-1 Huey, piloted by Richard, with the usual crew. Three other Huey helicopters are flying in a V formation, flanked by two Cobras on each side of the formation. They are flying fast and low, following a valley deep in the mountains. "Hawk" Anderson, with his map, followed their progress and gave them instructions.

"Make a left turn here, and drop down in this valley, stay as low as you can."

Richard nods and checks left and right, guiding his gaggle of helicopters down low, at tree-top level, following the terrain.

Richard talks on the intercom, "Doors! Guns! Go hot!"

In the well-rehearsed choreography, the doors of the Huey open, and the Vulcan miniguns are moved outside. Daniel is pulling down his flex gunsight for the miniguns in the front, while Richard is adjusting his gunsight for rockets.

Richard talks on the radio. "Uzies! Phytons! Go hot!"

This is the signal for all the helicopters to arm their weapons. The Huey formation armed with rockets and miniguns, and the Cobras with TOW missiles and rockets, and their turreted cannon in the nose.

Hawk goes on the intercom. "Let's hope that with this route we're taking, they will think we're resupplying. This way, whoever is listening or watching may not call us in."

Richard shakes his head, "Do they have eyes everywhere?"

Hawk nods, "Yes, they do, that's the crappy part about this place. There's always going to be someone willing to give you away."

Richard shrugs, "You'd think we're here for them, isn't it?"

Hawk replies, "Yeah, we are, but out of a hundred of them, you only need one to ruin it, one guy with a phone line or a little radio is enough."

Hawk chews on his mustache for a moment, looking up ahead, scanning the ridge, then continues. "And don't cast any judgment on the rest of them. Think about all these folks, generations and generations, someone came and either killed them or did something bad to them, Czar, Bolsheviks, Stalin,

Germans, Stalin again, and all the rest, can't blame them."

Richard nods, "Yeah, I guess you are right, all of you are philosophers like this?"

Hawk looks at Richard, "All of us?"

Richard smiles, "You and Angus are saying the same thing."

Hawk smiles, "We've seen enough, I guess, and we may have talked about it over a glass of scotch."

They continue to fly low, getting closer to the end of the valley.

Hawk speaks again, "Once we get to the end of the valley, turn right 210, and hug that low ridge, and we'll have a looksie and blow them to bits."

Richard grins, "Or we get blown to bits."

Hawk laughs, "Occupational hazard. You know how it's done. Just keep it moving and don't give them a shot."

Richard flexes his fingers on the stick and nods. His head on a swivel already, checking the land in front, looking up and checking the weather and the wind, a beautiful crisp day with blue skies and a few clouds at 6,000 feet, perfect weather to fly, ideal weather to attack.

Richard turns to 210, slowing down to 30 knots, hanging low over the trees, the formation of Hueys and Cobras now in Line Abreast formation. Richard pops over the trees and sees the Soviet base in the snow, six landing pads, four of them occupied by two Mi-8 and two Mi-6 transport helicopters, the Mi-6 with its sheer size, the blades almost covering two landing pads, one of the Mi-6 rotor is spinning, probably just starting its engines.

Daniel, the copilot, mutters, "Damn, that's a big sucker."

Richard nods, "Focus on the guns and APCs. We'll deal with them at the end." Daniel nods.

Hawk goes on the radio, "Uzies! Pythons! Clear in hot!"

At once, the Cobras pop up a few feet each, firing a TOW missile each, and the whooshing sounds and smoke trails from the Cobras converge on the Soviet base. The Hueys at once put their noses down, popping flares, accelerating towards the FARP, Richard aiming carefully at a line of BTR70s, mashing the button on his stick and firing a volley of rockets, walking the reticle of his sight over the line of BTR70s watching the impacts, all over the Russian vehicles, the Huey going now as fast as it goes, 100 miles an hour, Daniel is working with the flex guns, firing in long bursts, the sound of the miniguns, tearing the skies as a rain of bullets are hitting the Russians. Richard watches as a ZSU gun starts to turn towards him, as the bullets are hitting all around the gun, the gunners jerking in their seats, and the gun pointing down completely mangled. Richard turns left, watching the base, seeing the TOW missiles hitting gun emplacements, trucks, BRDMs, a violent explosion shaking the skies as a fuel dump is being hit, smoke and flames covering the base.

Mark, the Crew Chief, yells, "SAM, SAM, break!"

Richard jerks the helicopter around, cutting the power, reducing his heat signature, and popping flares, letting the Huey sink towards the ground,

"Kill him, Chief! Kill him!"

Mark is already firing his minigun towards the SAM launcher, hosing the poor Russian soldier with a stream of bullets. Richard turns the helicopter around. An Mi-8 in his sight, the pilots running away from it, firing a volley of rockets, again hitting the helicopter, the Mi-8 fuel tank exploding, and the helicopter sinks on its side, the landing gear broken as it becomes engulfed in flames. Richard cranks his head, looking for more SAMs, seeing more streaks of TOW missiles flying from the Cobras.

Hank yells excitedly in the back, "Keep 'em coming, keep 'em coming like this!"

Richard feels the shockwave of another explosion from a fuel tank, a wave of heat emanating from the nearby explosion that is being felt in the helicopter. *Christ! This was close!* The helicopter gains some distance, extending low and fast over the treetops, with the miniguns on each side firing continuously. Pulling up into the sky, going almost vertical, pedal turning the Huey around, and locating a spot of the FARP that's not hit. Firing the last rockets from his launchers as Daniel continues to hose the ground with his miniguns, Hueys, and Cobras streaking all around in a devastating strike on the unsuspecting Russians.

Richard gains altitude, circling the chaos underneath, surveying what was two minutes ago an operational Russian base, now reduced to a smoldering pile of junk, helicopters burning, BTRs mangled, fuel and ammo dumps belching black smoke, bodies, so many bodies on the ground, the white snow painted with red. Richard shakes his head, muttering to himself. *Poor suckers didn't stand a chance.*

"I think we got them."

Hawk keeps looking around. "Yeah, we did."

Hawk goes on the radio, "Uzies, Pythons, knock it off! Knock it off. We got them. Good show!"

Richard continues on the radio, "Uzies! Check!" Hearing that all three helicopters are checking in.

"Pythons! Check!" Richard is waiting for the same reply, "Form up on me, let's go home! Good show! Keep your eyes peeled for any stragglers."

Richard is turning away, following the route home, the rest of the helicopters joining in formation. The crews are grinning big and pumping fists in the air.

Hawk clasps Richard's shoulder. "Man, that was textbook, not a single scratch!"

Richard smiles, "Yeah, we caught them with their pants down. The guns were not even trained in the right direction."

Hawk nods, "I guess they were expecting something from the airplanes, not from the ridge we used. Ohh well, they will learn, next time probably it won't be this easy."

Richard lifts his shoulders, "Well, we always find a way, a better way to kill each other." Richard chews his lip. "I can't get used to seeing the aftermath. I feel dirty."

Hawk smiles, "Don't think about it, think about what they would do to you if they could catch you. I've seen the works of Russian interrogators."

Richard nods, "I've seen it too when the guys came back from the Hanoi Hilton."

Hawk continues, "I'd like us to land back and FARP Zulu, the one you dropped the supplies earlier, let's refuel and rearm there, and then we come back for a recon of this place. I need to get there on the ground."

Richard nods, "Roger that!"

Richard gets on the radio and lets the formation be led back to base by the number two Huey. He then slides under the gaggle of helicopters and turns right towards FARP Zulu, realizing that he is starting to know the area now by the back of his hand, not needing a map to get there.

FARP Zulu, Krasnodar Kray
February 10th, 1979

Richard is doing the final checks on the miniguns and the unguided rockets, tapping his boot on the skid of the Huey to clear away the snow before climbing in. He gets into the helicopter and puts on his helmet.

"Let's crank it!"

Going through the startup procedure, the turbine of the Huey starts to whine, coming to life. Hawk lifts his head, looking away, just like a dog is looking when sniffing something. "Get it up quick!"

The next moment, a thud in the snow and the explosion of a mortar shell some hundred feet away from the helicopter, a few more rounds hitting in quick succession, drawing in closer to them.

Daniel yells. "Get it up quickly!"

The next second, two shells hit the tents 40 feet away from them, the shockwave shaking the Huey, the tents where they had coffee not even five minutes ago, the tents where they took the wounded Marines two days ago. All gone in a fraction of a second. Richard pulls on the collective, lifting the Huey and gaining speed as it moves away from the explosions, where more shells are landing right on the spot they just left.

Hawk swears loudly, "They were zeroed in on us! I think they are firing from that clearing South-East of us! Go high, let's spot them!"

Richard is livid, his face white and his jaw set, looking ahead and glancing at the right side of the Huey, from the tip of it, right there where he always cleans his boot before stepping in the helicopter, a torn piece of bloodied uniform, and some human remains are flapping in the wind. "Will do! I'll keep them at my 3 o'clock."

They continue to fly in this manner, gaining altitude and

speed. Hawk points towards a clearing in the forest. "You got them? There! There's two, no! Three BTRs, some infantry, and six mortars! Those BTRs will tear us to shreds! Can you take them?"

Richard grunts. "To hell with them! Let's blast them to hell! Daniel, tell London! Chief! Open doors! Get ready, we make a rocket pass on the BTRs, then we take the rest of them with the miniguns!"

Hawk shakes his head, "If you miss, we're dead, you know that, right?"

Richard pulls down his sight and arms the rockets, "I won't miss! These bastards owe me a flight suit. I crapped this pair already! It's time to collect!"

Richard is making a gentle turn to the right, aligning the BTRs. Then, when they are lined up, he turns sharply and dives on the BTRs, always keeping it moving, varying the dive angle and direction, and not giving them a straight shot. Tracers are zooming past, big ones, 14.5 mm, the BTRs shooting in bursts of three bullets each. Richard aims and shoots his rockets, firing several salvos, walking the reticle over each BTR as Daniel shoots the flex guns at them. The minigun's small rounds do not do any damage but rather serve to rattle their brains and throw off their aim. The moment the rockets are hitting, Daniel is spraying the mortars with his guns, showering them with steel, as they zoom over the Russians, the door gunners join in with their miniguns, adding to the mayhem.

Richard calls on the intercom, "Hits on the BTRs! I told you I won't miss! Damnit, that was close! Chief, let them have it!"

A few dings are being heard in the Huey, and the helicopter shudders a bit.

The Crew Chief calls, "We got hit on the tail boom!"

Richard and Daniel are checking their instruments. Richard replies. "All green here and I have good pedal control!"

Hawk looks outside and speaks. "You got them! Those APCs made a big bang!"

Richard responds. "I told you, didn't I? Let's kill them all!"

Hawk looks at Richard, "What the hell got into ya?"

Richard grunts and points at his skid. "I have what looks like guts hanging off the skid on my side. A mortar round blew up a guy! I'm gonna get all these suckers!"

Hawk puts his hand on his shoulder. "Easy, buddy, take it easy. We're still alive, let's stay this way, okay? Compartmentalize, stay cool. We'll get them. I promise!"

Richard keeps cranking his head. "Anything moving out there?"

The Crew Chief responds, "Negative! Can't see anything. They either scattered in the forest or are dead. The mortars are silent."

Richard takes a deep breath. "Daniel, tell London our status! Look there in what's left of that FARP, there's a flare, someone must be still alive, we land there and get the wounded. We throw away everything we don't need and get as many wounded as we can. How many guys were stationed there?"

Hawk answers, "About twenty."

Richard looks at his instruments, "We may be a bit overloaded, but these guys won't stand a chance without us."

They fly towards the FARP, surveying the scene from the air. Hawk taps on Richard's shoulder. "Put it down there, next to that charred tent. There's no crater there. Just don't land on an unexploded one, that would ruin everyone's day."

As soon as they land, the Crew Chief and the gunner are jumping off, releasing the rocket tubes from their locks, pulling the miniguns away, dropping them in the snow, heaving and pulling the ammo boxes out of the helicopter, pushing them all away, throwing everything that they don't need, keeping just the med kits and the blankets. Richard keeps the turbine running at idle as they get off the Huey and start checking the wounded, helping them in, pulling them towards the helicopter, helping with a few dead bodies, cramming them in the small Huey, the Chief and Hawk already working on a wounded Marine, applying a tourniquet.

Richard gets back in the helicopter and looks at Daniel, "Tell London, we got seven wounded and three KIA, to have the medics ready."

Daniel looks back at Richard, "We're grossly overloaded. Can you lift it off the ground?"

Richard nods, "There's one way to find out."

He starts to pull power slowly, letting the rotor blades catch up. He feels the Huey getting light on the skids, pulls a bit more on the collective, and hears the beep of the low RPM warning. Grinning at Daniel, and pressing the left pedal all the way, the power that goes to the tail rotor is now available to the main rotor as the Huey starts to turn left, lifting, a foot off the ground, Richard nurses the Huey forward, accelerating like this while spinning away, gaining speed, and more lift on the rotor, finally making the overloaded Huey to fly, slowly lifting and transitioning into horizontal flight, enough speed now to have lift on the main rotor and fly away.

"There's always a way. Now, how are we gonna land this thing? That's a different story. I hope we will burn enough fuel, so I won't have to do this dance on the way down."

Daniel smiles, "Allow me to say that I'm damn impressed!"

Tanya, Misha, and Igor are moving slowly towards FARP Zulu. Twenty minutes ago, the commotion of a single Huey attacking was heard, maybe a kilometer away from them. What sounded like mortar shots, then followed by the distinct chopping sound made by a single helicopter, followed by the whoosh of rockets, the sounds of miniguns, and the following explosions on the ground. The small group of people moved cautiously through the snow, making their way towards their base.

A branch above their heads bursts, and a few other rounds are hitting the trees nearby. The group drops down in the snow as they hear the distinctive shots of an AK-47, and voices are being heard from the trees two hundred meters away from them. Voices in Russian are being heard as a sergeant guides his squad through the forest. Mischa looks at Tanya and Igor. They are frozen for a moment in fear, crouching low, as the training from Angus and Hawk finally kicks in.

Mischa speaks to the rest of the group. "Igor, pull back, that way."

Mischa motions away from the incoming soldiers, "Stay low, and if you hear us shooting, give us some cover fire. Tanya, come with me, we'll try to flank them."

Tanya shakes her head. "No, you go that way, I go that way. I can move quicker than you. I'm smaller. We'll flank them from two places."

Mischa looks at her, not wanting to let her go away. Tanya shakes her head. "Listen to me, it's the only chance we have. We have to shoot, and we must shoot properly. No need to worry now about anything else."

Mischa and Igor are nodding. "Be safe!" says Mischa as he

starts to move away slowly, keeping low and staying hidden.

Tanya checks her magazine, checks her safety, and starts to move away from them, looking through the trees where the Russians are. Time goes by quickly, and she fears that she has not moved fast enough and that the Russians are drawing closer. Steadying herself behind a fallen tree, covered by branches and snow. She sees a Russian soldier lifting his gun, not aiming properly. The Russian soldier let out a long burst from his AK-47, covering fire, maybe, or trying to scare them away. The moment he starts to load a new magazine into his rifle, Tanya clenches her jaw, breathing quickly a few times, then takes a deep breath, aiming towards the soldier, letting the air out, and steadying herself as she squeezes the trigger once, then the second time, then the third, in quick succession, like Angus told her. The recoil of the AK-47 kicks back in her shoulder as she keeps her aim through all those shots, watching with big eyes as the first round hits the soldier in the belly, the second in the chest, and the third one in the throat. A gargling growl comes from the mortal wounded soldier as he falls on the ground. Tanya bites her lip, watching this whole scene, not being able to take her eyes from the soldier on the ground, hearing him as he takes his last breaths. The final breath sounded like he was asking for his mother.

Tanya hears some shots, and the tree around her is riddled with bullets. She's snapping out of it, and she starts to move away to another covered spot as she hears Igor shooting in quick bursts and then another quick burst from Mischa.

Mischa yells loudly. "Hawk 1, we are three hundred meters West of your position, request support! We are attacking a squad of Russian soldiers!"

Tanya knows that there's nobody here in the woods except

them, but the Russians, who were probably just pounded by a Huey, have no idea about that. She takes another shot at a retreating soldier, hitting him in the leg as the Russians, with the sergeant in front, are peeling back on the double.

The moment the three reunite, Tanya is shaking all over, her adrenaline finally running out as she sits curled up in a ball with her back against a tree trunk.

Mischa is trying to help her, caressing her shoulder. "It's okay, Tanya, it's alright, they are gone now. You shot at someone?"

Tanya nods.

"You got him?"

Tanya nods again and puts her head down on her knees.

Mischa keeps rubbing her shoulder. "I know how it is. I got two too. But I need you, I can't hold it together much longer. We need to make it back to the camp. They will be all over us soon."

Tanya lifts her head and looks into Mischa's eyes, her eyes red with tears. Taking a deep breath. "Check your gear, that ruse was brilliant, and Igor saved my back with that covering fire. Sorry, I was such a weak girl. Let's go."

Mischa smiles and hugs her. "This weak girl is the bravest girl I know. Let's go!"

25

Chapter 25: The calm before the storm

FARP London, Krasnodar Kray
February 11th, 1979

Angus gets up on his pillow as he listens to the stories from Tanya and Mischa. He is still all alone in the MASH wing of the camp, the only occupant of the 20-bed recovery section of the MASH. Angus shakes his head, his eyes moving from Tanya to Mischa, then to Hank.

"You bloody left them alone there in the forest? Close to the enemy troops. They are not ready, Henry! They are not even close. That's too big a risk!"

Henry shakes his head, "Man, not a whole lot I could do, we had to strike that Russian FARP, and we were planning to go back and take them, we just got shelled, that forest was full of Russians."

Richard and Daniel step into the room, looking at the folks surrounding Angus's bed, the nurse hovering closely and monitoring the conversation.

Richard joins the conversation, "Oh, we got shelled pretty

good, Angus. I've never been so scared and so mad in my life. They had those mortars zeroed in on us at once. I don't know how I made it in the air. I still don't know how we managed to dodge all the lead they threw at us and tag all three BTRs and the mortars." Richard looks down, he is still tense from the battle yesterday, and the signs of strain start to show on his face, darker patches under his eyes, sleep did not come easily these days.

Angus looks at Tanya and Mischa. Mischa has a big grin on his face, but something in his eyes is showing that all is just a mask that he is wearing. Deep down, he remains frightened of what could happen and scared of what could have been if the Russians had caught up with them. Tanya is withdrawn, somehow looking even smaller today, her eyes red and tired, another sleepless night for her.

Angus, knowing what they went through, having heard all the details, looks at Tanya again. "You did good, there was no other way. It was either them or you. And it would rather be them. If the roles were reversed, do you think they would have shown the same remorse?"

Tanya lifts her shoulders, "I don't know. Maybe?"

Angus responds. "That's good, it means you are a good person, and maybe they would, but they had orders to hunt you down, and they were going for your wee little heads. That's the truth, and you saved Mischa and Igor, and they saved you."

"Does it get easier?" Asks Tanya, lifting her head up and looking at Angus.

Angus shakes his head. "If this gets easier, then that's the moment you should be worried. You will learn to hide it, just like the rest of us." Angus smiles and lifts himself up, letting out a grunt. "Bloody bed, I'm getting sick sitting here. Time to get out of here."

The moment he gets up, the nurse comes on the other side of the bed and puts her hand on his chest, pressing him down firmly. "Angus, no. You are not ready to be released, you heard the doctor, another week at least. There's no way I'm getting you discharged."

Angus looks at her, "Norma, errhhmm Nurse Dressler! Come on, I can't sit here when my troop is getting shot at. You can't keep me here, I'll sign the bloody waiver and the damn forms, I want to get out of here."

Richard and Daniel are exchanging looks. The way Nurse Dressler looks at Angus is not the way she looked at other patients. The way Angus looks at her, big and fearless Angus, looking at her with big puppy eyes. Daniel grins, "After so many sponge baths, I guess someone felt a bit more than just medical care."

Angus throws him a dirty look. "Oh, shut it, you know how it is, it turns out I'm lovable and cute, when I have to be."

Norma looks at Daniel and giggles, "That's the one scared of needles but with a cute butt."

Daniel turns red in an instant, "This is becoming that weird family that steers trouble at every Thanksgiving and Christmas dinner, it gets embarrassing really quick."

Angus takes Norma's hand and kisses her palm, squeezing her hand in his, "Norma, my sweet lass, look, I need to get up and start to move a bit. I reckon we have two or three days before it really hits the fan. You will need the bed, and I need to know if I can move around. I won't sit here in bed being useless. I have to get ready, and I'll be careful."

Norma looks at him and smiles. "If I have to pick more bullets out of you, this time I'll go light on the pain killers, so you feel every stitch. I don't want to put you back together again. I'll go get your clothes." She looks at him and caresses his cheek and his beard and turns around so the other people can't see her teary eyes.

Angus looks after her, and then he turns his head towards the people on the other side of the bed, "I think she might be the one. I'm not the one to be a big softy, but I'm turning to mush around her."

Tanya squeezes his arm. "I'm so happy for you, Angus. So very happy."

Angus smiles, "Thank you. Now listen up. I want you guys to get all your gear ready, always be prepared, and everything ready to go on a moment's notice. Eat and rest, when you are bored, out on the range, drill, and shoot. The next two or three days, that's all we have to do. I know what's going on, and this will turn hot quick, I can feel it."

Angus then looks at Richard, "Lad, you gotta keep it together. Compartmentalize, let the other guys lose their heads, that's when they will start to make mistakes. We're professionals, we shove all emotions back in and don't think about it. There will be time to heal later."

Richard smiles, "Or everything will come up later on the worst of times."

Angus grins, "Aye! That may happen, but what can you do? Now we must stay focused." Looking towards Henry, "You and I, let's have a talk with the Colonel and the General, and see what's what and how we tackle the next step. I think we have to get ready to save some pilots and slip behind their lines. But let's see what the big brass wants to do with us. I trust your guys are ready?"

Henry nods, "Yes, Angus, we're ready, get dressed, and let's talk with the big brass and see what the next days will have in store for us."

A few hours later, somewhere in the distance, you could hear the roar of a jet engine. Tanya looked up towards the ceiling, nestled against Mischa's chest. Sleep is not coming easily, not without another round of tears, but for the first time, she knows that she's not alone. There was Mischa. There's Angus, Nurse Norma, and Richard and Daniel, all now connected, over this patch of land, in the middle of nowhere. Strangers from every corner of the world, drawn together around this patch of land called Krasnodar, with nothing in common, and yet now connected more than ever, each battling their own pain, each fighting together for the same fragile hope.

End of Part 1 Krasnodar Rising

Glossary of terms

A

Afterburner – Jet engine system that injects extra fuel into the exhaust for additional thrust, used in combat or high-speed flight.

AIM-7 *Sparrow* – U.S. medium-range, radar-guided air-to-air missile.

AIM-9 *Sidewinder* – U.S. short-range, heat-seeking missile for dogfights.

Albert – Callsign of the C-130 *Hercules* transport formation.

Angle of Attack (AoA) – The angle between an aircraft's

wing and oncoming airflow; high AoA increases lift but can cause a stall.

Anapa – Town on the Black Sea coast; used by both Soviet and UN forces as a regional reference point.

Angels – Pilot term for altitude in thousands of feet (e.g., "Angels 25" = 25,000 ft).

Anti-G Suit – Flight garment that inflates during turns to prevent blackout from high G-forces.

Azovskaya – Forward operating area near the Caucasus foothills; staging ground for Allied helicopter missions.

B

Bandit – Confirmed hostile aircraft.

Bear (Tu-95) – Soviet long-range bomber and maritime patrol aircraft.

Bingo Fuel – Minimum fuel reserve required to safely return to base.

Black Sea Resolve (Operation) – UN peacekeeping operation to stabilize the Krasnodar region.

Bogey – Unidentified radar contact.

BTR / BRDM – Soviet armored personnel carriers and reconnaissance vehicles.

BRAA – Bearing, Range, Altitude, and Aspect; a format for reporting enemy position over the radio.

Brecon Beacons – Mountain range in Wales where SAS Sergeant Angus MacGavin trained prior to deployment.

C

C-130 *Hercules* – U.S. four-engine transport aircraft used for supply and troop movement.

Camp London – Allied base west of Novorossiysk housing

SAS, U.S. Special Forces, and helicopter units.

Chaff – Strips of metallic foil released to confuse radar-guided missiles.

Check Six – Pilot slang meaning "watch your rear."

Checkist – Colloquial Soviet term for KGB or internal security officer.

Code One – Aircraft declared fully operational after post-flight inspection.

Cobra (AH-1) – U.S. attack helicopter armed with rockets, TOW missiles, and cannon.

Comrade (*Tovarishch*) – Common Soviet address meaning "fellow member" or "comrade."

Contrails – Condensation trails formed by high-altitude aircraft.

Caucasus Mountains – Strategic range dividing Russia from Georgia and the Black Sea.

D

Defanovka – Coastal site of a major Allied helicopter assault on a Soviet forward base.

Dogfight – Close-quarters aerial combat between fighter aircraft.

Dustoff – U.S. military slang for helicopter medical evacuation (from "Dust Off" call sign in Vietnam).

Davaï! – Russian expression meaning "come on!" or "let's go!" depending on tone.

E

E-2C *Hawkeye* – U.S. Navy early-warning and control aircraft coordinating air operations.

Echelon Formation – Formation with aircraft arranged diagonally from the leader's wing.

Enfield – Callsign of James's F-5 squadron.

Ejection Seat – Pilot escape system that propels the seat clear of an aircraft.

FARP (Forward Arming and Refueling Point) – Temporary frontline base for helicopters to rearm and refuel.

Fencer (Su-24) – Soviet variable-wing bomber used for reconnaissance and precision strikes.

Fishbed (MiG-21) – Soviet short-range interceptor fighter.

Fitter (Su-17) – Soviet ground-attack fighter with swing wings.

Flare – Heat decoy used to confuse infrared-guided missiles.

Fox Two (Fox-2) – Radio call made when firing an infrared-guided missile.

Fragged – Slang for "mission ordered" or "assigned."

Frontal Aviation – Soviet air forces supporting ground troops directly.

Fuel State – Fuel remaining, reported in thousands of pounds (e.g., "Fuel 1.6").

G

G-Force (Pulling Gs) – Physical load felt by pilots during tight turns or acceleration.

Gelendzhik – Resort city on the Black Sea; secondary airfield for emergency landings.

Great Patriotic War – Soviet term for World War II (1941–45).

Guns Hot – Weapons are armed and cleared to fire.

H

Hawk (Henry "Hawk" Anderson) – U.S. Special Forces leader coordinating helicopter operations.

Hawkeye (The Hummer) – Nickname for the E-2C early-warning aircraft.

Huey (UH-1) – Iconic utility helicopter used for troop transport, medevac, and gunship roles.

I

Igor – Krasnodar local turned resistance fighter aiding Allied forces.

Instruments (Flying on) – Flying using cockpit instruments instead of visual cues.

J

James – U.S. Air Force pilot flying the F-5E Tiger II; central character of the air campaign.

K

Kate "Cali" Muller – U.S. Navy officer, Combat Information Center Officer (CICO) aboard the E-2C *Hawkeye* (callsign "Overlord").

Krimsk Airbase – Allied base in southern Russia used by U.S. squadrons.

Krasnodar Krai – Region of southern Russia and central theater of the novel's conflict.

L

London (Camp) – Allied forward operating base west of Novorossiysk.

M

Mach – Unit of speed relative to sound (Mach 1 ≈ 1,235 km/h).

Maykop – Soviet airbase in the Caucasus region; home of Vanea's MiG squadron.

MiG-21 / MiG-23 – Soviet fighters known by NATO code names *Fishbed* and *Flogger*.

Mi-6 / Mi-8 – Soviet heavy-lift and transport helicopters.

Minigun (Vulcan) – Electrically powered six-barrel machine gun used on helicopters.

Mischa – Civilian resistance member and Tanya's friend; part of ground resistance.

N

Nekulturny – Russian term meaning "uncultured" or "ill-mannered." A mild insult implying poor manners or refinement.

Novorossiysk – Key port city on the Black Sea and a central Allied logistics hub.

Nyet – Russian for "No."

O

O Club (Officers' Club) – Social gathering place for military officers on base.

Ogarkov, Marshal Nikolai – Senior Soviet officer commanding ground operations in Krasnodar.

Overlord – Callsign for the airborne controller coordinating Allied aircraft.

P

Pshada – River and crossing point of strategic importance in the Allied–Soviet conflict.

Python / Uzie / Hawk Flights – Allied helicopter units operating in Krasnodar.

Politburo – Governing body of the Communist Party of the Soviet Union.

Pulling the Throttle – Increasing engine power rapidly, especially under stress.

R

Radar Lock – Continuous radar tracking of a target, usually preceding missile launch.

Richard – UH-1 *Huey* pilot stationed at Camp London; close ally of Angus.

RTB (Return to Base) – Order for aircraft to return to home base.

RWR (Radar Warning Receiver) – Detects radar emissions and warns pilots of threats.

S

SAM (Surface-to-Air Missile) – Ground-launched missile designed to destroy aircraft.

SAS (Special Air Service) – British elite special forces; Angus's unit.

Secretary General – Head of the Soviet Communist Party (Ustinov in the novel).

Shilka (ZSU-23-4) – Radar-guided anti-aircraft gun platform.

Sidewinder (AIM-9) – Short-range U.S. air-to-air missile.

Sochi – Soviet airbase and resort city on the Black Sea; home to Vanea's rotating unit.

Sortie – Single operational mission or combat flight.

Sparrow (AIM-7) – Medium-range, radar-guided missile used by U.S. fighters.

Splash One – Confirmation that an enemy aircraft has been destroyed.

Strela – Soviet shoulder-launched surface-to-air missile system.

Su-17 / Su-24 / Su-25 – Soviet fighter-bomber and attack aircraft known as *Fitter*, *Fencer*, and *Frogfoot*.

Supply Convoy – Group of ships or vehicles traveling together for logistical support.

T

Tally Ho – Radio call meaning "enemy in sight."

Tanya – Civilian survivor turned resistance fighter; central ground character.

Throttle – Engine control regulating thrust or power.

Thud Ridge – Reference to the mountain area north of Hanoi; evokes U.S. Vietnam air combat history.

TOW Missile – U.S. wire-guided anti-tank missile launched from helicopters.

Tu-95 *Bear* – Soviet long-range bomber and maritime reconnaissance aircraft.

U

Ustinov, Secretary General – Soviet leader initiating the declaration of hostility against UN forces.

UH-1 *Huey* – Utility helicopter used extensively in Vietnam and in the Krasnodar operation.

UN Resolution 423 / 424 – Fictional UN resolutions establishing Operation *Black Sea Resolve*.

V

Vanea Gureevich – Soviet fighter pilot stationed in Sochi and Maykop; counterpart to James.

Vulcan Minigun – Six-barrel rotary cannon used on U.S. helicopters for suppression fire.

W

Weapons Hot – Clearance to engage and fire on enemy targets.

Wingman – Pilot flying beside or behind the leader for support and mutual protection.

Wobbly Pops – Slang for alcoholic drinks (usually beer).

Z

Zulu (FARP Zulu) – Forward helicopter base in the mountains north of Krasnodar used by Richard and Angus's crews.

ZSU – Soviet designation for self-propelled anti-aircraft guns, such as the *Shilka*.

Black Sea Resolve

Part 1

Krasnodar rising

To Brianna and Roya,

My rocks, my anchors, and my Northern Stars

Printed in Dunstable, United Kingdom

78349589R00178